Yaozu Cheng, a fifteen-year-old Cantonese boy, leaves his home in Guangzhou with his Uncle Ān Lì to navigate the Pearl River to Kowloon, where they embark on an historical journey to *Gum San,* the Golden Mountain. The gold rush of California has lured a hodgepodge of diverse characters from all corners of the earth. Unfortunately, Yaozu's ocean journey proves a horrific ordeal, and his new life as a miner becomes grueling and disheartening. When Yaozu meets a traveling stage performer from Europe, his luck takes a remarkable turn. Lola Montez, a worldly actress who introduces herself as the Countess of Landress, takes great interest in Yaozu's journal. She is fascinated not only with Yaozu's knowledge and appreciation of Chinese calligraphy, but she is intrigued with Yaozu's personal story. In an effort to improve his English, Yaozu translates his journal in exchange for the eccentric actress's autobiography, including her travels through India, Britain, Paris, Bavaria, New York and San Francisco.

Yaozu's journal is permeated with visions of Canton, Chinese folklore, and his knowledge of Chinese calligraphy. The reader is transported to his San Francisco of the 1850s and his Sierra Nevada mining camp adventures. Yoazu's friendship with a young Mexican named Diego leads him to a sojourn within a Maidu village. These native Californians and his friend Diego lend the narrative a genuine flavor of California history.

Set during the decline of a long era of Chinese Emperors, the Chinese have succumbed to British invasion during the Opium Wars. Queen Victoria reigns during her illustrious Victorian Age. California is a vivid clash of cultures in fierce turmoil. Frequently, however, a higher humanity succeeds in crossing boundaries with compassionate lifeblood, ushering in newly embraced inspiration. This chronicle is as entertaining as it is educational. The trials and lessons of this bygone era shed a hauntingly pertinent light on the tragedies and challenges of our own contemporary lives.

THE JEWELER'S APPRENTICE

a novel by
Walter Black

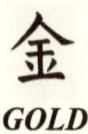

GOLD

THE JEWELER'S APPRENTICE

Library of Congress

This is a work or historical fiction. The Chinese main characters are entirely fictitious. While many of the California characters are historically accurate, the author has taken the liberty of creative fiction to enlarge upon and imagine interactions, dialogue, events, and personal details.

historical fiction; California gold rush, Chinese immigration, Chinese folklore, Cantonese culture; Guangzhou, Kowloon, Lola Montez, California history – 1850s, Cantonese history 1850s, Native Americans of California, Maidu folklore and history, *La Llorona,* Mexican folklore.

cover artwork by the author
back cover photo of Chinese woodcut by author

ISBN: 978-0-615-24807-3

Library of Congress Control Number:

2008908198

審

to flee

CENTRAL PACIFIC STATION,
MARIPOSA, CALIFORNIA

A cathedral-sized big-leaf maple formed a spectacular awning that nodded above the grand arched entry to the train station. I sat at the maple tree's base, wedged between exposed octopus tentacle roots. A gray squirrel nibbled nervously near my feet. His belly was white as a napkin stuffed under his chin. His long, bushy tail stood poised, but only briefly. A violet green swallow swooped low beneath the canopy of maple leaves, sending the gray squirrel scurrying and scraping up the rough-barked trunk.

A round-faced toddler in a frilly bonnet waved a plump hand at me. Her mother, dressed in a long drab gown and a similar bunched bonnet guided the unsure-footed infant across the yard toward the yawning entrance of the station. Nobody seemed to take notice of me. The street and walkway were jammed with carriages and buggies. Horses flicked their tails and bobbed their heads. Mules stood deadpan while boys and men unloaded bags, crates, trunks and luggage.

Among the faces of the world, the rich and poor, an image of my father appeared over my shoulder. His eyes were stern and penetrating. His mouth was drawn into a sneer. Whether he was ready to scowl or ready to grin, I could never predict. As if through a crystal ball, I saw through my father's eyes. He would feel shamed to see me, my queue shorn off, and my remaining hair matted with mud and grass. My hands were filthy, nearly black with grease. My lightweight Cantonese clothes had long since disappeared. He would have seen me in a floppy old hat and a fancy topcoat, now worn at the elbows. He would see my thick wool shirt, stained kneebreeches, and hobnail boots too big for my boy-sized feet. He'd watch me then, sauntering through the arched doorway of the train station, my hands in my pockets. He'd look on as I hid behind a thick support beam. "Hiding like a rat, like a scared animal," he would criticize. His tight-lipped sneer would have been unmistakable, and shaking his head he would turn away.

It was not my father's image, but my own conscience (inherited from him) sitting on my shoulder and anticipating what I was about to do. The previous year's trip across the Pacific Ocean seemed on that day a hundred years ago, and my life in China had been left far behind, a thousand years gone. I was truly a scared rat caught in a treacherous trap. There was a tightness clutching at my throat. Tears seemed long forgotten, and any form of comfort in my life had become long lost. I brushed caked grass off the shoulder of my jacket. My survival demanded action.

The station was bustling and raucous. There were beggars and farmers and merchants, and, no doubt, gamblers down-on-their-luck. The well-to-do were also mixed into the crowd. That's who I focused on, the wealthy ones. Apparently, even royalty wanted to find gold and become yet wealthier. I heard dialects and tongues from all corners of the globe, all babbling and gurgling in that mammoth room like a gargantuan soup pot.

A group of Chinese men had gathered in a far corner of the room. They appeared to be Manchurians from the north. I carefully avoided them.

The high arched windows of the room welcomed slanting sunbeams into the station. Like spotlights, the sunbeams singled out foppish dandies in the snaking mass of humanity. Three gentlemen had offered their assistance to a stately lady who twirled a fringed parasol above her head. She apparently cared less that an open umbrella was bad luck indoors. Two of the dandies shared the burden of her brass-handled cedar chest, while the other, eager-looking gentleman balanced two suitcases, a hat box, and a large handbag. The men's high boots were shined to perfection, their coattails were long, and their top hats were well kempt with black silk ribbons.

All heads turned to take in the splendor of the elegant woman twirling her white satin parasol, its black fringe in flight. She wore a massive hat of emerald batiste. An outsized bow on the hat matched her parasol. Her vermillion dress spread to the floor as if covering a Chinese funeral bell. A black netted shawl draped her shoulders and arms. A white gloved hand braced the parasol, while the other hand steadied a tiny booklet. Her face, through a veil, looked whimsical, even coquettish. Turning to double check on the gentlemen guarding her luggage, her dress whisked the wood floor like a shushing whisper.

As if eavesdropping, the crowd hushed. The dandy with too many bags arranged them neatly behind the lady on the floor, and ran off on an errand. As if this were the end of act one, the crowd resumed their various conversations in their varied tongues. I noticed that everyone was pretending to ignore the grand lady, with her tiny book and twirling parasol. Occasional quick side glances indicated that she had not truly lost center stage.

From my position, behind the wide support beam, I saw that the wide arched entryway was no longer blocked by the entering crowd. I took in one long breath and dashed across the room toward the magnificent lady, intently studying her tiny booklet. I snatched up the large handbag. Immediately, the stouter of the two remaining dandies bellowed out, "Hey, you!" The other gentlemen in his top hat cried out, "Thief, thief!"

As I flew through the doorway, I heard a woman's shrill scream. Turning left outside the arched entrance, I crashed headlong into a sturdy market woman. She whacked me in the head with a loaf of bread. It felt like a brick. I kept running. I heard the chorus of "hey you" and "thief, thief" close behind me and turned left again, ducking into Cassaretto's Store. I knew from previous experience that Cassaretto's had a back door. I could hear him yelling, "Filthy coolie, stay out my store," as I spilled out onto the dirt alley. Unfortunately, I was leaving a trail of dust in the air, so I cut across a weed patch beside the City Hotel, passing the Big Oak Tree, another well known tree in town.

My boots were too big, and they had blistered my feet so that blood had dried onto my socks. Needless to say, I hadn't bothered to remove my socks for several days. Despite blisters and clumsy boots, I ran like a terrorized cat. I crossed a field of grass that had grown so high that it was difficult for the men chasing me to see me. I still heard them yelling, "Filthy coolie" mixed with "thief," when I tripped on a large rock. Precisely as I tripped, I heard a rifle shot. I fell on my face, my hat flew off, and I dropped the handbag – all in one clumsy spill.

"Am I dead?" I had to ask myself, because I slammed my skull hard on the ground. I saw the stolen handbag lying in the grass. There was a pattern woven onto the bag of autumn oak leaves. The handle was brown leather. "Was this my life flashing before my eyes? Was this darn handbag the price I paid for my life?" As I crawled toward the bag, I could feel that my elbow was scraped. Blood dripped from my nose.

I knew that I had nearly reached the irrigation ditch, so I continued crawling. The yelling increased in volume. I crawled until I slid into the cold water of the irrigation ditch, and stayed low in the cold water. This kind of cold water will make your bones ache and turn your skin to a white mush if you stay under too long. I knew this from all my days of panning for gold in the river, up to my waist in cold water.

The voices sounded closer. I held my breath and lied motionless. My heart pounded so fast I was afraid they would hear its drumbeat. Another gunshot tore the air and harsh voices were cursing and calling out orders. I sensed by the location of the voices that they had jumped the ditch and started up into the woods. The voices faded gradually, so I started crawling again. Thinking back, if I hadn't tripped on that rock, I probably would have run into the woods. That might have been the end of me.

On this side of the ditch, I knew of a good hiding place where I had slept without being discovered.

to drag oneself CHAPTER TWO: MY HIDING PLACE

A northern spotted owl called, "Hoa, hoo-hoo," through the darkening trees. I shambled upon my hiding place as dusk drained the light from the sky. Coal-black silhouettes stood against witching-hour indigo sky. The circumference of a forgotten tree stump served me well as a night fortress. My circular room smelled of rotting grass and damp earth. I had collected tree bark and piled it in the middle of my small room to create a substitute for a wool blanket. At bedtime, I sat straight-legged as I covered my legs with dirt, twigs and grass. As an outer shell to protect from the chill of foothill nights, I placed the largest pieces of tree barks over the mound of debris. I liked to visualize myself as an Egyptian mummy, preparing myself for the afterlife. Part of me felt childish - playing a game, and part of me was pleased with the idea of dying in my sleep. Even the second thought was child's play compared to the tiger's spirit inside me that continually fought to stay alive. If I died here, *Gum San,* meaning Golden Mountain, was not my home. If my body was not returned to China, my spirit would become a ghost.

I knew better than to share my foolish fantasy with anyone here on the Golden Mountain. My fantasy involved my ghost spirit flying invisibly and mischievously haunting the foreign devils of *Gum San.* The Chinese have a saying: "For a gentleman to take revenge, ten years is not too late." My ghost would be a terrifying Tree-Stump Ghost, terrorizing the bullies, the miner's of the Golden Mountain who take what they did not earn, selfishly stealing the hard work of others. My tree limbs would undulate like snakes in the nightmares of those bullies. The bullies of Golden Mountain would never sleep peacefully again.

My fantasies are like kites, and I have to pull them back to earth by their strings. I pulled the Tree Stump Ghost back to reality, and continued to bury myself in rubbish. By then my chest was covered with dirt and mulch up to my neck. My arms and head stuck out like a turtle trapped on his back. I would tuck both hands inside opposite sleeves of my fancy European jacket.

My fantasies of avenging the injustice of the mining camp bullies faded into the night sounds of wind in the buckthorn and miner's lettuce and the gurgling of the nearby ditch. Tonight the insects of Gum San sang out with a tranquilizing pulse. Occasionally a sheep dog could be heard barking in the distance, but I felt safe and nearly warm.

The tedious part about sleeping inside a rotted out tree stump is that I tended to toss in my sleep, knocking off my protective covering. When I got cold enough, I'd have to rouse myself to remold my mummy cast. I dreamt one night that I had died and rotted here, and my ghost was too worn out to get up from the mulch and terrorize anybody. Another night I slept curled against the inside curve of the tree trunk. That night must have been warmer than of late. Usually, if I didn't mummify myself adequately, the nights became too frigid to sleep. The last night in my tree stump I had acquired new problem. I had in my possession a handbag with oak leaf design and a leather handle. The whole town must have combined forces for discovering my whereabouts.

The harsh call of crows awoke me in the middle of night. My plan had been to wake up at sunrise and disguise myself with gunnysacks. I had collected several gunnysacks for collecting and carrying loads of food, assortments of tools, and personal belongings. Lately, I had little of any of the three categories. I had learned to live on uncooked rice, which I kept in my pockets to suck on like candy. I chewed on grass, or stole corn and tomatoes from gardens. I felt no remorse for taking apples or cherries from the trees. Trees seemed, more than likely, to belong to the Gods. The stingy mining camp settlers liked to lay claim to every variety of handiwork of the Gods. All food is from the Gods and our ancestors, but I knew how protective a farmer feels about his crops, being a farmer myself.

As a result of living like a hunted animal, my nerves were pricked and my awareness enhanced with great caution. I woke well before sunrise, and the coarse cawing of crows startled me into a state of panic. My mind raced with thoughts of being shot or hung from a rope, or both. I located a candle that I kept in a matchbox. The darkness settled again into complete silence, and this reassured me that I was alone. With a fish knife that my father had given me, I sliced a hole in the bottom of a gunnysack to poke my head through, and cut two side holes for my arms. I made a gunnysack skirt that reached the toes of my clod hopper boots. I tore three strips of gunnysack to tie around my head, and stashed my hat in another gunnysack that would serve as my travel bag. The fancy embroidered handbag would be a dead giveaway that I was the thief, so I dumped out the contents onto the gunnysack, and buried the lady's handbag under the rotting mulch of my hideaway. The lady's belongings were quite feminine and several items gave off a luster, reflecting the dim candlelight. I moved the candle closer to the cache. Excitement and terror filled me simultaneously. (Worried that I had stolen Queen Victoria's handbag, there would surely be no avoiding it – my head will be chopped off.)

An ostentatious necklace of cameos and golden keys that dripped with tears of pearls was obviously not a likely possession for a filthy boy dressed in gunnysacks. A gracefully swirled ivory comb had been cleverly carved into the shape of a swordfish. A small velvet coin purse was bursting with clinking change, held secure by a glistening drawstring with a silver tassel. I loosened the drawstring and upended the small purse, releasing coins of various size and color. I had jolly well hit the jackpot! A small booklet, about the size of a woman's hand, had a crinkled cover the color of dried blood. In gold engraved print was its title, *Gem Rings and Jewellery for Every Enquiry.* On the backside it read: GEMMOLOGIST'S POCKET COMPEMDIUM. I had no idea what any of these words meant, but I decided that the booklet would come in handy for teaching me English. (I also had not yet learned that English books were read backwards – from left to right, so I didn't realize that the backside of the book was actually the cover and title.)

The coins went into my pockets, beneath the gunnysack skirt. I shoveled the remaining items into the gunnysack travel bag. If I had discovered a mirror, I would have checked my idiotic costume, but I'd seen the rich and the poor from every corner of the earth since I landed here. Every unexplainable and unexpected manner of costume was to be seen among the well-to-do as well as the impoverished. We all had come for the same thing, but we were every color of skin and spoke in tongues of many peoples. I never could have imagined the innumerable possibilities for dressing a torso, two legs, two arms, and a head. Gunnysack Man would merely be another in a parade of comical and fantastic costumes.

I left my tree-trunk home in the dimness of a cloud swept moon. I knew my way around the area in the pitch dark, but I was thankful to be able to make out any animals or persons I might want to avoid. Luckily, by sunrise, I was well outside of town, following the train tracks that followed the river and rounded bends on its path to Sacramento and on to San Francisco.

LUCKY

DAY OF LUCK FOR THE GUNNYSACK BOY

Tenuous trails angled, curled, and crossed like a fishnet draping the slopes of the mountain ridges. Miners had all but trampled the Mother Lode, including the hills and streams that lie west of the Sierra Nevada range. Even in the lackluster moonlight, I knew that this path departed from the settlement in an easterly direction before meandering north to cross a high perched gap between granite fists of mountainous bulkhead. The ascending glow of day had rendered the mountain pass more visible than my moonlight trek. I would be descending the north side of the ridge by the time a golden rim of sunlight would unveil the riverbanks that lie below. Along the north bank of the Merced River, modern railroad tracks followed the carved meanderings of the river.

Despite the chill of early morning, my gunnysack disguise over grimy European attire held in the body heat of my climb, drenching me in perspiration. Fear of angered townspeople stifled my inclination to discard extra clothes. If the stolen loot I toted belonged to Queen Victoria, her henchmen would be on my heels, so I suffered the extra layers of burlap. Fortunately, I soon descended the path that would join the river. As the first gilded gleam transformed the slate sky to azure, the river gave off the mercuric glints of a sword blade.

Laurel shrubs competed with small pines to overtake the trail, and the passage seemed overgrown with low hanging branches. I dragged the gunnysack beside me as I crawled like a crab on my stomach to reach a small clearing where it was a relief to stand up again. The nearby crunching of dead leaves caused my heart to jump in my chest. I froze like a deer in its tracks as a small, frayed woman with gleaming eyes sidestepped a wide tree trunk and appeared before me like a straggled ghost. Her mane of gray hair was so long and tangled with dirt that I initially mistook her for a wild animal. Her toothless smile gathered above a sparse beard and her sagging breast hung to her waist.

She seemed to reach for me briefly with her scabby claws, but her enormous eyes quickly lost track of me as she danced a small circle with frail arms extended like tree branches.

Wild animal or ghost, she appeared to be lost between worlds. Perhaps she had materialized to remind me that my frightening situation could have been worse. I continued down the path without looking back.

The sight of a river, that ancient ribbon that tossed and turned its way to the wide open sea, imbued me with a premonition of relief. The chattering songbirds and the dawn's canyon breeze were like seasonings dusted upon a meal of hope. Maybe, after all, I would escape alive. I was not about to drop my guard or let fate catch up with me, but the beauty of that early morning was like a refuge from a long, drawn-out nightmare.

The sun had claimed its throne above as I reached the river. The current was far too furious and deep for me to dare crossing the river at this junction. I splashed icy water upon my face, and cupped my hands for gulps of runoff from high elevation snow banks. I recalled an unusual bridge that would allow me to cross to the train tracks. A corridor-shaped A-frame protected the bridge, creating a tunnel for crossing the Merced River.

The tunnel-bridge would have served as a perfectly clever location for ambush. At once, I envisioned a posse sent from Mariposa, waylaying me as I entered the darkness of the tunnel crossing. In a delayed sequence, I threw several rocks and pebbles into the tunnel to test for any reaction. I hid my burlap sack of booty in a laurel shrub before venturing near the arched doorway to peer in. I mimicked the sound of a cat, but no response emitted from the inside. Confident that I was alone, I retrieved my hidden gunnysack, and entered the tunnel.

English words popped into my mind that prospectors repeatedly used. "The coast is clear" was usually declared when potential bandits had failed to raid the camp. "Hallelujah and God Almighty!" were cries of success when a miner hit pay dirt or spotted a healthy specimen of the opposite sex. The A-frame covered bridge smelled musty and sour, like an outhouse where drunks had upchucked their dinners. I held my breath, hastening my pace through the sunless corridor, my boots crunching the gravel that pierced like needles pricking my blistered feet.

Encountering the train tracks on the north embankment of the river, I turned toward Sacramento to the west. As morning heated up, my enthusiasm faded sharply. Plodding lethargically from one rail tie to the next, I fantasized a *dim-sum* breakfast followed by a long nap on a goose-down mattress. After doggedly rounding several curves along the tracks, a massive, rust-colored house came into view, guarding a flat, horseshoe-shaped gorge. Glistening stalks of corn formed diagonal rows, interrupted occasionally by looming spires of hemlocks. From a distance, a dog barked wildly, causing me to scan the ground for a hefty stick to offer the beast before its hostility turned against me.

A boy's voice called out, "Calm down, Frosty, I said quiet!" His shouting echoed back from the gorge. I stopped dead in my tracks, feeling nervous to encounter humans so near to Mariposa. The enthusiastic youth ran out toward the rails. I heard Frosty barking frantically, and the raucous sound doubled back with the resonance of a noise in a deep well. Upon spotting me, the boy froze. I could only guess that he had heard of the famous thief pursued by residents of Mariposa. I prepared to backtrack like a jackrabbit hearing the fire of rifle shot.

The lad called out, "Good Morning," and waved his hand like a surrender flag. I felt a change of heart in his cheerful tone and welcoming gesture. I was a few years older than the kid, but we were nearly the same size.

"Where yah headed?" he called out as he approached me.

"I go Sacramento," I responded, pointing in the direction of the train tracks. My English (in those early gold rush years) was limited, and I resorted frequently to pantomime for conveying unknown terms. I intentionally lied about my final destination to protect myself from criminal hunters.

"You're not from around here, are yah?" He smiled and I could see his unassuming friendliness.

Casey had been left to watch the farm while his "Papa" had gone into town for some coal, a new bucket, and some oats. I felt relieved to discover that Frosty was fenced in. Casey explained that you can't let animals wander around on the train tracks. He invited me to play Hide-and-Seek. I apologized for being far too tired and hungry to play any sort of game. (I didn't yet know what Hide-and-Seek was, but I didn't choose to admit

it.) Casey offered to prepare a strawberry jam sandwich. I told
him I didn't want to "cause problem" for his mother or sister.
"No problem." Casey explained that his mother and two sisters
had stayed behind in Missouri. I didn't want to appear like an
idiot, so I didn't ask where or what was "behind-in-Missouri".

He fed me bread with strawberry and apricot preserves. I
learned a new word, "butter," but I refused to eat it. He also
poured me a glass of milk. I had already experienced the frothy,
white liquid several weeks earlier, when I discovered I was
allergic to it. Casey acted dumbfounded that anybody could live
without butter or milk. "Maybe that's why you're so darn
skinny," he deduced. I didn't know how to explain that I didn't
enjoy the flavor anyway.

He wasn't allowed to invite overnight guests without
permission, but he decided that if I slept in the loft of the barn,
his "Papa" wouldn't find out. After climbing a rickety ladder to
the loft, Casey wanted to know what I had in my gunnysack. I
decided, with extreme caution, that I could show him the coins in
the velvet purse. My intention was to purchase some food from
him for the trip to "Sacramento." He sold me a dozen apples
from his tree and several ears of corn from the field. He also dug
out a secret stash of hard candy, which he divided up between
the two of us. "No charge," he added. I benefited from the deal
with an unexpected boon. After I had dumped the collection of
coins on the wooden floor of the loft, Casey inspected the velvet
purse and discovered an interior pocket stuffed with folded paper
money. Casey was flabbergasted by the sum. This enthusiasm
made me very apprehensive. Surely such a phenomenal amount
of cash would turn Casey into a blabbermouth. I decided to
bribe him. I offered him five dollars to keep his lips sealed about
me and the money. He looked at me with a look of awe mixed
with suspicion. "Ten dollars," he demanded, upping the ante.

Shortly after taking his two five-dollar bills, Casey realized
that everybody he knew would be suspicious for his carrying
paper money. He rarely had occasion to carry more than pennies
or nickels. I ended up paying him off with pennies, nickels, one
dime, and several one-dollar bills. "I'll save the dollar bills for a
special occasion, like when I get married." I carefully restrained
any look of astonishment that might have given away my
ignorance. I had no way of knowing how much money I was

holding. I knew the approximated worth of Chinese money, but I had no experience with foreign currency.

Casey left me alone in the loft while I designed a makeshift bed of gunnysacks and dried grass stalks. He returned with a chipped plate of jam sandwiches stacked precariously. He warned me to not light a candle. "If you leave in the middle of the night, my Papa won't see you, but be extra quiet."

He left me there in the twilight beneath the cobwebs and rafters, contemplating my good luck. There were plenty of Chinamen haters among the gold prospectors and plenty more teenagers and children who would laugh and jeer at anyone foreign to them. Occasionally, though, California offered me these rare souls, people who could see a fellow spirit and not think of me as an animal or a slave. I knew that I was looked down upon when I heard the word "coolie," and many of the white devils called us by the demeaning name. It would be years before I learned that *coolie* was a word the British had used to describe the poor servants taken in India, and the word had made its journey to the Golden Mountain to be a chain around another man's neck.

Casey was naïve of all this one-upmanship. He would have alarmed my family with his ice-colored eyes, his pepper-sprinkled face, and that wavy hair, like the washed out color of a water chestnut. It was our smiles that bonded us, reaching from the Canton farm across the wide Pacific Ocean to the California farm, wedged between mountains and railroad track. The smile was a link between us, despite our different cultures and our contrasting appearances. If I had been asked to design the flag of California, I would not have chosen a gold nugget or a brown bear as the emblem. I would have selected a smile, that emblem that you see in every country, of every race, on any face from any tribe. It would be the smile you see in California when a Mexican laughs with a black man, or a Chinaman admires the artwork of an Irish child. It's the smile that means to me that we are all people, side by side, capable of helping each other and caring for each other. I didn't see this shared smile on all the faces of Californians those days, but when I did, I felt a sensation of hope for the Golden Mountain, for this new state that had so recently been added to the union. My hope was that the smile would beat out over all the cruel forms of one-upmanship.

Lulled by the rattle and clatter of the train bound for San Francisco, I dozed off with my head vibrating against the window pane. A circle of condensation marked the glass with my warm slumbered breath. I dreamt of Manchurian banner men, galloping on their glossy black stallions. The banner men sought my execution for stealing the jewelry of the Empress Tz'u-his, and I had ensconced myself in my hollow tree stump. An apricot satin robe, embroidered with emerald and gold peacocks with lavender feathers, served as a sack for my cache. I marveled at the Ordos headdress with rows of coral and malachite beads. Blue and green turquoise formed swirls and arabesques of enameled fungi. There were hair fasteners, amulet boxes, snuff boxes and bracelets, a needle-case and large finger-rings. Long silver nail-covers rested on the apricot satin, resembling ornamental fangs of saber-toothed tigers.

A din of clanging bells, squealing brakes, and the train's powerful blast of steam stirred me from my dream and rescued me from capture. I had shed my layers of burlap, and although my face and hands were scrubbed clean, my frock jacket and kneebreeches remained tattered and soiled. Not a soul had dared to occupy the seat beside me, although the cabin was clamoring with the hubbub of passengers sardine-packed with their excess of belongings underfoot and overhead in storage cubbies. My possessions, along with a few of Queen Victoria's, all fit in one large sack.

The squealing of brakes announced out arrival. The cramped file of humanity in the narrow aisle debarked at a snail's pace, while the shock of morning light outside the smudged windows created a stage light for a theatre of waving hands, bouncing hats atop heads, long embraces, and hen-peck kisses upon cheeks.

You might have guessed that after hiding in brush and brambles, San Francisco would have been a beckoning lap of luxury. In my case, you would have guessed wrong. San Francisco was a ferocious jungle of contrasts and fierce competitions. By 1853, prices had soared to unheard of cost. People paid ten dollars for a thumb tack and sheets of paper went for one hundred fifty dollars each. With the excess of wealth, businesses that catered to high society lined the boardwalks.

Playhouses, haberdasheries, barbers, tailors, and jewelers shouldered purveyors of mining equipment, churches, dry goods merchants, banks, and mortuaries.

The excess of wealth had failed to reach some areas of city planning. Some of the muddy streets were treacherous as quicksand, swallowing up dogs, drunks, and even mules. Wooden crates and beer barrels served as steppingstones for crossing.

A notorious group from Australia called themselves the *Sydney Ducks.* These jail birds and ex-cons wandered the streets, murdering and stealing to acquire quick riches. In opulent taverns the Mexican *rancheros* in *zarapes* stood next to Chinamen in wide-brimmed, mushroom shaped reed hats and their waist-length braided queues down their backs. Irishmen in fisherman hats shouldered up to the bar with Frenchmen in top-hats, and professional gamblers wearing tuxedo tails. Outside the bars the separate neighborhoods were portioned out by nationality; a Little Chile, a Chinatown, and a French quarters called *Keskesdee.* Passing through the wrong part of town could as easily go unnoticed as end up deadly, depending on the time of day and whoever was celebrating a special occasion. These celebrations were transplants from far away lands.

I noticed that among the hodgepodge of outlandish businesses in the surge of city growth, many of the Chinese had given up on gold mining, and resorted to laundering shirts and pants. It you were not of European descent, and there were many of us who weren't, the white devils were hard pressed to depart with the least amount of the pocket change for your services. This is what I heard from the various non-whites. Blacks, Latinos, Native Americans, and Chinese were all shortchanged for their hard work. (My father would later point out that well-trained, specialized, and educated workers always acquired more wealth than common laborers.)

Unfortunately, adding to this dilemma, there were so many Chinamen laundering clothes that the price of cleaning a dozen shirts was driven down to three dollars. The Chinese, were, and still are, accustomed to working long hours and spending little, so I'm sure the Laundromats were prosperous with time.

Laundering clothes, as it turned out, was not to be my fate. My destination that day was Montgomery Street. A Chinese agent for Asia-Pacific Sea Merchants had purchased my ticket for crossing the ocean. The contract agreement was that I would pay off the debt by working in California. The contract had been arranged by Uncle, who signed one (for himself) identical to mine. The ticket to cross the ocean was so expensive, that it generally took eight to twelve years for a Chinaman to pay it off. Most Chinese, myself included, had purchased round trip tickets to assure our safe return home. The contract required that the debt be paid in full before issuance of the return boarding pass. A fellow prospector on the train had informed me that if I paid off fifteen percent of my debt or more, that I would be readily assigned a new mining camp, no questions asked. They would merely move my name to the top of the list.

THE FOUR TREASURES OF
THE ROOM OF LITERATURE

Seaweed and barnacles, exposed and then submerged in salty sea, added to the damp musty stench of fish markets and rotting of remnants attacked by winged scavengers; lanky seagulls and plump pigeons. In addition to the changing aromas of my street walk, I encountered mysterious women beneath their concealing hats and engulfed in flowery perfumes. Hirsute gentlemen left cigar trails of abrasive smoke, and babbling lunatics their foul odors of aged perspiration and soiled pants. A boisterous clique of miners spilled out of the Trivole Tavern, whopping and walloping. These cowboys and prospectors jostled various self-absorbed businessmen from their quick-paced, direct-lined gait. A clenching sour, yet sickeningly sweet odor bonded the inebriated companions like a yellow dust cloud.

Montgomery Street remained two blocks down the wooden plank walkway, beneath a cirrus-streaked, cool blue sky. An endearing vision appeared beside me through a thick glass display window. Resembling a museum exhibit, I beheld a revered tradition from my homeland; a *Ch'ang-T'iao-Cho,* a long rectangular table. A coarse textured paper was draped midway over the tabletop, beside a brush stand, brush, ink-stone, ink and a water-pot.

I made a quick detour from my intended destination, stepping into the Chinese calligraphy shop. A wind chime announced my entrance, and a round-faced man lifted a finger above his head without looking up from his work. I recognized the scent of jasmine incense, and marveled at the vertical wall hangings, Chinese poems written in the ancient picture-characters *Hui-T'u-Wen-Tzu,* which we call *Piao-Shih,* meaning sign or symbol. Reading the verses, I envisioned the movement of the wrist, fingers, and the right elbow. The brush strokes evoked a rhythm, extending to the left, fading away to the right, pivoting, pirouetting, and balancing. It brought to mind the satin-shoed feet of a ballerina, posing on one toe, twirling, leaping, and then abruptly poised motionless on the other toe. If the brushstrokes were fluid, we called them the Running Style,

17

but if the strokes were diminutive and swift, we referred to them as the Grass style. The more regimented and formal stroke were categorized as the Regular Style.

I was swept away by a yearning for my journal that I had unintentionally left behind in Sacramento. A pride and emotion swelled within me recalling the gift of my formal training. The subject of Chinese calligraphy is infused with history of the Middle Kingdom. I greedily bought a full set of calligraphy supplies. It wasn't until I reached inside my burlap sack, digging for the velvet coin purse, that I felt self-conscious about handling and spending stolen currency. I felt embarrassed and shamed to hand the store attendant a handful of coins, having absolutely no idea if the amount was either insufficient or far exceeded the amount of the total bill. The clerk gathered four large silver coins and one gold coin without the bat of an eyelash. In my hand remained plenty of the same. I returned them to the coin bag in which they created a rhythmic clinking against the pile of coins inside the bag.

Later that night, as I reclined upon a well cushioned bed with a down-filled pillow, I realized that the shop attendant must encounter many an inexperienced Chinaman with newly acquired wealth. A sound businessman would consider it poor etiquette to question the purchaser's source of income. Prices were so over-inflated, that most shops catered to the well-to-do of the gold rush, and "well-to-do" did not always equate with persons of class, refinement, manners, or even a reasonable knowledge (for the customer's part) as to the quality of the purchase. I may have been a poor farmer-turned-miner, down on my luck, and guilty of theft, but my familiarity with the tools of Chinese calligraphy assured me that I had purchased high quality merchandise.

Rather than purchase a large, expensive roll of porous, coarse-woven paper, I purchased a blank journal book. A relatively small book would fit comfortably in my lap, although I preferred to place the booklet on a flat top table. The later allowed me a comfortable setup for my brush-stand and brush, ink-stone and ink, along with the water pot. I had readily discovered that my calligraphy skill made me a popular Chinaman among my people, as many fellow prospectors lacked my skill. They willingly paid for my services as a correspondent to their families across the Pacific. This work was a bit tiring after a day of gold panning, but I felt honored to link family members for a humble fee. Several letters were written free of charge after hearing their stories of harsh luck and grim circumstances. This was all before my own life had taken a similar severe turn for the worse.

Perhaps the most enjoyable aspect of my Chinese calligraphy skill was the lure it held for curious souls of non-Chinese descent. I learned more English, and new acquaintances would marvel at the intricacies of Chinese writing. I came to learn, also, that the curious personalities from any part of the world were generally the most open and endearing of spirits. Very rarely, a very clever person would disguise his trickery behind a mask of curiosity, but the fearful types were more likely to be spiteful and suspicious upon encountering anything new. Some folks actually believed that their own way of life was obviously the best. They liked to look down on others and berate the practices and traditions of strangers.

During my early days of the gold rush, I considered these people hateful and closed-minded. My perception may have been partially accurate, but it hadn't yet occurred to me that some people have been exposed to severe suffering and degradation of their own. I hadn't yet imagined that if a person was pushed into quicksand, he may have a hard time seeing others without suspicion and hatred. This later realization came to me decades later and enabled me to observe the selfishness of others while maintaining at least an ounce of forgiveness in my own heart.

But forgiveness was not my forte in those days. That day as I left the calligraphy shop and hurried to the Asian Pacific Ser Merchant's agent on Montgomery Street, fear, disgust, awe, confusion, curiosity, and elation were some of my many reactions to the variety of humanity that crossed my path on those wooden walkways of San Francisco. Some of the women shocked me as thoroughly as the outrageous men. Women in bonnets carried woven baskets, covered with checkered napkins. Some were lighthearted, but many walked stiff as a bed board, their eyes straight ahead and faces barely visible between the folds of their bonnets. Other women, more Parisian or European, strolled evocatively with their tasseled parasols, great plumed

19

hats, their huge bell-shaped skirts and high-heeled, laced boots. There were women that lived like men, carrying rifles or holsters with pistols. These were the Calamity Jane types, wearing raccoon hats or flattened cow-poke hats. They tended to chew tobacco or long stalks of dried straw, and could spit in the spittoons with the best of the tough guys.

On these walks, I never could guess who would nod, maybe offer a smile or a "Good Day." Of the men, though, I soon learned who was least likely to be civil. I could see or hear the anger long before I approached the person. Unfortunately, this talent had to be learned, like most talents. That particular bright day, one block from my destination on Montgomery Street, an old prospector stood leaning against the doorframe of Kelly's Brewery. His dirty hat was pulled down over his face, and a rifle rested on his shoulder, the barrel touching his ear. He had one straight-angled leg jutting out upon the walkway, and the other knee bent, with his boot bottom flat against the wall. Without warning he lifted his rifle and yelled out, "Damn Chinaman, I'll send you back home where you belong!" His voice was rough like a snarling dog. He fired the rifle three times. Each bullet splintered the boards at my feet. I felt the wind of my soul jumping up and nearly out of my chest. Surely, I must have jumped three feet into the air.

Without changing my pace, I continued walking, half wondering if I carried a bullet in my foot. The harsh laughter of the man at the door rang out like a crazed soldier's ranting. I knew that a junkyard dog would bark more wildly if you showed your fear. A dog likes to hear you talking calmly to him. I tried to hide my fear by walking, not running. I didn't look back once, and the old dog did not fire another shot.

PAYING THE SEA MERCHANT AGENT

From the outside, the door of the Asia-Pacific Sea Merchants on Montgomery Street was dark stained wood, with an oval window that served more as ornament than a peep hole. Having just survived the madman's bullets without a scratch, my pulse continued pounding and the anxiety had flushed my face. I felt self-conscious of my squalid appearance at the sight of the opulence of the sea merchant's doorway. I paused to regain composure. Once inside, the beveled glass of the egg-shaped window created prisms that refracted the setting sunlight into shafts of rainbows about the foyer. I calmed immediately upon closing the elegant Victorian door behind me, sealing out the unpredictable city street. Steeping into the lobby, lovely French davenports with scrolled legs and clawed feet invited me with blackberry velvet cushions. Positioned strategically above the davenport was a bold painting in a frilly golden frame. The painting seemed lifelike and yet motionless, a rosy-cheeked gentleman in a white powdered wig and a double-breasted Chesterfield overcoat.

Being Chinese, I held a reverence for my own ancestors. Even remote and ancient ancestors had power and sway over my life's course, as they witnessed the worth of my deeds on earth. Although the sea merchant's lobby stood silent and vacant, the proud austerity of the painted face cast a spell of obedience upon me. If the painting had come alive, and initiated an interrogation, I would have surely felt obliged to confess my recent crime of grand theft. (My guilt must have lain heavily on my conscience, causing me unusual perceptions of paranoia.)

A brass plated sign directed clients to room numbers for various departments of the building. I recognized the Roman numerals, but the department titles were as good as Greek to me. The English language was so bewildering. I entered a hallway, and knocked upon the first open door. A corpulent, bald man looked up from his desk strewn with paperwork. Directing his uncaring gaze at me, he said, "Yes?"

I froze in confusion. This single word, yes, served as an answer for a question, but I had not yet asked any question.

21

After a few squeamish seconds the man spoke again, "May I help you?"

"Pay bill," I stated, reaching for my pocket, pantomiming a search for money.

Using his free hand to push himself up from the desk, he pointed his fountain pen down the hall, "Room 104, Billing."

"Thank you, sir," I replied, nodding my head like a bouncing ball. Of my repertoire of English words, this was my one and only entire sentence in English.

The sea merchant's office had west facing windows, and the descending sun lit the room with a blinding copper sunset. Fortunately, my agent's cashier was Chinese. He explained my currency's worth and gave me specific information that I could grasp. When I paid for several months at one time, the merchant looked at my name on a roster, and said, "One moment, please. I return." He left the room for several minutes. I worried that he might have information leading to my arrest, so as my heart pounded I gnawed on my index finger. He returned with a brown envelope in hand, which he placed in mine. It was a letter from my mother in Guangzhou. She was glad that Uncle and I had arrived safely on the Golden Mountain, and she trusted that I was helpful to Uncle and she tried not to worry about me. Father thanked me for writing, and added some news from Kowloon for Uncle. My brother wished me best of luck and my sister said she looked forward to seeing me home again soon. Mother said that the local revolutionaries were not faring well against the Manchu, and the entire Middle Kingdom was suffering from the British onslaught of invasions and their continued trading of opium from India for Chinese tea. The Middle Kingdom was losing its reserve of silver, and the increase of opium smoking was crippling the entire nation. "We are all proud of you for venturing out with your Uncle Ān Lì. May our ancestors grant you prosperity and longevity. The only prosperity and longevity left in out homeland is enjoyed by the Empress Dowager and her son, the very young Emperor Tung Chih." I was glad that my first letter had arrived in China, but I had to marvel how nearly a full year had passed since I mailed the letter, and only now did I receive a response.

I left the office with instructions to report the following day at noon with a gathering of miners at the North Pier, where I would be assigned a new work order from a small man named Samuel Thurston.

Outside the doorway of the merchant's office, a withered stick of an old man sat on a milk stool with a banjo on his knee. I remember his amusing little battered straw hat, and a black patch covering one eye. A diagonal cord crossed his forehead and cheek like half of the letter X and secured the patch to a blind eye. He sang a capstan shanty about Sacramento, a seaman's song that told the tale of the ship's journey around Cape Horn toward the El Dorado of the Sacramento River. He sang of "them Dago gals he so adored, all drank vino and 'ax for more, and them Spanish gals ain't got no combs, they comb their locks with tunny-fish bones." The lively song ended with the mention of "ninety days to Frisco Bay, ninety days is damn good pay." I could only make out a word or two here and there and missed the drift of the story, but the banjo and cranky voice had a bounce that made people want to kick up their heels. Next to his tapping toe was a tin mug into which listeners who stepped forward dropped a few coins with a clink, clink.

I stood by listening to several tunes. I had yet to correlate the gruff voice, melody, and the banjo pickings to a feeling of convivial elation, although I took in the crowd's lively reaction. My stance revealed nothing. Likewise, my face was without expression. I could have easily been in a classroom, witnessing the dissection of a cadaver. I would have felt ridiculous feigning amusement. Nonetheless, I dug out a handful of *pfennings* to add to his brimming cup. Feeling less a foreigner for hearing my stolen coins tinkle with the others, I continued down the walkway in search of a room to rent for the night.

A disheveled newspaper bristled in the sea breeze, and scurried across the walkway planks like a chased mouse. I captured it before it blew into the muck and clutter of the street. Any help with learning English was bound to improve my relations and standing in the mining camps, so I tucked the newspaper into my burlap sack. At a glance, I noticed that the advertisements included intricate illustrations of undergarments, elixirs, carriages, kerosene lamps, and gadget that I had never laid eyes on before. A picture is said to be worth a thousand words, and I looked forward to learning a thousand words in English.

My image reflected in the gleam of the shop window. I looked like a child. The English speaking prospectors had referred to me repeatedly as "Shrimp." I had wondered if I smelled like a fisherman. Did my backbone coil into the shape of a swirl? Perhaps they were insinuating that I had a thin shell. I stood outside the window, trying to focus my attention on the display. Shiny lanterns and new candles, candlestick holders with finger-hole handles, portable assayers' kits, magnifying glasses, mortars and pestles, nickel-plated letter openers, decks of cards with scenes of miners' camps, miners' picks, Argonaut and bowie knives, a derringer, a Wesson percussion piston, and a short-barrel Colt handgun with ivory grips – all were arranged on a drapery of deep blue velvet to enhance the artistic allure of the display. I pondered, instead, my boyish physique, a short and harmless creature, nonetheless determined and bold in facial features. The passersby drifted behind me, a crisscrossing of multiple paths, big fish gracefully dodging each other. At that moment it hit me! Among the big fish, I was a miniature, a minnow or a shrimp. Having heard this nickname over twenty times, I finally grasped the insinuation there on the street.

"Only dreaming, or looking to buy?" a deep voice came from my left. The man's derby hat and head reflected above the red letters FT painted upon the display glass. The words spelled out FINELY CRAFTED MINER'S SUPPLIES. My forehead was visible beneath the letters E and R of the word MINER'S. The gentleman wore a monocle and a white silk scarf tucked into his starched vest. His long dark coat narrowed at the waist and flared outward to the knees. I wondered if he might be the shop owner or a dignitary of some sort. "My name is Gifford. Do you speak English?" (His manner was quite subdued and refined compared to the miners and gamblers I tended to encounter.)

"No, oh...yes, little bit. I name Yaozu." I pointed to myself to compensate for my broken English.

He reached for my right hand. I had seen this gesture among more genteel and well-bred gentlemen. Occasionally two miners would grasp hands, but crude exchanges were likely to follow. Mr. Gifford's hand bounced quickly up and down with my small paw in his large palm. His smile widened his perfectly trimmed mustache and his teeth were unusually shiny and white. "*Yow Soo,* pleased to meet you."

I smiled timidly and looked at him with wonder and surprise. His sincerity seemed disarming.

Mister Gifford showed an interest in Chinese calligraphy and details concerning my homeland's customs, my parents' livelihood, and the Chinese people's attitudes concerning the Empress, the Opium Wars, and the Chinese reaction to Great Britain's invasions and trade stronghold on China. I offered him my limited perspectives based on my parents' and relatives' reactions. My schooling had offered me a wealth of knowledge concerning calligraphy and our customs and status within our village's social hierarchy.

I spoke with vagueness about the Opium Wars and Great Britain's invasion of the Forbidden City. Realizing that I sat on a very sharp edged fence between two cultures, I avoided revealing any hatred of the British or of Queen Victoria and the English in general. My English was so obviously lacking in vocabulary and structure that I felt assured that I had safely sidestepped the political issues that he inquired about.

Mister Gifford's family name was Gifford, of course, and his personal name was Geoffrey. I was astounded that English names listed their family name last. Chinese names always commence with the family name, a tribute to our respect for our ancestors and a clear indication that family operated as a unit. The individual was merely a branch on the tree, easily broken off and relying entirely on the whole tree for sustenance and support.

Mr. Gifford invited me to join him that evening to attend the performance of a play at the American Theater. The play was a benefit for the San Francisco Fireman's Fund on June18, 1853, which was that evening. The play to be presented was *Yelva* - whether the name was a woman or a country, I didn't know and I failed to ask, but the performance was well attended, being that fire was a reoccurring threat in San Francisco.

Mr. Gifford met me at the very spot we met, in front of the Finely Crafted Miner's Supplies. He wore a shiny black top hat and carried a walking stick with a golden falcon handle. He wore a Prince Albert coat, an elaborately brocaded waistcoat, and narrow-legged trousers over boots that shone like obsidian. I felt self-conscious in my coarse jacket and my dull, heavy boots, but Mr. Gifford assured me that the spectators would be diverse. The miners had infused the population of San Francisco, had in fact created the population, and public events drew diverse crowds spanning from aristocratic crème de la crème on down to tramps, scoundrels, and swindlers. I would fit in there somewhere, and I knew that my stay in California had seen me living out various categories.

The fund raising event did indeed draw an interesting crowd. Crowding Montgomery Street outside the theater were the usual ruffians and gamblers I had grown accustomed to in the mining camps, along with the Hispanic-Californians, and the more upstanding and cultured foreigners from countries I had yet to locate on a map; the Spanish and South Americans, Czechs and Turks, Russians, Germans, Irish and Brits, and numerous Chinese dressed in their silk robes and tasseled silk hats. I felt proud to see my own countrymen looking so respectable.

Mr. Gifford informed me that the variety of nationalities had introduced a diversity of amusements, sport, and recreation to the fiber of San Francisco. There were bull fights, cock fights, dog fights, fencing, racing, gambling, and boxing, along with charity balls, extravaganzas, parades, social picnics, fiestas, operas, and the theatre. Opera stars and stage personalities were the darlings of the public eye, and Lola Montez, starring in *Yelva*, the featured performance of the night, was a recently arrived actress from the east coast and Europe.

Much of his knowledgeable chatter flew past my ears like bees in pursuit of cherry blossoms. Pretending to understand gave me a minor headache and trying to keep up with his galloping pace made my temples throb. Fortunately, that crisp cool evening, a Cantonese couple was stationed ahead of us in the line. In gold rush days, women in general were few and far between, but a Chinese woman was a rare, jade jewel among the flocks of male gold seekers. During Mr. Gifford's dialogue, the couple turned their heads, nodding in agreement with his

27

observations. The Cantonese gentleman noticed my bewildered expression and generously offered a condensed translation.

The play was highly entertaining and colorful, but I dare say I was unable to follow the story and failed to react with appropriate cheering, laughter, and the frequent mannerism of slapping flat palms at the pace of a woodpecker's rapping, directly in front of one's face. I easily appreciated the character portrayed by Madame Montez, as she portrayed a mute girl in pantomime. Her character was without language entirely, leaving my overworked brain a welcome break from my failed attempts at deciphering the enigmatic English language of the other performers.

And to sugarcoat my appreciation, she reappeared between acts in a tarantula costume and proceeded to perform her scandalous "Spider Dance." Loud hoots and piercing coyote howls emanated from the audience along with a variety of earsplitting whistles. The spider lady wore layers of tinted chiffon that insinuated a spider web. As she twirled and wrestled with the webbing, the dance mounted to a frenzy of shedding spiders and stomping them to death. Then, in spider fashion, she spread her arms and legs and pounced left and right, crossing the stage grotesquely. It seemed the women found it offensive, while the men found it erotic. Either way, I must say, I found it thoroughly captivating. The performance marked a turning point in my California enterprise, and a lasting impression.

Mr. Gifford, I was soon to discover, proved to be more than interested in my cultural background. Among a cornucopia of cultures and clashing behaviors, I took no personal offense to his fascination for my youth and innocence. His social standing and wealth afforded him the luxury of such freedom, but I was well aware that due to my standing as a "guest," or visitor, I was deprived many liberties. My welfare upon the Golden Mountain was dependent on a careful footing on delicate eggshells. I was not alone in this precarious state.

The moon was a partially eroded sand dollar upon a clean and sparkling black sea. I rented a room on the second floor of the New Helvetia Hotel on Sutter Street. The rooms facing Sutter Street had a narrow verandah. These rooms rented at a higher rate and were occupied, of course. The boarders could be seen smoking cigars, or leaning on the rail of the verandah as they held tiny saucers of spicy cake drizzled with molasses. Forks bobbed from saucer to mouth as the guests peered down upon the animated passersby. A cigar smoker dragged his chair onto the balcony and propped his feet upon the rails. He practiced blowing smoke rings directly above himself.

The street crowd sauntered and lollygagged, some daring to show off lustrous pearls and gleaming jangles. San Francisco may have been a magnet for extraordinary and outrageous women, but a woman rarely walked alone at night. Portly men wearing top hats and eyepieces sported walking canes and ostentatiously checked their flip-open time pieces before tucking them handily into miniature watch pockets upon their vest. Other less fortunate men wore their gnarled hats and breeches with knee patches, though many had scrubbed their grimy faces and hands, hoping that the fresh scent of soap might add appeal to the lady folk. It was a rare occasion for the common laborer to scrape out the black dirt rings from beneath his fingernails.

My window shutters opened upon an alley barely the width of a man's shoulders, cleaving the hotel and a honky-tonk next door. Shortly after dusk, when I thrust the shutters wide open, the syncopated clatter of a lively upright piano and the chatter and cheering of gamblers and drunks tumbled into my room. This odd, unfamiliar uproar wrapped me with a tingling sensation of mirth. San Francisco's air was crisp and charged with its alluring and lurid ether.

A misty sea breeze seeped into my tiny room. My spirit was Chinese tea brewing in bubbly California water. Carefully, as if initiating a ritual, I lit the two oil lamps on the nightstands at the sides of the wide glorious bed. The desk clerk had offered, for additional fee, the use of the downstairs washroom. An attendant (who would expect a tip – the desk clerk warned me) would pump basins of water to be heated over a wood-burning stove. The large pans of steaming water were then poured into a large zinc washtub. Given a long-handled scrub brush, a stack of scrim (most likely laundered dishcloths), and a black brick of soap, I gladly surrendered the added cost. A crooked beam of hand-worn wood served to latch the door of the washroom from the inside. The room was tight, the size of a closet, but I didn't feel cheated.

After several minutes of dipping toes and fingers, I dared to submerge my entire foot in the near scalding water. By the time I had both feet on the washtub's bottom, the steam gently warmed my knees and thighs. I bent forward, slowly sliding my fingers, hands, wrists, and arms up to my forearms into the stove heated water. I carefully lowered my rump onto the steaming surface. Fortunately, my extremities had been more sensitive to the change of temperature than my torso.

I scrubbed and scoured stubborn black stains from my elbows and knees. My feet were filthy beyond recognition. The blisters had left dried blood in my toenails. By soaping the dishrags and wrapping my feet in them, I hoped to chase away diseases and demons that might infest my poor battered feet. Beads of sweat gathered on my forehead and shoulders, drawing out the tension that I held between my shoulder blades. Droplets of perspiration fell from my nose and rolled into my navel. My mind cleared itself of clutter and concerns until I nearly fell asleep in the tub. The water lost its bite, cooling to lukewarm. I roused myself from my stupor, and rose up reaching for the stack of dishcloths. Slightly lightheaded, I stepped from the tub, and quickly dried. My mud-packed clothes lied wadded on the floor, flopped over my dilapidated hobnail boots. My clothes gave forth a wretched stench, triggering recollections of encounters with lost souls, lunatics, and horrifying brutes who screeched and scolded, growled and babbled nonsense. If only I could have burned my shameful rags that night. Having lacked the foresight, I would have to don them in the morning, before venturing out to purchase new duds. I no longer owned a spare outfit. I caught myself before I nearly tossed the whole pile into the bath water. If I were to hang out these pitiful clothes to dry, it would most likely take the better part of tomorrow. My appointment at the North Pier was at noon. I wrapped one large scrim around myself, and tied two others at their corners to form a laundry bag. I bounded up the staircase, two and three steps at a time, clutching my hobo bag.

The halos of the oil lamps welcomed me like the warmth of a campfire. A torrent of exuberant piano music spilled through the window. Savage yelling and blood-thirsty bellowing of intoxicated men trampled upon the serenity of my solitude. I yanked the shutters closed tight, and locked the miniature latch. Parting the opening of my burlap bag, I located the discarded newspaper. My body-wrap scrim was damp, so I hung it on the doorknob. I was not in habit of sleeping nude, but freshly washed skin against the laundered sheets and the warm blanket brought to my mind a Chinese silkworm wrapped in his cozy cocoon.

I puzzled at the mysterious and unaesthetic shaped words on the pages of the newspaper. Straight lines, loops, and repetitious angles and sharp diagonals like knives – the awkward calligraphy of this demanding language, English. Odd little cross lines and occasional pinpoints of ink hung here and there like pellets, ears, hats and stick figure shoes. Many of the straight lines had tiny budding twigs, as if to signify the existence of a floor and ceiling, but some of the loops had odd little sprouting bumps, like goiters. I would require an instructor to make sense of all of this.

The newspaper illustrations were, however, charming, imaginative and amusing. Two cats sat side by side, one wearing an ominous grin, his eyes averted toward the partner. The other cat wore spectacles, which magnified his eyes to a comical size. The pair made a clownish duo.

Another illustration of an anxiety-ridden gentleman caught my eye. The poor gent wore a tie and jacket, his mouth and eyes sagged, while three leafless trees grew from his head like a thorny headdress. A closer look revealed that the three spreading trees were actually tiny demonic figures; dancing savages with horns and pointed tails, each brandishing sledgehammers. I could only guess that the suffering businessman had a curse place upon him, or that he was imagining his worst nightmare.

I awoke to the clanging of a cowbell outside my room window, sat up groggily, crossed the room, my bare feet chilled at the touch of cool varnished wood floor, and retrieved the scrim hanging over the doorknob. Wrapping the long ecru clothe, still slightly damp, around my torso, I reopened the shutters, letting in fresh morning air. The freshly painted wooden wall of the saloon served as my meager view from across the alley. A small oval mirror on the wall near the unmemorable door offered a warped reflection of my puffy morning mug gazing back at me. My straight black hair jutted out above my left ear like a raven's tail stuck to the side of my head.

Gingerly removing the framed mirror from the wall, I turned toward the large porcelain bowl that stood upon a Victorian walnut corner-whatnot. I tilted the swallow beak jug of clean silvery water, filling the porcelain bowl. Placing the mirror at my feet enabled me to watch my elongated reflection as I pulled handfuls of water from the bowl to flatten my disheveled hair. Water splattered upon the floor, the mirror, and my damaged feet. I had no shortage of bathing towels for cleaning up.

I couldn't bear to pull my filthy socks over my freshly cleaned feet, so I wrapped my sensitive toes in dishtowels before dressing in my rancid outfit. The sickening aroma had barely thinned from one night of airing. Except for placing the folded newspaper back into the gunnysack, I had not one thing to pack.

I checked out and settled my tab, leaving the suggested tip for the washroom attendant. The morning desk clerk slid the tip coins into a brown envelope. I would have enquired about a clothing shop, but this clerk was not the same one as the evening desk clerk, who had spoken to me in Chinese. Fortunately, shops displayed their goods behind sparkling widows, painted with cleverly designed titles that conveyed no meaning to my Chinese brain. I was deterred from entering two dry goods markets. First a clerk and then an owner would not allow me to enter with my burlap bag and my filthy, reeking outfit. I was unable to hold this against them.

Perhaps some Cantonese ancestors had found their way to the Golden Mountain, after all. Were they watching over me?

After a third refusal to be allowed entrance, it occurred to me that standard pioneer clothing, or ever better quality European style finery, would only re-enforce my identity; the thief from Mariposa. I felt at ease in San Francisco, but that very day I would be reassigned a new work location. No telling how close I would be sent to the mining camp where I had become a criminal. After purchasing light cotton Chinese clothes, I arranged for a quick sponge bath, purchased brand new long johns, a wool-lined jacket, new boots, gloves, a warm hat, and a thick, hand-woven blanket. After the second bath, dressed in my new gray Chinese smock and pants, I was able to sit down among fellow Chinamen to eat chrysanthemum soup with slivers of chicken meat and large white flowers, along with a fresh pot of green tea. I purchased a small linen bag with a draw string in which I stashed a supply of sesame seed cookies and some dried squid. I devoured three fried fruit puffs as I stood outside watching the hustle and bustle of the crowded street. The fruit puffs reminded me of my mother's cooking, with their blend of ground dates, apricots, orange peel, raisins, coconut, sesame seeds and almond butter all dipped in beaten egg white.

I was able, outside of the tiny restaurant, to make brief use of a wooden bench. I pulled out my ink and ink stone. The owner's wife allowed me to bring a teacup of water outside, for wetting the ink. In my blank journal book, upon the first clean page I painted a small horizontal stroke, followed by a longer vertical stroke that intersected the first, making a cross. It resembled the Christian cross I had seen as grave markers and pendants worn on necklaces. The next stroke, painted to the right of the first, began similarly, with a horizontal direction, but turned downward, ending with a small tail-like upward twist. This third stroke resembled the open mouth of a serpent, baring only a lower fang. The upper jaw of the serpent was crossed by another long vertical line that curved toward the base of the first cross. The two symbols looked like one man beside his crippled companion, leaning on a cane. Two small dashes were added aside the man with the cane.

The crippled man is actually a symbol of strength, a man with his arm on his hip. The two dashes are shorthand versions of two men beneath him, stacked like a pyramid. The first cross is the symbol for the number ten. This Chinese character is

33

called *Xie*, which means together, or co-operate. The effort of ten persons, working in unison toward the same goal, creates a wholehearted cooperation. This symbol, *Xie,* combined with other symbols, creates such words as agreement, unify, consult, coordinate, harmonize, agree, and assist.

I felt that *Xie* had recently abandoned my life. Except for the small farm boy who allowed me to sleep in his father's barn, I had felt the absence of agreement, harmony, and unity. Words carry within them a power. Some words poison us and other words strengthen us. This word, *Xie*, together, co-operate, became the title of my new journal. The owner's wife stepped outside to retrieve her teacup. She glanced at my open journal, nodded with a singular dip of her face, adding a small upturned smile of approval. Before she turned away, she gently patted my shoulder. I felt like a dehydrated desert traveler, drinking up this small gesture like a small sip of cool water.

I repacked my calligraphy utensils. After my purchases and preparations, there remained more than an hour to appear at the North Pier. My gunnysack bulged with the weight of calligraphy supplies, the Queen's stolen valuables, new long johns, wool socks, and a new blanket. My cash supply was enduring longer than I had expected. I proceeded to improve upon my traveling by purchasing two decent sized suitcases with brass latches and leather handles.

As I paid for these new travel cases, I noticed, within a glass case, a striking zigzag pattern etched upon a shoulder bag. (I learned later that the bag was handmade of deerskin by a Maidu, a native of the Golden Mountain. Many of the prospectors and new arrivals referred to these people as Injuns, or Indians.) I told myself that enough was enough. My accumulated belongings were weighing me down. On second thought, though, I visualized a quick paced thief snatching my suitcases, ending up with the coin purse and the extravagant jewelry. I bought the deer skin bag for hiding the valuables underneath my wool-lined-jacket. My jacket pockets were already stuffed with snacks.

As I approached the North Pier that day, I looked not only clean, but successful. I had hoped to be filled with confidence, but my background and youth deprived me of this luxury. With apprehension, I felt sure that my ancestors knew of my erratic behavior. I half expected to be trampled by a horse and carriage, or shot dead by a drunk miner.

The sun sailed high in a cloudless sky. A sea breeze curled the shining bay into foaming seahorses. Among the sailors, fishermen, and common merchants, several aristocratic and impeccably dressed men and women gathered along the wharf that led to the North Pier. I wondered if by chance the better dressed of the crowd had arrived at that moment and destination by way of deceit and crimes against others. To the grimy looking or desperate souls, I must have looked like an upstanding citizen. But no, I decided. Deceit and honesty were not detectable by the poverty or wealth of the clothing. All these traits and histories were mixed higgledy-piggledy like a colossal caldron of stew. We were good, bad, fashionable, common, and destitute, side by side and rubbing up against each other. We were, each and every one of us, being changed by the nature of where we were and who we came in contact with.

BARGE TO SACRAMENTO

The supervisor of the North Pier, Samuel Thurston, was a tall gruff man with a Havana cigar and a wide brimmed felt hat. Tangle muttonchops splayed from his enraged face, giving him the appearance of a bulldog. After checking my name from pages on a clipboard, he yelled out, "Ching-Ching," pointing his fuming Havana in the direction of an assemblage of Chinamen. Of these Cantonese men, most were new arrivals. Only a handful, including me, could claim to be experienced miners. The leader of the Cantonese group was *Cheng Shongshi,* a robust, no nonsense, squashed-faced, short character with kind eyes and a worn doorknob of a nose. English speaking co-workers referred to him simply as Ching-Ching.

Our group was herded aboard a drab, weather beaten freight barge. We were treated like oxen, prodded with long splintered poles. The crew of the barge barked and growled their orders. It was a four man crew, gruff and grungy each of them. The two Irishmen were bulky, the mustached Italian was tall and thin, and the stone-faced Russian had the suspicious glare of a hot-tempered murderer. The cargo beneath us was as European as the crew; barrels of barley and oats alongside wooden boxes packed with brightly labeled bottles of gin, scotch, whiskey, and vodka.

The barge left the northern piers of San Francisco, facing the bay, and slightly within the official Golden Gate, where San Francisco and Tiburon (Spanish for shark) nearly closed in on the bay. These two fingers of land each pointed to the other, protecting the port docks from the wilder waves of the Pacific Ocean. The bay was always less likely to be as windy as the western oceanfront coast. The ocean would have been a short rowboat trip from where we launched, but we traveled east, away from the ocean into a series of bays connected to each other by wide passageways.

Fishermen on small tugboats or solo in canoes, cast their nets and lines. Only a few bothered to tip their hats or wave their arms. As we headed north into a wide open bay, an abundance of Chinese shrimping vessels huddled together along the west shore of San Pablo Bay. The sight of the brown rectangular sails, the large, cone-shaped shrimp nets, and the mushroom silhouettes of Chinamen in wide-brimmed reed hats – all these sights brought back visions of Canton and Kowloon and the ubiquitous fishermen of my homeland. Cheng Shongshi pointed out China Camp, the sprawling ramshackle coastline of shrimp and seafood merchants from Rat Rock Island to Jake's Island and the shoreline hump of Turtle Back Hill.

Out upon the wide San Pablo Bay, large paddle-wheelers glided by, jammed with passengers dressed in their finery. The giant water wheels churned the water steadily, a gentle motion that appeared effortless. The newest of the paddlewheelers were modern steamers with coal burning ovens, but the older steamers burned cottonwood, river oak, and bull pine, which soon became unavailable when the fast-growing railroads bought up most of the favored pine.

Most of the coal came from Mount Diablo and was unloaded at Black Diamond, a small town we passed before reaching the Sacramento Delta. A fellow Cantonese miner named Wing Li informed a small group of us about the steamers, the fuels, and delta transport in general. He had recently worked on a coal barge, but had been replaced by the captain's son, who had journeyed by "prairie schooner" from Oklahoma. Wing Li explained that a prairie schooner was a miner's term (no doubt coined by a sailor) that meant covered wagon.

The sluggish water transport took the better part of the day. The Cantonese passengers were not offered food, drink, or any semblance of passenger accommodations. Many of us attempted to sleep as the sun beat relentlessly down upon us. Our shirts stuck to our backs, soaked in sweat. I rolled my new jacket into the shape of a headrest. The dry barren riverbank scrolled past, interrupted occasionally by a cluster of oak saplings or a poorly assembled fence. Lanky, drooping black cows grazed on the dead grass and farm women beat wet laundry with wooden paddles.

The blinding light of day subsided as evening crept upon us. The river put on its ribbons of silver and vermillion. A cooling marine layer caught up with us, deepening the colors of the arid landscape. The fragrance of apple wood smoke triggered recollections of my mother – her long black braid, wafts of loosened hair around her head, and that work-worn look on her face as she stir-fried *bok choy* with a long wooden spatula. White froth sputtered from her massive pot of rice. In my mind I heard the sound that frequently woke me from my morning slumber, (the sound also announced her presence in the kitchen). It was a gentle dawn sound of uncooked rice pouring into her clay pot.

I looked about the deck at the miners being transported. Every crowd had its talkative, outgoing types. As usual, I was reserved – the onlooker. Even with my advantage of acquired expertise on the subject of mining on the Golden Mountain, I remained self-conscious and awkward among my own kind aboard the freight barge. It was true that these were fellow Chinamen, but I felt transparent and fraudulent. My outfit was proof that I was becoming Americanized. I felt convinced that among these down-to-earth Cantonese, one or two of them would be quick to smell a rat amongst them.

Being surrounded by my own countrymen brought to light within my self the conflict that I carried. My logic begged to pardon my criminal action as a drastic measure to assure my survival. My behavior had, in fact, carried me to this very day, alive and well upon this river barge. The familiar Chinese faces surrounded me. Each face seemed to hold a voice from my previous life back home in my family's village. My feeble logic was losing battle against my ancestors. I felt outcast and ashamed to face my own people. I wore my well practiced expressionless face and kept to myself. Separating my self from the others failed to avert the dogs from attacking. Comments sprang up about my clothes. "Who buy all this fancy thing for you, boy?" "You sure you Chinese?" "Why you on boat to mountain if you already find gold?" These questions drew an audience along with chuckles and laughter. My failure to respond only enlivened the heckling and laughter.

An old hunched gentleman with sparse gray beard and deep-lined wrinkles leaned close to my ear and said, "Smart Chinaman," in a soft raspy voice. A swollen mole on the side of his nose stood out like a blueberry. He grinned, exposing opium stained crooked teeth, and he looked me directly in the eye. His gaze was friendly and warm with a lighthearted sparkle. Without saying so, he seemed to know my secret, and yet I felt that he accepted me with generosity and forgiveness. He was merely one among the whole clan of countrymen, but his elderly bright eyes lifted my mood in some unexplainable manner. Did he perhaps shine a lantern into my own spirit, inviting me to join him in his generosity and forgiveness of myself? I felt somewhat relieved of my burden of guilt. I began, also, to feel a little less self-conscious.

I drifted into memories of the Dragon Boat Festival back home in Guangzhou. I envisioned the colors of the five elements – red, yellow, azure, white, and black. The summer weather would be hot and humid. The young rice plants would have already been transplanted and the torrential summer rains would be soon to arrive. Upon the Pearl River the river parades would be drifting by, along with the dragon boat races. We called this day the "double fifth" because it was the fifth day of the fifth moon. There would be *zongzi,* rice offerings to Qu Yuan, China's earliest known poet. Originally Qu Yuan was a minister to a king. Qu Yuan tried to advise the king to keep peace with neighboring states, but his advice was rejected. When Qu Yuan later learned that the capital city had been destroyed in war, he wrote his famous elegy, the *Li sao,* (Lament on Encountering Sorrow). He threw himself into the Milo River and drowned. The local people jumped into their boats, seeking to find him. They threw rice into the water to keep the fish from eating his body. This day marked the end of the yang force, the growth and ripening. The beginning of the yin force thus commenced with a decline and decay of nature as autumn approached, ushering in the sparseness of winter.

I missed my home in China. I felt a longing to go home. I pictured the long slender dragon boats like undulating water snakes in the river. Long colorful flags would trail in the breeze and the twenty-foot-long oars would rise and fall like centipede legs. Smaller boats might have forty rowers, while the longer boats held up to eighty rowers. A gong tied to the mast was used to set tempo for the rowers. A flute musician and firecrackers were kept onboard to encourage the rowers with additional excitement. Clans from various regions would compete against each other, and the competition became fierce. Different strategies were employed for blocking an opponent's boat or tricking the enemy. Oars were broken and occasionally a boat would capsize.

I pictured in my mind the various types of *zongzi*. Originally *zongzi* was prepared by filling bamboo tubes with sticky rice. It is said that Qu Yuan ordered that the rice-filled bamboo tubes be enclosed in lily leaves and tied with multi-colored strings. This wrapping prevented the dragon from stealing them. There are many kinds of *zongzi*. The knotting and manner of winding of the string indicated the ingredients inside – gelatin pudding, yam, fruits, melon seeds, walnuts, pickled egg, or dates. The Guangdong *zongzi* that I pictured had either a sweet bean filling, walnuts, dates, or a salty filling of mushroom, ham, egg, chestnuts, duck, chicken, or salted meat.

Missing out on such a festive day gave my arrival to Sacramento a sad footing.

舛

OPPOSITION

SACRAMENTO

Swiss-American pioneer, John Sutter, acquired a land grant from Mexico in 1839, and established the colony of New Helvetia. A successful trading post, New Helvetia beheld the completion of Fort Sutter in 1844. Nearby, at Sutter's Mill, gold was discovered in 1848. News spread round the world, and the onrush of wealth seekers brought about the founding of Sacramento, situated where the Sacramento and American Rivers converge. Between 1849 and 1853 the rapidly growing settlement suffered three ravaging floods. In 1852 a large section of the town was consumed by fire.

Cheng Zhongshi escorted our entourage of miners to our temporary barracks. Sacramento lacked the opulent and theatrical European flair that was molding the reputation of San Francisco. Nevertheless, Sacramento was located near the famed discovery of gold at Sutter's Mill, and served as a fork in the journeys to the northern mining camps and the southern settlements of the Mother Lode that spread along the west slopes of the Sierra Nevada range.

The population of Sacramento was diverse, and the hardships of disasters along with the overflow of unlucky gold seekers had divided the various sectors of cultures into suspicious and ill-at-ease segregation. It was only natural for communities to develop, based on the similar customs, foods, and the easy comradeship of the same language. The earlier idealism of anxious arrivals was accompanied with open-mindedness, respect, and a sense of marvel at the various guises, mannerisms, differences in rituals and celebrations, and unheard of dietary practices of the barrage of newly arrived cultures. As disillusionment clutched at the hearts of many suffering miners, a new sentiment was closing people's hearts. This stubborn

41

selfishness, as a self protecting armor, comprised itself of hatred and resentment. What had started out as a lighthearted celebration of diversity and compassion for all was turning it heels to racism and intolerance. People's ability to trust others blew away like hats in a flurry.

We walked as a group, led by Cheng through the dusty streets to our barracks. This was not my first time in Sacramento, but I felt overcome to see the reactions of shop owners, street salesmen, passengers in horse drawn calashes, bankers, miners and gamblers hanging on to the street rails of taverns. I knew that these people had seen an abundance of Chinamen, time and time again. Many of the shirts on their backs were laundered by local Chinamen.

We passed a wide open lot of shaggy grass and old oak tress. A gathering of men stood near a solitary tree. They were cheering and smoking cigars as two horsemen stood at opposite ends of a stretch of dry dirt. One of the horsemen galloped wildly toward the tree, where a goose had been hung upside down with a rope tied around its feet. The horsemen were taking turns galloping past the squealing goose, attempting to twist its head off. "Cruel game call *gander-pulling,*' explained Cheng Zhongshi. "Whoever pull off head, win hat full of coin. Two new rider take turn – new duck or goose hang upside down. Hat pass again." In China, we eat duck and goose and many animals, but I never saw a heartless game like this. I turned my head away, but the tortuous squealing filled the thick air of the dirty town.

The atmosphere over Sacramento hung heavy with a putrid dust. The whole town was charged with discontent. I saw in the faces of these local citizens a hardened anguish that had turned to a sour contempt. They looked at our newly arrived ensemble as if diseased cattle were parading their streets, threatening them with pestilence. My stomach hardened, constraining the beating of my heart and stifling the passage of oxygen to my lungs. Dismal neighborhoods of charred walls and boarded up windows offered foreboding of ghost towns to come. Mold and wood rot left houses and buildings lopsided and unstable. Nauseating odors of decaying rubbish and decomposing animals permeated the rancid atmosphere, and many of our group covered their noses and mouths with a handkerchief or buttoned their shirt collars, pulled up over their nostrils. In the recent passing of a few years, the muddy delta had behaved like an outraged monster greedily devouring the trampling newcomers' feeble attempts at homesteading.

If only Samuel Thurston had dispatched us directly to our mining camp, we could have bypassed Sacramento altogether. We had been instructed to wait here as another agent made his way down lists of crews, each to be directed to their separate locales. The possibility, though slim, still remained that I would be dispatched for a second time to Mariposa. I would have to sabotage my trip, if it came to that.

Within the walls of the barracks, my company of Cantonese miners loosened up. We were treated to a hearty meal of steamed squid and scallops over fluffy white rice with *bok choy* and seaweed soup. Laughter filtered into the conversations. After the meal, several of the newcomers approached me, this time without teasing me about my new clothes. After our dreadful walk through town, my status had improved. I was seen as an experienced survivor of this harsh new environment. Rookies now looked to me for insight and tips about negotiating with these white devils. I had survived nearly a year of the Golden Mountain, but I felt lacking in insight, and avoided giving advice. Negotiating with the white devils was not a skill I had acquired, so I directed our conversations to the task of mining and the tools of the trade.

I had been involuntarily separated from my Uncle Ān Lè Cheng for over a year. During that time I heard from coworkers that he had taken up residence in Sacramento. I asked my supervisor if he knew my uncle, but he had no recollection of the name. I inquired at the post office, and they were able to locate his name from several deliveries over previous months to 484 Adeline Avenue. Having a day or two of downtime while waiting for news of my assigned mining camp, I obtained directions to the address, and proceeded by foot. The going was rough. Patches of dried mud created illusive passageways. The dry mud crumbled and sank beneath the weight of a foot, and before that outing, I had sunk more than once into the thick ooze halfway up my shins. Large stones that would have offered secure footing in a creek sank as easily and deeply with the weight of a small man. I learned to rearrange planks that were strewn haphazardly about town, or I carried long planks under my arms for impassable crossings. This made my mile-and-a-half walk rather tedious, but I finally came upon Adeline Avenue. Some of the oak and pepper trees of Sacramento were gargantuan and I could envision a more inviting, romantic appeal to the neighborhood in less devastating times.

484 Adeline was a two story wooden house, with two chipped white spindle chairs on a large porch beneath a low, overhanging roof. Beside the double doors, a rope with a rounded knot handle hung from a bell above the door. I rang the bell, not too boldly, but it clanged four times quite loudly, irregardless of my slight pull. I heard a loud clomp, clomp, clomping of hard soled shoes on wooden floor, and the oblong doorknob turned slightly before the door opened inward. A young woman with stout features and pink skin, peppered with red freckles, stood gazing sternly at me. Her eyes were a pale shade of blue that looked like shattered ice. Her defiant anticipation of my announcement unnerved me.

Finally, she broke the stone silence, "Young lad, kindly state your business!" I must admit that I was the intruder, but her tone seemed to indicate annoyance.

"Madame, very sorry. I finding Uncle. Name of Yaozu Cheng."

"Who, may I ask, is calling?" she tipped her nose down as her startling blue eyes continued to survey me. I noticed that her golden orange hair had been braided and coiled upon her head like a rope on the deck of a ship.

I pointed to myself. "Name...Yaozu Cheng."

She crinkled her forehead between her eyebrows with a puzzled expression. I had grown accustomed to this reaction to my name.

I pointed to myself again, "Yaozu."

She tipped her head briefly to the side, shrugging her shoulder. "One moment, please," She nearly smiled before gently closing the door. I felt foolish standing there on the porch staring at the door, as I had seen the pet dogs of these fair skinned people do. The animals would stare at the door with their tails wagging, as they whined impatiently. After a short interval an older woman appeared in a long straight black dress. She wore a white apron over her dress and quickly wiped her hands with a washcloth that she then folded and tucked into her large apron pocket.

"Yaozu?" she asked.

I nodded, "I find Uncle."

"Please step inside, Master Yaozu."

"So sorry," I said pointing to my feet, "Very mud feet."

She looked at the thick, caked mud upon my pants and boots.

"Dear me, I should have guessed. Please be seated on one of our porch chairs," she said, pointing to the white chairs.

"Not necessary, thank you, Madame."

"Nonsense, I insist, she said. "Mary Louise, where are your manner? Please offer the young lad some refreshment." The freckled girl's face appeared over the older woman's shoulder briefly, and then disappeared.

None of these words made any sense to me so I remained standing at the doorway. "I have something for you, Master Yaozu," said the woman in the apron as she left me standing there. A moment later, the freckled girl with a braided rope of hair returned with a small glass of sugary lemon drink. I drank it graciously, and Mary Louise led me to sit upon the padded chair.

The woman in the apron returned with a booklet in her hands. She stepped out onto the porch and approached the padded spindle chair.

"I'm sorry to say that your uncle, Mister Cheng, is no longer residing here. I have no information as to his whereabouts, but I do have something that belongs to you, I believe."

"She presented the booklet to me. I recognized the green canvas binding of the booklet, and quickly glanced into the pages at my own calligraphy. This was the journal that I had begun writing in China, at the suggestion of my grandfather. The pages included my accounts of my horrifying journey across the Pacific Ocean, my first impressions of San Francisco, and my early experiences in the mining camps. When I was unexpectedly separated from my Uncle in a small river town, I had lost track of the journal.

"Your uncle enjoyed reading this booklet during his short stay with us. I had asked him what he was reading, and he told me it was the story of his nephew Yaozu. It was the only available Chinese literature in his possession as nothing in the household is written in Chinese. He seemed very proud of his nephew, and now it is my pleasure to meet you in person."

I smiled and nodded in recognition, hoping that I had absorbed the correct meaning of her words.

I looked down at the journal and back up in to the woman's kind eyes.

"Thank you, Madame," I said.

"My pleasure, young man. I only regret that I am unable to lead you to your uncle, but I offer my blessing to you in finding him."

As I descended the steps of the porch, I tucked my journal into my shirt for safe hiding and negotiated my trip back to the barracks. As I relocated the beams of wood for avoiding the muddy mess, I thought how embarrassed I felt to think of the woman in the apron reading my personal journal. There was nothing I felt inclined to hide from my uncle – at least not in this journal. But a woman was an entirely different matter. Surely, the woman knew nothing about Chinese. My writing was as

46

much a secret code to her as an English document would be to me.

Little did I know that one day the translation of my journal for a light skinned woman would one day open up a new world of joy for me.

The memories of my life are small shoelace holes. I am able to peer through the tiny openings upon vistas representing pronounced moments of my scattered past. A long leather bootlace might trace the sequence of events that I can no longer string together in proper sequence. Children, so ready to discover new sensations, play a simple numbered game of connect-the-dots, but an old man plays with pinpoints of his memories that fail to be connected properly. This loss of clarity to recall can be a mixed blessing for an old man.

But my story is not about an old man. I was once a fifteen-year-old set loose in a frightening, confusing, enchanting and fascinating new world. I had carefully hidden my journal inside the deerskin bag along with the stolen treasure that I had frequently considered abandoning. The jewelry and feminine accoutrements would surely point a finger of evidence at me. If discovered, I would become another voiceless, defenseless gold seeker, another outsider left swinging from the noose of a lynch rope in this land where everyone seemed to have been an outsider in the recent past. My overactive imagination had conjured the image of Queen Victoria herself ordering my head on a platter.

The Native Americans had been pushed aside and massacred by the Atlantic outsiders, who now claimed to be the only non-outsiders. My spite at this barbarian rule, coupled with my clan's hatred for the British, fueled my foolish persistence in holding onto the incriminating items for the sake of their monetary value. Fear for my own survival accounted for my remaining motivation, but the sight of the glittering articles aroused my fear of being caught. The scales seemed to tip with the direction of the wind.

I considered hiding the deerskin bag under my bunk-bed, but thought better of this in such a public residence. I wrapped the bag around my waist under my shirt and strapped a belt around my chest to secure it to my torso. I wore my thick coat over the shirt to hide bulky lumps that showed through the shirt.

The large room full of beds was empty except for old White Owl, who slept more in the day than the night. I felt unsafe about reading my journal there. I preferred finding a place where nobody would see me. I stepped outside the front door, where several fellow-Chinamen had set up their game of Pai Gow Tiles upon wooden crates. The ivory dominoes created a familiar array of red and white dots. Gambling was a favorite pastime, and there was plenty of time to kill that day.

The sky was overcast, but the windless day was pleasingly cool. Across the wide street a commotion of laughter or an occasional jovial roar heralded a winning hand of Black Jack or Poker from the Blue Bell Saloon. Two aristocratic looking women drifted by, both wearing ribbon-festooned hats. They lifted their oversized skirts so as to not trip on the laced hems. One wore all black, the other dressed in ecru with a lavender hat and shawl. Long trails of their dresses dragged in the dirt behind them like foxtails. A strange screeching sound seemed to come from the Blue Bell Saloon as they passed the doorway. Two drunkards appeared from the darkness of the saloon and stood pointing at the women's hats. Multiple screeches were followed by the appearance of a monkey from beneath the large hat of the lady wearing black. The monkey climbed to her hip bouncing and screaming, pointing a mimicking finger back at the drunkards in the doorway, who slapped their knees and guffawed.

The women ignored the drunken men, but the woman with the monkey turned her head briefly to look at me. I knew in that instant that I had seen her before. A crow perched above in an oak tree let out its harsh "Caw, caw," which seemed to say, "Go, go," and I knew that an ancestor spirit was speaking to me. By the time I crossed the street the two hourglass figures were well ahead of me. I quickly removed my overcoat and unbuckled the belt so as to remove the deerskin bag.

"Ma'am!" I called out. I walked quickly toward the women calling out, "Ma'am, please stop!" Of course, the monkey started up with its screeching and bouncing and finger pointing until the two women turned to face me. "Ma'am, I have thing belong to you." I held out the deerskin

49

pouch with the Maidu zigzag pattern. The two women looked at each other with puzzled expressions and the monkey jumped down and ran up to grab the pouch. I would not have handed over such valuables to a monkey had the creature not been so crafty and quick. A wild animal might have easily dumped the cache there on the street, but this monkey seemed very clever and carried the shoulder bag upright and handed it over to the woman in black. The creature then climbed up her dress in quick tree-climbing fashion until positioned on her shoulder under the enormous hat.

"Sorry," I said, "One thing belong me." I pointed toward the bag for clarification.

The impressively attractive woman handed the deerskin bag back to me. I noticed that she wore long black silk gloves. Spotting my possession, I pulled it out before handing the shoulder pouch back to her. She raised one eyebrow, anticipating an explanation.

"Journal," I explained. She smiled as she opened the deerskin bag.

"Oh, goodness, Sarah, look at this!" she said pulling out a necklace. I had inspected the necklace many times. Cameos of a woman and golden keys were arranged among tear shaped pearls. Her friend pulled out the small burgundy velvet coin purse with the silver tassel. As her friend peered inside the coin purse, the woman in black pulled out the oxblood booklet titled GEMMOLOGIST'S POCKET COMPENDIUM. (My English had progressed since the day I had stolen these – I had learned the word *pocket*.)

"Young man, where did you find my belongings?" She looked at me directly with large brown eyes. Before I could respond her friend had found more.

"Will you look at this charming comb!" and she held out the swordfish comb made of swirled ivory.

"My lost comb!" cried out the woman in black, "You must tell us where you found these."

"I take bag," I confessed. The woman in black handed me the deerskin pouch.

I realized that my English was failing here, so I tried to be more precise.

"I take every thing," I said pointing to the retrieved valuables.

"That's impossible," said the woman in black. "The thief was a common street urchin. I saw him with my own eyes. He was a dirty, filthy animal."

"I dooty, filthy animal," I responded, to which they turned their heads to each other and giggled.

"But you are a charming young man," said her friend in my defense.

I messed my hair quickly and raised my arms in a monster pose, then turned entirely around for her inspection. The monkey started screeching at me, and when I turned full circle, the woman in black looked more closely and her mouth hung slightly open.

"A thief returning the booty? Unheard of," she sounded more amazed than angry.

"Always first time," I replied.

She smiled and reached out her right hand. I knew how to shake hands by then, so I reached for her black, silk gloved hand, and we shook hands.

"Lola, are you crazy?" asked her friend in amazement.

"I never claimed otherwise," said the one in black as she turned defiantly back to me.

"I am the Countess of Landress. With whom is it my pleasure to make this acquaintance?"

I paused for a moment and decided she must be asking my name.

"My name Yaozu Cheng."

And so it came to pass that I would not be beheaded after all.

The remainder of waiting in Sacramento escapes my memory. As a matter of fact, I don't clearly remember the journey up into the northwestern Sierra Nevada Mountains. Sierraville, my new assignment, was a high altitude mining camp. Sierraville was high above and north of Sierra City on the North Yuba River. The views down the slopes of the mountainside were impressive, but daily life was bleak for most of the townspeople. The gold had been panned out and there was barely little dust to be found in the icy cold and frequently frozen-over streams.

By early 1853 the Chinese miners were frequently singled out as one of the least welcome groups of immigrants to the California gold rush. Newly arrived Europeans and those who traveled from the Eastern Republics of the United States had laws written in the English language that favored their own interests. Chinese, especially those who could not speak English, were not allowed to testify in court. A small handful of Chinamen, including myself, were sent back to Sacramento, where I was reassigned to Grass Valley. Fortunately the journey to Grass Valley was shorter and easier. The citizens of Sierraville had exiled me, but unwittingly had initiated my transfer to a much more successful mining town. "Grass-root gold" was discovered in Grass Valley in 1848, and a rich strike in 1850 became the deepest mine in California, the North Star. This mine turned out to be over a mile deep, but nobody was aware of this at the time I arrived in Grass Valley in 1853. Grass Valley was south of Nevada City and lay east of the confluence of the Middle Yuba and South Yuba Rivers.

Ancient ancestors from China must have coerced with ancient ancestors from Europe to improve upon my fortune. I had barely spent two days at my new worksite, when gossip and rumors flourished about the arrival of the notorious dancer, Lola Montez. This was the very woman I had returned stolen belongings to in Sacramento, and I had also seen her famous Spider Dance in San Francisco. It was said that this Parisian courtesan had charmed the King of Bavaria, Ludwig I. She had lived like a queen in Bavaria before moving to New York and then to San Francisco where she appeared on stage as an actress and dancer.

By 1853, my English had much improved, but vocabulary tended to bog me down. I had heard of Paris, but the word Parisian sounded like Persian and the word courtesan sounded like it might be a dressmaker for royalty. I had no idea where Bavaria was, but I had tasted Bavarian cream, a rich custard dessert topped with sweet whipped cream. (My life since teenage years has been an ongoing battle to acquire and retain more English vocabulary. Fortunately, a wise elderly woman in San Francisco pointed out that she had spoken English all her life, and she still continued learning new vocabulary nearly everyday.)

The miners of my work team seemed enthusiastic about attending the arrival of such an illustrious persona as Ms. Montez. I had no feeling of enthusiasm for a large crowd, but I had learned that following the pack of wolves could lead to amusing surprises. I agreed to join them on Tuesday morning. The Grass Valley Chinatown was a small section of narrow alleyways not far from Main Street. The treetops of poplars and cottonwoods waved in the wind that day, and the businesses of Main Street looked tidy, with bright colors of paint. Small open spaces with benches were shaded by catalpas and ailanthus, better known as Chinese Trees of Heaven. The russet-red blooms of the Trees of Heaven joined the welcoming committee for this infamous Lola Montez. The whole settlement of Grass Valley seemed to have crowded Main Street as if waiting for a parade. First on everyone's mind was catching a glimpse of this so-called Queen-of-Bavaria-turned-stage-actress. Passing judgment upon her was second.

A dusty claret Concord stagecoach jostled into town, and we awaited the opening of the side doors, expecting Ms. Montez to step down from the coach dressed like a queen. Perhaps she would have a ruby studded gold crown. I imagined her holding a scepter topped with a bronze phoenix handle embedded with glaring blue diamond eyes. Her violet velvet cape would be carried by her maids in waiting. The crowd would drop to their knees and press their foreheads to the ground. Several minutes passed and the door was not flung open. The driver sat quietly with erect spine. He did not dress appropriately for someone employed by royalty. He wore a bowler and a plain vest. He was so thin he looked like a puppet and his large nose reminded me of a parrot. Nearby spectators were interrogating him, but he merely shrugged his shoulders and shook his head.

A voiced called out, "Messenger!" and an arm from the crowd pointed down the street. Faces turned in the direction of a rising cloud of dust that warned of an approaching rider. I watched the smoky cloud of dust trace its path in our direction, and made out the distant pounding of hooves. A night-black Arabian stallion pulled a small buckboard driven by a man dressed completely in black, wearing a top hat and holding a long handled horse whip. The black buckboard reminded me of a Greek chariot, but in contrast the driver was seated comfortably. The well dressed driver pulled up beside the stagecoach, halted, then stood to step down from the buckboard. It was then that I realized the driver was a woman. She wore tall, black boots and riding pants. Everything including the buckboard and the majestic horse was shimmering ebony-black and the effect was quite theatrical. The woman waved her whip in the air to create a hypnotic and menacing whirring above our heads. After coiling the whip and hanging it over her shoulder, she placed her hands on hips, preparing for an announcement. "My name is Lola Montez, the Countess of Landress." She bowed with a flourish and turned to step back aboard the buckboard.

I knew this was the woman to whom I had returned the stolen accessories in Sacramento. She rolled calmly down Main Street drawn by the grand, muscular stallion, and the Concord stagecoach followed her path. Some of the crowd applauded and several of the men whistle. Some members of the crowd followed behind the stagecoach, making the appearance of a small parade as they marched down Main Street.

MOON GATE
(first entry in my journal)

It is the eighteenth day of the first lunar month. The New Year Celebration is over and once again Father, Uncle, Older Brother and I have set aside a day for worshipping the Star Gods. Father and Uncle had constructed a small alter in the courtyard of our house with offerings of sugar coated rice balls. A picture of one of the Star Gods, Lu Xing, the God of Wealth (depicted riding a deer) was placed on the alter along with a picture of the Rooster, one of the cyclical signs. A sealed envelope held a chart of lucky and unlucky stars. Father made a special prayer to Shou, the star that presided over his birth and lit the red and yellow paper lamps filled with perfumed oil arranged around the alter. I remember the paper lamps burning out quickly. Ching Hah, my older brother, came forward to relight three of the lamps to honor his own star. The flames burned brightly, signifying that Ching Hah would have good luck in the coming year. I followed my brother's example, relighting three colored lamps, but the flames were quickly met by a burst of wind that extinguished the flames. My immediate sense of doom led me to close my eyes, while a second burst of wind cause a commotion of noise from my older brother and Uncle. I opened my eyes to see brightly lit flames within the lamps, reignited from the second burst of wind. Uncle explained to me later that afternoon that a severe hardship can often be the door that opens to the best of luck. I looked to the wall that stood behind the Star God's alter. The top of the wall was curved like a swelling wave on the water. In the middle of the wall beneath the highest arch was a wide circular opening for entering the courtyard. We called this round entrance a Moon Gate. As if guarding the Moon Gate to the left and right, sturdy empress trees stood outside the wall. Across the curve of the dirt path outside the gate, honey locust hugged the path like ferns to a stream bed. I envisioned my approaching new year as passing through a Moon Gate.

Mother and Younger Sister never joined us in the ritual of the Star Festival as women were forbidden to participate. We returned to the small dining space adjoining the kitchen. The humid heat of late spring and summer would arrive much later in the year, at which time Mother and Younger Sister would prefer to boil rice and cook meals upon the stone fireplace positioned outside in the courtyard. The last chilled breaths of winter still made the shadows of the willow trees and walls uninviting. The small wood fire in the kitchen was a comforting source of heat in the early mornings while Mother and Sister prepared the morning rice and egg flower soup.

The evening of the Star Festival was an occasion for a special meal. In more well-to-do years we might have enjoyed turtle soup or shark's fin soup. I remember a few years ago being served sweet and sour chicken liver along with a whole braised grass carp in a rich soy sauce with sherry. Chinese flowering cabbage, snow peas and bamboo shoots were my favorite vegetables, and one of my favorite soups for this time of year was a broth with pigeon, winter melon, and mushrooms. Stir-fried bean curd with mushroom, onions and soy sauce was also especially delicious. In Guangzhou during the winter, snake meat was considered a remedy and a delicacy because the snake was potent with yang energy, giving the body hot energy during the cold season.

This winter, however, had been a lean one, and our special occasion meal consisted of thin onion soup and rice noodles with slivers of cucumber. This may sound meager to some, but for our family this was a lavish feast after the long winter. New Year's Celebration is always occasion for the best of food, so we were not feeling malnourished that evening.

We sit shoulder to shoulder on long wooden benches while the instructor lectures about history. Today is not about Confucius or the Tang Dynasty (I am thankful to say). The instructor wears a long wheat-colored smock. With his arms at his sides the long sleeves cover most of his veined hands, but his bony fingers stick out below the wide cuffs. He wears spectacles, which look unusually modern on such an old, bent-over man. His beard is long and graying except for a clustered trio of long dark hairs that have sprouted like wild grass from his left cheekbone. His face is sunken, and he shuffles about the room as if he might not make it from desk to door. His feebleness is deceiving, and we quickly learned to not be caught off guard by his self-absorbed, whimsical appearance. When he raises his voice the lion roars, so to speak, and worse yet, if he directs his gaze and lowers his voice as he taunts a student personally, a chill passes through me as though an evil ghost has touched my spirit.

I sit erect and direct my attention entirely, so as to avoid his attack. Fortunately, he does not read from the scroll draped over his arm as he taps randomly on the inside of his open palm. He is telling us about our city history, "Guangzhou is a beautiful old city located in the southeast of the Middle Kingdom. The people of Guangzhou keep a legend alive that tells of our city's beginnings. In ancient times arrived five immortal beings dressed in different colors, each riding a goat with its own special color. The immortal beings came to Guangzhou from the South Sea. They presented local inhabitants with a head of rice as a symbol of their blessing and their wish for bumper harvests from then until far into the future. Guangzhou therefore earned the nicknames "Yangcheng" (City of Goats) and "Suishi" (City of Grains). It is also how the statue of five goats happened to find its home on the Yuexiu Hills that lie in the city center and how the goat became the emblem of Guangzhou."

"Guangzhou lies in the province of Kwangtung. This province includes the offshore island of Hong Kong, a major port city for commercial trade with Portugal, India, Arab countries, and most recently Great Britain. Foreigners consistently find the pronunciation of Chinese words difficult, if not impossible. As a result, words and names are mangled or deformed to fit their native tongues. The province of Kwangtung, famous for its diverse food and tea, silk and porcelain, has become known to foreigners as Canton, a simpler mispronunciation of Kwangtung. Chinese from this province have become known worldwide as Cantonese, and all students of this province are well advised to become familiar with this foreign terminology."

Second Moon: Day 3
Birthday of the God of
Literature, Wenchang,
represented holding an ink
brush and book. On the
book is written the phrase:
"Heaven determines
literary achievement."

scholar

STAYING AFTER CLASS FOR SPECIAL PRACTICE

This morning I walked to school in the rain. Father loaned me one of his umbrellas made of wooden frame with waxy cloth. I know from experience that if I take care of something he has loaned me, he will feel confident to give it to me in the future. Today is just a test of my reliability. Mother reminded me to wear my wooden soled shoes and carry my lighter slippers for changing at school. She needn't have said a word because I was already dressed in my wooden sole shoes with my slippers in my pocket. I told her thank you for reminding me, though, because Father does not allow any disrespectful comments to Mother or to him, but especially to both Uncles we are expected to show exemplary manners. In general, anyone older than me deserves my respect. Those are his exact words. My brother fits into this category, but there are times that seem not to apply to him. These times are when the two of us are left alone.

I had guessed that the best part of the day would be walking to school in the rain. I didn't know that a better part of the day would happen later. The morning was not windy, so the rain seemed to come directly down. I liked looking up at Father's umbrella as I walked. The rain hit the canvas noisily like many fingers tapping frantically, and the water poured out in even rows around me. The stones of the roads were shining and the dirt in the cracks had darkened to black and all the colors of the trees and the wooden shops and their makeshift awnings were rich with a wet sheen. I could easily pretend that I was a stranger visiting a far off land, because everyone's face was half covered by bobbing umbrellas or newspaper tents they held over their heads. Everyone out walking kept to themselves and not a single acquaintance called out my name. I walked in the privacy of my very own turtle shell.

Even the vegetables sold by the vendors had taken on deeper shades of colors; the crinkled kale alongside long thin broccoli rape with its yellow flowers, the oblong tomatoes; shiny red, and deep purple of polished eggplants. The gray branches of the banyan trees posed like elephants coming out of a bath. A bald vendor held up a tiny, shining silver carp for a tiny, well-bundled woman while an energetic man behind him scraped off the scales with a special tool with round holes. My mother loves to buy fish heads. At home, she chops them in two with a hatchet, and then oils and steams them with spring onions and ginger. She claims that the fish heads will make me intelligent, but I like how they taste.

Today's lesson at school is about Chinese poets. We are currently studying poets who lived nearly a thousand years ago. Our instructor, Mr. Yi is a small stout man. He would make an excellent Buddha in a theatre production. He even has the long ear lobes and the perpetual smile on his face. His good mood is contagious. It spreads to the students and to anyone in the room like tea seeping into a hot water kettle. Today he reads a poem by Li Bai from a long scroll:

"At dawn I left Baidi towering in the midst of colorful clouds,
And reached Jiangling a thousand Li away in a day.
The screams of monkeys on either bank went on and on
While my light boat passed by ten thousand hills."

Mr. Yi explains that the description of the boat rushing down the river through the gorges is a description of the poet himself. He asks us to comment on the calligraphy of the scroll. I have a comment, but keep it to myself because it is about a dream I remember of walking along a gloomy road with wild monkeys screaming at me from the trees.

When class is dismissed, I ask to stay longer so that I can copy the poem. Mr. Yi agrees to let me stay, and even though the morning walk in the rain was a joy for me, the opportunity to stay after class for special tutoring in calligraphy is now my favorite part of the day. Mr. Yi had already informed our class that he encourages us to copy the classic calligraphy after class. This involves setting up the long table with a fresh scroll of blank paper, as Mr. Yi does not have enough room for the whole class to use the table at once.

The table we use for calligraphy is called *Ch'ang-T'iao-Cho*, a rectangular table that is quite long. We prefer to stand when writing a large calligraphy. The paper is porous and coarse in weave, the same paper used for painting. This paper is best for the rapid, lively alternation of heavy and light strokes of the brush. Of course, for learning, we practice with cheaper paper. The paper is draped over the front and back, slightly right of the table's center, leaving room to the left side for the brush, the brush stand, the ink and ink-stone. These writing instruments are called The Four Treasures of the Room of Literature, *Wen-Fang-Szu-Pao*. Every calligrapher, painter, and scholar considers The Four Treasures essential.

I look up from the table at one of the banners that Mr. Yi has suspended near the doorway. On red satin, in a column that reads down from the top, Chinese characters form the proverb: "One written word is worth a thousand pieces of gold." Near the window another proverb sways in the breeze: "Falling leaves return to their roots." Near the back of the room is the third banner that reads: "Three inches of immortal tongue." We see these words daily, so that meaning might sink in slowly, but depending on the day, a new interpretation might occur to us. I feel these proverbs surrounding me like sentinels or ancestors, guarding my lesson and impressing upon me the importance of my task.

I look back down at the table with its calligraphy paper, and the Four Treasures. Mr. Yi tells me about the ink with detailed knowledge. "The ink is not made in liquid form. The soot of burnt pinewood or of oil smoke, called lamp-black, is mixed with a type of gum, warmed, and then left to solidify. It

61

is molded into flat or round sticks that might be decorated with carved designs and characters. Expensive ink is frequently perfumed to add desirability."

"Just before writing, a calligrapher grinds the ink stick upon the ink-stone with a little water added. The ink-stone is flat with a hollow scoop in the middle, where the ink is ground and mixed with the water. Ink-stones tend to be made of red-stone, a special rock that can be cut and polished. Smooth rocks, like jade or glass, are not used for ink-stones, but bricks and roof tiles have been used."

Mr. Li shows me how to grind the ink, holding the ink stick perpendicularly with the left hand, between the thumb and forefinger, twirling it slowly but firmly into the water in the hollow. The right hand is left free for writing. "During the grinding of the ink-stone," says Mr. Li, "make your mind calm. This is a time to meditate or to study the original piece, looking for expressive or beautiful strokes in the work." He advises that I grind a little more ink than I expect to use. A long pause in the middle of the writing may result in an abrupt or unwanted change in the style. "Always grind fresh ink," he added, "as ink left on the stone in hot weather becomes affected and flows harshly, unevenly, or may turn an unsightly brownish color."

Mr. Li shows me that an extra layer of paper had been draped beneath the top paper to prevent the ink from bleeding through to the table. "Take extra care to move the backing sheet when you move the writing sheet, or wet spots from the underside will make your calligraphy blotchy." The writing paper is usually a long scroll, which makes the finished work handy for carrying.

Mr. Li always pleads with us to continue using a Chinese brush made of animal hair. The hair is tied together and fixed into a hollow reed or thin bamboo stem. A pen can be fashioned merely from cutting an angle of reed or cane, and then the tip can be whittled to a point. Unfortunately, the point of the pen is not pliable like animal hair, and loss of style and beauty of the strokes is sacrificed. Rabbit's hair is considered best for small, delicate characters, while sheep's hair tends to be best for rendering bold characters. Of course, a calligrapher may prefer or make use of a variety of animal hair: deer, mouse, fox, wolf, sheep, or rabbit, depending on the writer's taste or availability.

I look at the original poem by Li Bai. The characters that describe "the screams of monkeys" are bold and sharp edged, while the characters for "light boat passed by ten thousand hills" look softer and more elegant. My imitation of these strokes is disappointing, but Mr. Yi assures me that Li Bai had practiced more than I could imagine before doing any better than my attempt. He asks me to paint the characters again, but this time he dictates the poem to me, and he stands in front of me, blocking my line of vision to the original calligraphy. "A true artist must develop his own style, and yours can only be drawn from your own vision." After I finish, we both look admiringly at my second draft. "Of course," he adds, "the day will come when you fashion your own ideas into the characters that you create with your own calligraphy."

I know that at times I have my own ideas, but I have yet to imagine creating my own poetry. Mr. Yi has supplied confidence that my day would come.

A LETTER FROM KOWLOON

Father had received a letter three weeks ago. I remember Mother was excited to make special preparations. She always aspired to being a gracious host for visitors. Our home was simple, but cleaning and cooking were activities that she took with great seriousness and vigor before a visitor's arrival. Flower vases were emptied and soaked in strong smelling cleaning concoctions. The walls were mopped and the rafters were swept for spider webs and collected dust. My sister, Lotus Flower, could be found in the courtyard, soaking the window linens in lye mixed with water in wooden buckets, and I would be expected to soap down the courtyard wall and whitewash the moon gate. Father trimmed the empress trees and the sumacs along the sides of the house. My brother, Ching Hah, was sent to purchase new packages of incense, and Mother asked him to keep an eye on the prices of litchis, loquats, plums and dried candies.

As I soaped down the wall, I would turn to watch Lotus Flower rinsing and wringing out the window linens. She squatted beside the bucket, a position that kept the backbone limber and prevented poor posture. From my stance at the back wall, the tall top of the Katsura tree in the front of the house could be seen reaching above the wood tiles of the roof. The corners of our roof curled up like boats in the Dragon Boat Festival. At intervals throughout my life, I have memories of myself as a small boy, standing at the open front door, watching the winged seed pods descending from the Katsura tree. The seeds looked like dragonflies twirling dizzily to the rock garden that decorated our small walkway to the street. I loved the time of year when the samaras fell, their gentle twirling always entranced me.

Lotus Flower looked over her shoulder at me, catching me daydreaming. She was not the scolding type. Her personality was gentle like her name, and I thought to myself that it was unfortunate that her face had a scornful, disciplinary severity acquired from Father, no doubt. I was old enough to know that a good mask of one's feelings could come in handy when needed, so I didn't think of Lotus Flower's stern looks as any real disadvantage for her.

The letter that had set us all into housecleaning mode was from Father's older brother, Ān Lè from Kowloon. This was my favorite uncle and his name, Ān Lè, meant Peace Happiness. He was more easy-going and entertaining than Léi Yǔ, Father's second older brother. Léi Yǔ was the loudest and the quickest to anger of the three brothers. In this way he was a good example of his name, which meant Loud Thunder. Unfortunately, the size of his roar was not matched by the size of his success, and he seemed to be the moodiest of the three. Loud Thunder had taken the opportunity at a young age to move inland to purchase farmland that was "a real steal." Unfortunately, the salesman had failed to mention that the topsoil was a mere thin layer over a thick layer of granite rock shelf. No crop could endure the wind, rain, or lack of deep soil for taking root, and even the goats and oxen that could endure the cold winters were too thin and bony to be slaughtered for meat.

Father said that Loud Thunder had surrounded his entire life with bad luck and ill fate, so that the failed farm was no real surprise. I noticed that Loud Thunder was the most critical of our neighbors and complained that our manners failed to show the respect that he deserved. A visit from Loud Thunder was like walking a tightrope in a strong wind, I never knew what would annoy him next.

Uncle Ān Lè was nearly the opposite of Loud Thunder. He said that life as a merchant in Kowloon had changed his narrow thinking, and he frequently said that there was more than one type of horse and many ways to tame them. Father had to explain to me that life in Kowloon was influenced by the huge import-export shipping trade that poured in and out of Hong Kong, Kowloon's next door neighbor. The influx of foreign goods from India and Arabia and Portugal were now being matched by the growing trade from Great Britain. Such exposure to peoples of the world and their peculiarities and habits had indeed made Uncle Ān Lè an outgoing and adaptable spirit, but once again Father claimed that his eldest brother had always been the adventurous and generous brother, and it didn't surprise him that Uncle Ān Lè had welcomed success and interesting persons into his life.

Father's observations proved to be valuable to me. Without telling me exactly who he expected me to be, he was warning me that how I relate to others and how I treat them effects who I am and who I become.

PROSPERITY IN GRASS VALLEY

The Bread Basket was a cramped little adobe and brick supply store on the corners of Avenida Quinta and Camino del Rio. The owner wisely considered food to be a miner's supply. The aroma of fresh loaves of baking bread and sugary, snail-shaped pastries meandered out of the small bakery where the fragrance lured passers to follow their noses from the street into the supply store. A rickety, splintered bench outside was frequented by pipe smokers and newspaper readers. The tiny shop barely held more than eight customers at a time, and several times per day the overflow waited outside while the first-come-first-serve regulars completed their purchases and exited through the open wrought iron door.

My mining camp's crew leader, R.J., had sent Big Mouth McClatchy along with me to purchase some lard, dried beans, and chewing tobacco. These essentials, along with coffee, provided the mainstay of diet for these miners. The preparation of the coffee always smelled inviting, but the taste was so bitter and offensive that I had to doctor it up with molasses or lumps of sugar. That day, we were lucky enough to arrive at the Bread Basket mid-afternoon, when only two other customers were inside the store. The owner, Ben Lanky, liked to lean on his shining silver register while talking shop with babbling customers. As usual, one stood by the counter; a short, stout man wearing striped suspenders. His long sideburns hung down to his shoulders.

The conversation continued between Ben and the little round man while Big Mouth handled the money transaction. Big Mouth McClatchy handed me the bag of beans to carry back to camp. As we turned to leave the counter we were met face-to-face by an elaborately dressed woman in red.

"My dear friend, Yaozu!" said the woman with astonished enthusiasm. It was Lola Montez, and I recognized the very dress that she wore at the train station the first day I laid eyes on her.

67

"So please to see you," I said proudly with a practiced bow.

"And this is your friend?" she asked.

"Yes, ma'am. My name is Morris McClatchy," and he bowed nearly as awkwardly as I did.

"The Countess of Landress," she responded, offering her gloved hand.

Big Mouth McClatchy leaned forward to kiss her hand, but she removed her hand from his, leaving him face down in his own hand.

"Yaozu," she said turning abruptly to me. "I would like to briefly talk business with you, if you wouldn't mind waiting outside while I complete my purchases."

I turned my head to Big Mouth, hoping for assistance interpreting her request.

"I'll make sure that "Yahoo" waits outside for you, ma'am," said Big Mouth with exaggerated eagerness and his toothless smile that failed to charm her.

"Thank you, Mr. McClatchy," she said as she turned back to the counter. The wide trails of her red dress twirled with a swish, barely fitting within the thin aisle.

The "business" that Ms. Montez had in mind took me by complete surprise. She distinctly remembered my journal, and was curious about the contents of it. She noticed that I looked a bit dumbstruck, so she assured me that her real intention was to learn about Chinese writing and Chinese lifestyle and customs. She invited me to her home the following day for lunch at three, and encouraged me to bring the journal if I so pleased. We stood to shake hands, and once again I turned to Big Mouth McClatchy for extra insight into the nature of her business. Without explaining anything to me he said, "He'll be there at three o'clock sharp. You have my word."

"Thank you," was all she said, offering me a delightful smile before turning to walk away.

Big Mouth McClatchy made an embarrassing fuss about the whole thing, telling everyone in our mining crew that I had a hoity-toity girlfriend. He didn't explain to me very much about what she had suggested, he just said, "Bring your good-for-nothing journal, for God's sake, bring it. The ol' gal seems to like you, sonny boy. This is your chance of a lifetime."

It was hard to go to sleep that night. My mind was full of thoughts that the nighttime tends to exaggerate out of proportion.

I arrived at Ms. Montez's house fifteen minutes early, wondering if it would annoy her to knock on the door a few minutes early. A man with a dark mustache and a large straw hat was kneeling in the front yard, arranging small cacti among daffodils and roses that bordered the brick path to the doorstep. He noticed me waiting outside the fence and lifting a finger he said, "*Un momento.*" He dropped his hand shovel to go knock on the door. He turned and gave me a hand signal to come on into the yard, but I stood apprehensively at the little white gate. The door opened and Ms. Montez stepped out into the sunlight, dressed in a lightweight yellow dress. She also wore a straw hat, but hers had a yellow ribbon tied around it that hung down the back of her bare neck. She walked out to the gate to meet me, and inviting me in as she pointed out the gardening work that she and Javier had completed that morning.

Her house had two levels, actually three, including the cellar. Although it was certainly larger than my family's small house in Guangzhou, it was by no means a castle. California had plenty of desperate miners living in ramshackle dwellings, but there were also plenty of decent homes like hers and I'd seen much larger in San Francisco and Sacramento.

"I'm happy to see that you brought your journal. I have a new idea that I'm hoping you might like. I noticed that you are learning English and I thought I might be able to help you. In exchange, I thought you might not mind teaching me a little Chinese and helping me to understand Chinese writing. I am also curious about your journal. I have met a number of authors in Paris, and I've grown fond of reading their stories. I thought that you, too, must have an unusual story to tell, about your life in China and of crossing the Pacific Ocean. I'm sure that your personal reactions to the whirlwind of peoples and cultures here in California would be interesting to hear. What do you think?"

I looked at her with a blank expression.

She realized that she had lost me with her wordiness and simplified the proposal, "I teach you English, you teach me Chinese. Yes?"

I smiled at her and said, "Yes, I like idea."

We met two days per week, for three hours a day, after which we were served lunch by her servant. The food was more refined than I had experienced among the miners, so the meal was usually a language lesson in itself. Of course the going was slow at first. I opened my journal to show her my calligraphy, and she marveled at the rows of Chinese characters in columns. She couldn't read a word of it, so she would point to a character and I would reconstruct it for her on a single piece of paper. I didn't know the English word for many of the characters, so I began with characters that I knew how to say in English. She showed me how to spell words I had never written. Of course, she was surprised to learn that the Chinese symbols did not stand for individual phonetic sounds, nor did they belong to an alphabet. Chinese characters were actually pictures that signified individual words, and some English words required two characters to represent

71

the one word. The English alphabet seemed so simple in comparison – only 36 letters in all. Of course, the combination of letters was as infinite as the number of Chinese characters, so I wasn't certain that one was simpler than the other.

Ms. Montez was able to locate a dictionary for translating Chinese characters into English. I had never seen one before she presented it to me. The second half of the book translated the English words into Chinese characters, along with Pigeon English. I had seen Pigeon English before. My Uncle in Kowloon had explained to me that English speaking shippers and tradesmen had been unable to make sense of Chinese, so the Pigeon English had been developed to help them converse with Cantonese merchants.

I decided that an excellent Chinese symbol for her to know is the character meaning *to learn*. This symbol shows at the bottom a child under a small shelter, a child in darkness, and two hands pouring knowledge in, symbolizing the master pouring knowledge in. I put the character on the left and drew a simplified ancient version on the right.

Modern character: learn

Ancient pictograph: child in darkness, master's hands pouring knowledge in.

Eventually, as the weeks passed, we began the task of translating my journal to

English. This was tedious at points, and hilarious at others. Sometimes our accumulated knowledge carried us through several symbols without resorting to the Chinese-English dictionary. Ms. Montez appeared to be fascinated and captivated by my story as it unraveled. One day, it occurred to me to ask about her story. I wanted to know about her life before arriving in California. She said that her story would be quite lengthy, involving several countries and various languages. "It would be a daunting undertaking in the telling," she insisted.

After several lessons, it became apparent that after reading a page of Chinese script out of my journal, and translating it to English, it would only be fair for her to write out a page of English describing her own history. The accumulation of two days per week of lessons turned to months, and individual pages of our stories turned to chapters of our personal histories. The lessons continued for slightly less than one entire year. Fortunately, after she moved to Australia and I returned to San Francisco, we managed to maintain contact by letter, so our personal histories were further developed and traded.

During an early lesson at her home, Ms. Montez made a poetic observation about the moon gate that I had briefly described as a large circular passageway in the back wall of our family's courtyard. She said that she found the image delightful and intriguing. She added that during her life she had stepped through various moon gates, leaving one life behind and discovering herself transformed by the new life that she had stepped into. This reminded me of the types

73

of poetic commentary my calligraphy instructor, Mr. Li, would make. I understood perfectly what she meant, because I had experienced this myself. The Cantonese boy who stepped onto the ship to cross the Pacific had been transformed somehow by this new environment called California. I did not, however, consider myself the type of person who was looking for moon gates to step through, but it seemed to me that Ms. Montez was an unusual sort of personality. She seemed to thrive on stepping through one moon gate after another. She never really stayed put for very long in one place. Within a year or two, she would pack her many bags and move on. This tendency made her very multi-faceted. The result was that I rarely knew what to expect while in her company. This was unsettling at first, but I grew to like it. I learned, in fact, to look forward to the spontaneity.

WORDS I HAVE LEARNED IN ENGLISH TODAY

1. Bonnet: a fan shaped headdress, resembling a flower. This headdress allows women to hide their faces from onlookers and protects them from wind and rain.

2. Mutton chops: bushy, wavy hair worn in front of the ears of men.

3. Smile: a happy mouth.

4. Daisy: a knee-high plant with a blossom shaped like the sun.

5. Look: pointing the arm and finger to direct someone's attention.

6. See: knowing something with the eyes.

7. Walk: following a leader with slow feet.

8. Run: following a leader with flying feet

9. Goodbye: I am leaving, you are staying.

LOLA MONTEZ -- MY LIFE AS A YOUNG GIRL
(Mz. Montez begins her biography)

I don't think that a single soul knows my birth name except for my immediate family, all of whom I no longer have need for maintaining contact. I survived my early years with the dreadful name of Marie Dolores Eliza Rosanna Gilbert. Now that you've heard its mention you can drop it squarely in the waste can. As a small child I lived near the atrocities of war. My father, Edward Gilbert, was a soldier. We lived in India, so, being very young, I was quick to learn Hindustani and Bengali along with the English spoken at home. I remember the filth and misery and poverty of the cities. Each city has its flip side of the coin, and I beheld the jewels and palaces as well, along with maharajahs, snake charmers, and shrines depicting Shiva and Vishnu with multiple arms. In India, I was tended to and supervised by nurses and maids called *ayahs.* Upon occasion, the Indian soldiers, called *sepoys,* were also asked to look after me. The ayahs and sepoys were timid at being strict with British children, or so I perceived. As a result, they tended to spoil me and I learned at an early age how to get my way.

Both my parents, in fact, had difficulty controlling me, but especially my mother. She would not tolerate this and not tolerate that until I would turn blue in the face and throw a magnificent tantrum. My father liked treating me like a princess, so he quickly ran into a brick wall whenever he decided to break the spell. I grew accustomed to being waited on and not the least receptive to being ordered about. If somebody tried persuading me, I considered the person entirely out of line.

I remember the lush countryside of India – the exotic flowers, magnificent plumage of wild birds, and huge leathery elephants. Apparently, I was exposed to snakes at such a young age that I never learned to be squeamish or to scream hysterically like some of the silly brats or lightheaded women I have come across. The children of India found in me an eager pupil for mimicking the graceful, languid ritual dances.

In India, however, my heart was crushed by the tragedy of my father's death. He died of cholera, a horrible and painful way to pass away. On his death bed, he had requested that his friend, Captain John Craigie, take charge of his wife and daughter. A few months after my father's death, my mother married this Captain Craigie, and I was furious. I resented the remarriage of my mother and rebelled against either one's attempt at authority.

There was a thick clustered area of giant banyan trees where I was forbidden to go, because of the venomous and deadly snakes to be found therein. My stepfather had caught sight of me heading in that direction on an afternoon that I recall with clarity. The pathway was pebbled, but I ran barefoot like the children of India. Before Captain Craigie caught up with me I had disrobed and dipped myself into a small, hidden pool of water. He was unable to see me through the canopy of tiger lilies and shrubs, but he ordered me to cover myself properly and return immediately home to my mother.

I was eight years old, and it was decided that I should return to Scotland. I was to be educated and molded for a more proper and civilized social life. I left India in 1846 and arrived in Montrose, on the coast of the North Sea. Captain Craigie had taken to calling my mother Eliza, short for her actual name, Elizabeth. My own father had called me Eliza, but Captain Craigie began referring to me as Dolores, and then, Lola.

After such an independent and colorful life in India, my new life in Montrose was unbearably drab. My nursemaids and instructors were at their wits' end with futile attempts at disciplining me, and I was at times despondent and at others explosively outraged. Finally, on one cool day in summer, after endlessly dull tables of multiplication followed by a wearisome lecture on etiquette, I lost all control. In a fit of rebellion, I tore off my clothes and ran naked out the front door and down High Street. An otherwise quiet day was stabbed by the sight of a nine-year-old girl, stripped bare, her long hair flying behind her.

77

The girl had intense dark eyes blazing with fury as she ran like a wild pony down the Scottish road.

Irrevocably, the memory of that mind-shattering moment is embedded deep within the core of who I am. A flame flares up within me, insisting that the boundaries of who I am and what I choose are not at the mercy or whims of others, but guided by the very spirit that dwells within me.

My brother Ching Hah suffered two misfortunes in one afternoon. While passing through the fish market a heavy table-display collapsed, spilling cod and herring across the ground. Women in the crowded market released shrill screams as the fish slid onto their shoes. The display table dislodged a support beam supporting the corner of the roof, which seemed to fall in slow motion. In the midst of all the pandemonium, my brother slipped and fell, landing on his elbow and breaking his arm. The double misfortune was that Uncle Ān Lè from Kowloon had arrived only two days earlier with the intent of convincing Father and Brother to join him on a Pacific Ocean journey to the Golden Mountain. Father had no intention of leaving China, but Ching Hah was overwhelmed with excitement. Even after the accident at the fish market, my brother insisted that he would be entirely capable of the venture, but Doctor Wu advised against it. Doctor Wu had heard horror stories about dreadful conditions at sea, and he pointed out that a strenuous journey was poor medicine for the proper healing of a broken bone.

A change of plan was arranged by my father and uncle. The new plan was that I would join Uncle Ān Lè on the journey. I had to hold my joy on the inside, keeping an outward appearance of indifference. My older brother had always been more physically ambitious and capable than I was. He could run faster and, being larger, he could lift larger and heavier objects. My talent had been with calculations and calligraphy. Of the two brothers, I was less likely to loose my temper. I knew from experience that my brother would resent being replaced by me for this trip to the Golden Mountain, so I carefully played the role of "unenthusiastic boy facing his fate".

The journey to Kowloon was more beautiful than famous watercolor paintings of the Yangtze River. We paid the driver of an ox drawn wagon to deliver us to the Pearl River where we shared a sampan with an old fisherman named Da Shui, who was very lean but strong. He smoked a long handled pipe and wore a wide-brimmed sunhat of woven reed grass shaped like a gigantic cone. With a long crooked pole he gauged the depth of the river and managed to steer clear of sharp boulders that would have splintered our sampan like the shattered shell of a trampled snail.

Han Yu, a Tang scholar, wrote, "The river is like a green silk belt, and hills are like turquoise jade hairpins." The spectacular hills rose up like giant fingers of the gods, sharp pinnacles and cliffs of karst limestone. Trees sprouted from the vertical cliffs, their trunks curling to straighten upright in the sunlight. Occasional wafts of the sweet perfume of cassia blossoms would pass through us like invisible ghosts. Beneath the looming rock formations, subterranean caves and caverns created a labyrinth of dark chasms and underwater passages. We arrived late afternoon in Kowloon, an amazing port, bustling with noise and smelling of sea and marine air. We took a rickshaw to my uncle's merchant office. We jostled over crowded, narrow lanes paved with slabs of red and gray stones. Incessant traffic had worn the stones to a hollow ditch in the center of the road, which served as a means of runoff for rainwater and waste. We turned down Fortune Teller Street where a multitude of bright red banners hung from brick walls or gently swayed midair, suspended from wires that crisscrossed overhead. We passed porcelain shops displaying massive vases and jewelry stores and tea tasting rooms. Fruit stands galore displayed persimmons, plums, apricots and cherries. A wild-eyed thief knelt at the side of the road. A chain had been wrapped around his neck, and a cangue (a huge collar of wood) balanced upon his shoulders. His disheveled head of hair stuck through a hole in the cangue, and cards telling his crime, his name, and his residence were attached to the cangue. This poor thief begged for food, chained to the ground before the jewelry store where he had failed to escape with a silver ring in his pocket.

Uncle Ān Lè directed the rickshaw driver to the hills of Woo-E. Hidden behind a thick veil of trees and shrubs we approached the Temple of the Silver Moon. Uncle explained that the temple had been inhabited from time immemorial by a family of the 'Tea Sect.' During the season when the tea leaves mature, the family makes offerings to the patron saint of fine tea. As if guarding the temple, three small tea trees surround the doorway. It is said that divine hands planted the trees thousands of years ago. Each tree produces one catty of tea. The tea is kept in tightly closed earthen jars for at least two years before using. This divine tea is black tea, the preferred tea of well-to-do Chinese. The choicest of all teas was 'Padre Souchong,' named after a famous monastery of priests who grow the tea. This tea was sent to the Emperor, who gave as rare presents small amounts of the tea to his favored high officers. The officers would offer the tea as New Year gifts to Hong Kong merchants in return for pearls, snuff-boxes, valuable watches and 'smellum water' (the Chinese nickname for lavender water and cologne).

My Uncle's merchant trade office dealt in cargoes of teas and silk. The teas were packaged in crates labeled in Prussian blue and Chinese yellow. The satins varied in production from handkerchiefs, lutstrings, pongees, to satin fabric, including crapes, levantines, and sinshews. Uncle told me that the silkworm feeds on the Tree of Heaven and produces a silk of lesser quality than mulberry silk. The cheaper silk is more durable, but inferior in fineness and gloss. Uncle was a treasure trough of these types of insights. The fascinating and admirable articles for exchange were symbolic tokens of the variety of humanity involved in the trading. Merchants from India and Arabia had found their way to the ports of Canton, and the Portuguese had been influential here long before the recent boom of British influx. All these languages and personal items of both necessity and luxury swirled around my Uncle Ān Lè, making of him an endearing character and a wealth of odd information.

My trip to Kowloon would have been a fulfilling adventure in and of itself, without the thought of an ocean voyage to the Golden Mountain. I saw in Uncle's eyes a sparkle of joy in sharing with me the ins and outs of his business. I would have gladly volunteered to apprentice with him. His work seemed far from any drudgery that one might think of as work. The larger venture lying ahead seemed mythical, even magical. Imagine a fantasy mountain so strewn with nuggets of gold that any visitor could fill his pockets to his hearts desire. Somehow, by a shuffling of strange fate, I had been chosen as a rare guest to join my uncle on this fantastic voyage.

Third Moon – Day Three:
Birthday of Xuantian Shangdi,
the Supreme Lord of the Dark
Heaven, who presides over the
North Pole and is worshiped as
a controller of floods and rains.

ALL ABOARD

The day before our departure Uncle asked me to join him for tea on the wharf. I knew from experience that when a Cantonese relative or friend invites you out for tea that you had better be prepared to experience a seven or eight course meal. The restaurants of the wharf were lined up like a river bank beneath a looming cliff of rigging, masts, and numerous long trailing flags dancing on the wind like brightly colored kites. On the exterior, the Golden Phoenix was a low bungalow of dark stained mahogany carved into trailing dragons rising above tiers of clouds. Gnarled branches of miniature pagoda trees that twined like ropes formed vertical arches that framed a huge red double door. Intricate arrays of patterns cut into the door emitted twinkling candlelight from within the restaurant. The effect was that of a red sky strewn with sparkling constellations. Massive brass door handles formed separate halves of a moon riding on mahogany clouds. Pulling the heavy doors open revealed a mantel of thick candles spilling waterfalls of wax tears onto the vines and fronds of hanging ferns. Upon entering, the trickling of water was obscured in shadows beneath the ferns, but as one crossed the lobby the glisten of refracted candlelight upon the bubbling surface of the fountain was unveiled. We were escorted from the lobby, and descended several carpeted steps that circled downward to a dining room that resembled the hull of an elegant ocean liner.

The dining room was a maritime museum of valuable artifacts. A British grandfather clock with a bronze pendulum ticked out English seconds and western-world minutes. A gargantuan aviary constructed of bamboo and grass reeds exhibited toucans, macaws, and peacocks, among small darting swallows of iridescent greens and blues. The screeching and chattering of the birds created a wildly animated atmosphere. A massive varnished steering wheel from a Portuguese vessel dominated the center of the dining area. Nautical charts, compasses, astrolabes, cross-staffs, back-staffs, and quadrants were secured to wall space, tables, and even chairs. A glass showcase exhibited pagodas of carved ivory alongside models of ships that had been miraculously assembled inside bottles with narrow spouts.

Our table was a large round table capable of seating sixteen customers. There were three men seated at the table, awaiting our arrival. When they noticed Uncle Ān Lè approaching, they all stood. We all offered ceremonial bows and greeted each other with wishes of good fortune and longevity. One gentleman had a bald head like a skullcap circled with long graying hair that hung over his ears and collar. His eyes bulged profusely like a bulldog's. He was an herb and medicine doctor named Yaozong. (Yaozong, the mandarin pronunciation of my name Yaozu, means to bring glory to one's ancestors.) Another small man with a narrow angular nose and a kindly expression stood near Yaozong the herbalist. The small man was a Buddhist monk from the mountains of central China. His name was Zhe, meaning wise sage or philosopher. This name may have been given to him by acquaintances later in his life. A Chinese name does not necessarily resemble the nature of the person who is bestowed it. A very tall thin man wore a thinly braided beard. If he turned his back to you, his long braided queue looked the same as the beard on his chest. This man's hands and face were extraordinarily large for a Chinaman. His name was Mochou, which means "do not worry". It was hard to say if this slow moving, lanky man was worried or not, as he rarely engaged in conversation. These three men; Yaozong the herbalist, Zhe the Buddhist monk, and Mochou the giant, would be boarding the ocean vessel with my uncle and me. The five of us as a group would be heading to the Golden Mountain. It was Yaozong the herbalist and Uncle Ān Lè the merchant who had agreed to create a gathering of "friends" who would join in a pact to assist each other on this journey and endeavor.

Uncle had warned me that the ocean voyage could last two to three months, and not to expect appetizing food. He was not a rich man, or so he claimed, but we would be storing up our strength at the Golden Phoenix by enjoying a luxuriant meal before our sendoff. The banquet was rich and excessive, with several Cantonese dishes and samples of regional cuisines such as Sichuan, Peking, and Huaiyang. We enjoyed shark's fin soup, Yue fish meat balls, pork steamed in lotus leaves, Duck with Eight Ingredients, Phoenix in the Nest, Sichuan pancakes stuffed with sweet-bean paste, Thousand-Layer cake, quick-fried Mandarin Fish, stir-fried bean curd with mushrooms and onions, steamed five-colored Huntun, and cubes of coconut milk jelly.

A young waiter dressed in a red and black silk robe wheeled in a cart with a large rectangular box draped in a painted canvas coverlet. The waiter unfastened the small hoops from ivory buttons shaped like mushrooms. Pulling off the coverlet, he exposed a cage containing three snakes. Swiftly, he opened the cage door, and with his bare hands grasped a cobra. His elbow pushed the door shut and he laid out the live cobra on the floor. Placing one foot on the snake's head and the other on its tail, he pulled a dagger from his belt, slit open the snake's belly, and extracted the gallbladder. A second waiter approached with a small tray with a flask of rice wine and an empty carafe. The first waiter cut open the gallbladder sac and drained the bile into the carafe, which he mixed with rice wine. The second waiter circled the table with the flask, offering each of us a shot of snake bile wine. Uncle and Yaozong nodded yes, signaling that we were all to be served. I had never tasted snake bile wine, but it would have been rude to refuse it. The dissected snake was coiled into a pewter bowl and hauled off while the snake cage upon the cart was wheeled away.

"Does it taste bitter?" I asked Uncle.

"No, it's actually sweet," he said. Yaozong explained that snake bile fights off "wind-evil" and "wet-evil." He said that snake bile will sharpen a man's eyes, strengthen his liver, eliminate coughing, and clear away phlegm. Snake bile wine is sought out by people with arthritis and asthma as well as many who have lost their ability to walk without assistance.

We ate and drank strong green tea, talked and gorged ourselves, oblivious to the contrast this scene would soon make to our upcoming voyage. Yaozong, the herbalist talked of the difficulties that foreigners faced with their feeble attempts at learning Chinese. "Local government," he said, "has enforced severe laws forbidding the teaching of Chinese to foreigners. A

84

Chinese teacher was recently beheaded for giving such lessons. Foreign students determined to assure their own safety have been known to study at night as they carefully screened any visible light in their rooms from outside scrutiny."

The waiter returned with a soup he called "Porridge of Chrysanthemum, Dragon, Tiger and Phoenix." It was actually a thick soup consisting of the butchered cobra, cat meat, and chicken with chrysanthemum petals and shreds of lemon leaves added to the broth. The soup was delicious. The slivers of snake meat were ivory white and very tender.

Conversation continued about the various foreigners we would soon be encountering. The Cantonese had an array of clever names for sorting out the various foreign nationalities. "Fan Kwaes," meaning foreign devils, was a term that lumped together all the foreigners. The English were referred to as "Red-haired Devils," the Dutch became "Hu-lan", the French were labeled "Fat-lan-sy," while Americans were called "Flowery-flag Devils."

Uncle Ān Lè had purchased a handful of pamphlets from bookshops near the Factories. These pamphlets were frequently seen being read by shopkeepers, servants, and coolies in general. At the cost of a penny each, they were well worth the entertainment and education. On the cover was an illustration of a foreigner wearing a pirate-type dress of the recent eighteenth century; long stockings, shoes with buckles, a coat with wide shirts, lacey sleeves, breeches, and a three-cornered hat. The script began with "Yun," its barbarian definition directly below, a Chinese symbol with the sound for the word 'man'. As Uncle passed out the pamphlet round the table for our inspection, he warned us that he would collect and discard them before the journey, so as not to create harmful animosity of the ship's "Fan Kwae" crew.

to go – to leave

EMBARKING ON VOYAGE

The ocean trader we boarded was known as a "kettle bottom" in America. It was a heavy, deeply U-shaped, slow moving vessel. The ship was a gigantic village-sized monster named the *Seringapatam.* Three masts supported rectangular sails piled five high with triangular sails angled on ropes. "Kettle bottoms" were some of the largest wooden ships built in Britain. The *Seringapatam* weighed 818 tons.

British soldiers with rifles strapped to their shoulders formed two lines funneling the boarding mob of passengers into a single file up the gangway to the boarding pass inspector upon deck. I had ridden junks and sampans, but the excitement of boarding such a monstrosity of creaking wood filled my anticipation to a high pitch. Above me the flapping flags and rippling sails, along with the harsh calls of circling gulls created a chaotic drum roll that accompanied my racing heartbeat. Uncle Ān Lè boarded ahead of me and Mochou stood like a massive, silent guard behind me. We were directed to a hatch built into the planks of the deck. A rope ladder had been lowered into the dark, dank hold. The hold was actually a storage area, originally intended for cargo and storage. We climbed down into stacks of bunks. Actually these bunks were merely shelves. The air inside was warm with a putrid odor of something rotting, perhaps garbage or dead rats. Many of the men quickly made a habit of tying a shirt or cloth over their mouths and noses. I imitated their example. We looked like bandits attempting to hide our identities. Breathing was hindered by the cloth over my mouth, so I was forced to lift it at intervals.

Uncle instructed us to select bunks as high and near to the hatch entrance as possible. I selected a bunk shelf above Uncle. I crawled inside the narrow space and noticed a spider web in an upper corner. I wondered if I had a stick or a cloth for removing it. Mother frequently said that a spider web left undisturbed might be for our benefit. The small bugs, flies, and mosquitoes captured by the spider might be more of a pest to humans than the spider itself. I left the spider web untouched, and his end of the shelf became the foot of my bed. No bedding or mats had been supplied for the narrow shelves, so we did our best to pad the planks with our carry-on clothing. The only saving grace of the claustrophobic shelf space was a thick vertical support beam that prevented me from falling off the shelf in my sleep. Lying down, the support beam stood next to my hip. Attached to each beam beside the bunk a chain dangled a tin can which served as a food bowl. From my dimly lit bunk near the open hatch, I could detect a build up of dried food and residue on the cup. I vowed to never touch the filthy thing.

We were all aware that the voyage could take several months, and the type of food stored by the ship's owner for the cooks was limited to items that were unlikely to spoil. The widespread poverty of the Middle Kingdom had forced many Chinese to adapt to similar cuisine, cured and salted fish, pork, and beef, along with dried fruits and herbs – all of which were mainstay in Chinese kitchens, in addition to bags or caldrons of ubiquitous rice. The four staples aboard the Seringapatam were beans, rice, hardtack, and salted meat. Hardtack looked like a rock hard, dried-up rice cake. It was actually a densely baked biscuit made from wheat flour. The palm sized discs would have better served as hand weapons. One could pellet an enemy in the head with a hardtack, braising the skin and leaving a purple bruise. The biscuits were best enjoyed by dunking into tea or coffee, turning one's drink into an odd soup of soggy flakes. In times of worse depravation, pieces of the biscuit could be slowly dissolved in the saliva of a starving man's mouth.

Twice during the first month we were treated with pudding. The crew called it duff, consisting of suet and flour and sweetened with bits of dried fruit. We saw this treat only twice and then settled into a dreary repetition of beans, rice, salt meat and hardtack. Passengers called the salt meat "old horse." There were days when the beef was as tasteless and dry as chewing on a piece of bamboo. The coffee was bitter and hard to finish, but amazingly as the days passed, I began to long for it. The smell of coffee was always deceiving, appealing to the nose and distasteful to the tongue.

Immediately after the last Chinaman had boarded and descended the rope ladder, the British crew on deck had been ordered to roll up the ladder. An alarmed roar of dismay rose up from the Chinamen in the dark hold below us, and several Chinese passengers grabbed onto the rope, hoping to overpower the crew above. The rope continued to ascend, dragging two Chinamen up to the hatch. A crew member kicked one Chinaman in the head, and another crew member yelled, "Filthy coolie!" as he stomped on the fingers of the other Chinaman. The first to fall was caught by hands that reached out from the shelf bunks below us. The small man hit one of the shelf boards, resulting in a broken rib. The other was less fortunate. On the way down he broke an arm and split open his lip. Crashing to the floor below, he landed on a barrel and crushed his hip. Above us a roaring voice gave the crew an order. A group of them chanted together, then groaned and growled as a huge metal grate was lowered over the hatch. Two huge locks were secured from the outside. This was an ominous beginning on the day of our departure.

The second day was uneventful. Salt meat and beans were lowered down by wooden buckets tied to a rope. A voice from below me was yelling, "Doctor, doctor, please!" There was no response to this plea, although the man with the broken arm had moaned and cursed all night. The man with the crushed hip had apparently turned delirious and was barely able to mumble. We quickly realized that we would have to tend to our own wounds, as best we could – without supplies, medicine, or sufficient light.

The wooden buckets of porridge were lowered to the bottom level, divided up, and then handed up to the level above them. When the bucket was empty, a Chinaman would tug two times on the rope, which signaled a crew member above to pull up and refill the bucket to be lowered again. The process was slow, and Chinamen on the lowest levels learned to pass messages attached to the bucket to those of us at higher levels. I had torn a page from my journal and fashioned a funnel. I did not pass messages at first. By folding the pointed tip of the funnel, I could place it inside the tin cup which had a handle. Without chopsticks, I had to pour the thick soup into my mouth.

Needless to say, the porridge dribbled onto my shirt and down my chin. I wiped my chin with my sleeve, and accepted my messy fate.

Human waste was dealt with in pretty much the same fashion as food. Fortunately, wooden buckets were used for food, and metal tubs were used for the waste. Once a day the sailors would lower empty metal tubs into the hold, and haul up the used ones to be emptied.

We were being held like prisoners in a jail. Many of us had paid our ways for this journey, while others had signed contracts for paying off the voyage by working on the Golden Mountain. We were not criminals; we were passengers being treated like animals.

ZHE, THE SAGE AND PHILOSOPHER

Uncle resided in the bunk below me, directly across from Zhe, the Buddhist philosopher. Below Uncle, Mochou the Giant had bunked, and somehow the herbalist had not been able to bunk near us. I could not easily see Zhe if he was lying down, but I could hear his voice when he talked. It was our great fortune that Zhe was an excellent storyteller. The first story he told was a famous story, well known to my family, called The River God's Wife.

THE RIVER GOD'S WIFE

A new commander was selected as the leader of Ye. His name was Ximen Bao. Ximen Bao called upon the local elders to inquire about the failing economy of their city. Collectively the town elders responded. "Our poverty is the result of the marriages that have been forced upon us by the River God."

"How is this possible?" asked Ximen Bao.

"Every year the taxes are collected by the high officials. When hundreds of thousands of coppers have been collected from the people, the coppers are divided. About three thousand coppers are used to pay for a wife for the River God. The rest of the coppers are divided among the high officials, while a small pile of coins is saved for the female shaman who assists with ceremonies."

"The female shaman goes from family to family, inspecting the attractive daughters. When she has discovered an especially beautiful daughter, she informs the family, 'Your daughter is honored to become the wife of the River God.' After taking the daughter from the household, the beautiful girl is bathed, dressed in silken robes, and then expected to fast. A fasting pavilion is built by the river. Silk curtains are draped on all sides of the pavilion, and the beautiful girl is left inside in seclusion. After ten days, an exemplary meal is prepared using the finest meat, wine, and rice. Upon the river a mat is placed and the meal is arranged upon the mat. The beautiful girl is led from the pavilion down to the river, where she is asked to sit upon the mat with the elegant meal. The girl on the mat with her sumptuous meal is sent down the river. The gathered crowd watches as the mat floats down the river, but after a few dozen *li* the mat slowly sinks. The crowd watches as the beautiful girl's head sinks into the water."

"Every family with a daughter has fled Ye. They fear the dreaded visit by the female shaman to their home, so they all moved far away from Ye. As a result, the population of the city has dwindled and the remaining residents have plunged deeper and deeper into poverty. This has been the sad fate of our city for a very long time. There is a well known saying here in Ye, 'When the River God has no wife, he is angered and the river rises up and floods the entire land.'"

"Ximen Bao thought about this dilemma. 'I would like you to inform me the next time a wife is chosen for the River God. When the female shaman and the local officials are ready to send her down river, I would like to also see her off.' They bowed, 'Yes, Honorable Commander.'"

"When the day arrived Ximen Bao was notified. He arrived at the pavilion near the river to join the elders and officials, who awaited the ceremony. The crowd that had gathered was huge. The female shaman was an old woman, at least eighty years old. Behind her were ten younger women, dressed in fine silk. These ten women were the shaman's novices."

"Ximen Bao ordered the guards to summon the River God's new wife. 'I would like to know if the old female shaman is a good judge of beauty.'"

"The girl was released from the pavilion and led before Ximen Bao. After examining the girl, Bao turned to the elders, the female shaman, and the high officials. 'I must inform the shaman that this girl is not worthy of the River God.' The female shaman was escorted before Bao who told her, 'Please inform the River God that we are selecting a more suitable bride. Please tell the River God that we will deliver her in a few days.' Bao then ordered his attendants to throw the female shaman into the river."

"After a lengthy wait, Bao became impatient. 'Why is the shaman taking so long? One of her novices must be sent to hurry her up.' The attendants threw a novice into the river."

91

"After another delay, Bao was upset. 'The novice seems to be as inefficient as the shaman. Send another novice to speed up the process.' Another novice was thrown into the river."

"After tossing three novices into the river Ximen Bao said calmly, 'We have sent only women, and they are incapable of completing the task. We need three officials to take care of business.' Without hesitation, three officials were thrown into the river."

"As Ximen Bao stood gazing at the river for a good length of time, the remaining elders and observers began to fear that they too would end up thrown into the river. 'Not one of the shamans or a single official has returned. Who can I rely upon to return?' Surely, Bao was about to order that some of the local elders be sent after them, but they knelt down, kowtowing frantically, knocking their heads so fiercely upon the ground that blood dripped down their foreheads, and their faces were drained of their color."

"Ximen Bao paced back and forth, tapping the side of his nose with his forefinger. 'Rise up off the ground, all of you. The River God is delaying his guests. I declare the closing of the ceremony. It is time we all return to our homes.'"

"From that day forth, the people of Ye vowed to never again speak of the River God taking a beautiful daughter as his wife."

....

Then the seasickness consumed us. Worrying about dripping food on my clothes was nothing compared to the mess that followed. Men who were not sick cursed and threatened the ones who were. Vomit spilled from upper bunks to lower bunks. The stench of bile, of sickeningly sweet and soured, regurgitated meals mixed with the smell of dead animals. Men who were not seasick were taken ill by the horrid fumes. Nausea, vomiting, dizziness, and throbbing headaches were all ailments that I had experienced beforehand on land, but this was a multidimensional horror. Compressed together in an airless hull were over a hundred sick men. Out came the bandit scarves again. The smell of vomit and the turmoil of queasy stomachs were mercilessly provoked by loosened bowels and toxic perspiration and urine that dampened clothes and then dried, only to be soiled again by the endless poisons that bodies are capable of excreting.

"Death, give me death." These were the words that I heard more than once. I thought of my unlucky brother, Ching Hah, with his broken arm. Maybe he was the lucky one, to be left behind.

In the early afternoons an additional smell filled the hold, rising up from the lower deck to the upper deck. It was the smoky, sweet, musty smell of opium pipes. For the few of us who didn't smoke opium, the smell was a sad reminder that the British had successfully weakened the will and the power of the Middle Kingdom. By trading opium from India for tea from China, the British had fanned the fire of addiction that now crippled our country. If I felt well enough to write in my journal, the early afternoon was a well lit time for seeing my paintbrush and grinding the ink. The light spilling through the hatch helped me to see my journal as I carefully painted the intricate strokes to form Chinese characters. I would lie on my stomach, with my shoulders propped up by resting on my elbows. This was terrible form for executing Chinese calligraphy, but I really had no alternative. The dreary smell of opium smoke would frequently remind me to pull out my journal. I don't know if the procedure of journaling or the smell of opium settled my stomach, but the opium was like incense that helped to mask the nauseating fumes of our seasick bodies. Given the hardship of the situation, I learned to feel more forgiving of my fellow Chinamen for having succumbed to such a nasty habit.

It would be weeks later, long after the seasickness had subsided, that a tropical storm would bring deadly weather. This storm took the worst toll of all on the Chinese passengers.

Third Moon – Day 23: Birthday of the Queen
of Heaven, Tian Hou, popularly
known as Mazu, Goddess of the Sea.

A RARE DAY OF THE VOYAGE

It was during the third week of our journey that I awoke
to the familiar sound of the locks being jiggled open and the
"Heave-ho" and groaning of sailors pulling the metal grate aside.
A group, consisting of approximately twenty of us, was ordered
up on deck. Several men on the deck were heaving the huge
handle of a large pump up and down. I felt blinded by the
sharpness of the sunlight. The ocean spread about us endlessly
like a huge field of scintillating silver. The sky was unreal, like a
dome of blue jade feathered with dragon's breath clouds. A cool
breeze filled my nostrils and lungs with a brisk freshness as clean
as cool water. I doubted that these sailors had been instructed to
treat us with any respect. At first I suspected that they would put
us to work like slaves.

A grimy man with a beard like a lion ordered us to take
off our clothes. We looked at each other in dismay until several
sailors lunged at us, ripping our clothes off, tearing them with
their hands or cutting them off with knives. We knew they
meant business, but those of us who failed to disrobe entirely or
moved too slowly were attacked again. When we all stood naked
before them a great howling and hooting and laughter came from
above us, where an audience of crew members had stationed
themselves upon the masts and ropes above us. This was
terrifying, to have a jeering audience as we stood stripped bare.

Then, as the men at the pump continued to work the
handle, a large hose was aimed at us and icy, salty sea water
blasted us, knocking several of the weaker men down. A
crescendo of howling and laughter filled our ears as we dared not
open our eyes or attempt to breath. As abruptly as the blast had
started, the spray was turned upon our pile of clothes. We were
then shoved and ordered to redress in our soaking clothes and
then forced back down the hatch. I imagined that if we had kept
weapons hidden in our bunks, we would have planned retaliation,
but we had been carefully searched the day we boarded the ship.

As I climbed into my shelf space, I carefully wedged my journal into a gap beneath the bunk above my head to spare the pages from the seawater from my clothing and hair.

Another group of twenty men from the bunks directly below us were ordered up on deck, and we listened to the harangue and jeering ridicule. We were forced to relive the humiliation in our minds, over and over again, as each new group was hauled above to be degraded. It was perhaps the fourth group that included the Chinaman with a broken arm. He wore a sling constructed of torn cloth, but he was able to climb up the rope ladder by leaning against bunk shelves as he reached for each higher rung. I cannot imagine how he undressed with only one arm. I lay in my bunk wishing him the best. The man with the broken hip was unable to climb. He was so sick that he was not able to stand up. Two sailors who stood at the edge of the hatch were yelling down at us, insisting that the sick Chinaman had to be brought up onto the deck. After much commotion, the two sailors descended the rope wearing scarves wrapped over their noses and mouths. A cot was wrapped around the ailing Chinaman, tied with rope above his head and below his feet. Sailors above dropped a long rope down to the two sailors below, who connected the long rope to the knot above the Chinaman's head. He was hoisted slowly but surely up to the deck. The sight reminded me of a large fish being pulled from the river. After the final humiliating seawater bath, the last group descended the rope ladder in their dripping, soaked clothing. The Chinaman with the broken hip was never returned to the hold. Word soon reached us from the group below us that the man had been rolled out of the cot and dumped into the ocean. "Drowning in the sea is faster than the way the poor man was slowly dying down in the hold," I heard someone say in the darkness. I could only think to myself what we all knew – that even the man's ghost would not be able to return home, as the body would end up at the bottom of the ocean. For days after, I felt sure that I would never care to put this story in my journal. It was my Uncle who convinced me that the most revealing and interesting of stories include the best along with the worst of any experience. In the end, I decided to swallow my pride and follow Uncle's advice.

Fourth Moon – Day 8: Birthday of Sakyamuni Buddha,
Founder of Buddhism, whose teachings
on the release from suffering through
meditation and the search for enlightenment
spread through China beginning
in the first century A.D.

ABOARD THE *SERINGAPATAM*

Monotony on a long sea voyage turns in upon itself, and idle time brings out some of the calming, and aimless activities of voyagers and sailors alike. The Chinaman in the bunk across from me took to whittling a piece of driftwood into a dancing monkey. An invisible sailor up on deck could be heard in the lull of afternoons playing harmonica tunes. As if to accompany Chinese Opera, the singing strings of a qin filled the hold after a dinner of hardtack and tough, salty "old horse." The qin is a beautifully designed wooden instrument, shaped into a pentagon. The flat part of the instrument represents earth, while the rounded part represents heaven. Round coins with square holes could be heard as they fell from an untied string, to be restrung with a clink, clink, clinking. I reread in my journal about my last days in Kowloon, and days before with my family in Guangzhou.

Days grew more peaceful, the swelling of the sea rocked us gently in our shelves like infants in cribs. Zhe continued to tell more legends and folk stories. He held us spellbound with a long story about a handsome youth named Ma Chun. The well known tale was called *Land in the Sea.*

Ma Chun was fond of singing and playacting, but his father was a merchant who warned him that he couldn't eat his books or cut them into clothing. His father would have rather that Ma learn the trade of a merchant, but Ma wandered off on a sea voyage. His voyage went off course, and he landed upon a mountain village where the inhabitants were incredibly grotesque. As it turned out, the mountain people were astounded by his unusual appearance, and everyone feared him. After meeting a variety of people who shied away from him, an old man of one hundred twenty years took him to meet dignitaries and then a diplomat, who asked Ma to sing and dance. After being very impressed with Ma's performance, Ma was given a position of high office.

He soon grew tired of his high office post, and seeking to be relieved of his duties, pretended to fall ill. He was returned to the mountain village to recuperate, where he showered them with gifts of gold and jewelry. The little people vowed to return the favor when they returned from the sea-market. Ma was curious about the sea-market. The villagers explained that the sea-market was in the middle of the ocean, where mermen of the four seas kept their treasure and where twelve nations engaged in commerce. Ma asked to accompany them, but they refused. Ma insisted that he was an experienced sailor, that wind and waves did not intimidate him. He prepared for the voyage and boarded the ship.

After landing at the sea-market, Ma encountered a prince riding a purebred stallion. The prince escorted him to meet the King. The King requested that Ma compose a few verses of poetry about the sea-market. Ma was given an ink-slab of marbleized quartz, a paintbrush of tiger bristles, bright, clean rice paper, and fine ink the scent of lilac. He produced a lengthy poem about the sea-market. The king was overjoyed with the verses. To acknowledge the favor, the King offered the hand of his daughter in marriage. Ma accepted the offer.

Zhe described the King's daughter, the jingling of her jewelry and ladies of the court in elaborate detail, painting vivid pictures in our minds. I could see the drifting gowns of maids holding painted candles, the dark hallway where Ma was led to the inner quarters. The bride, in lavish splendor upon a bed of coral and precious gems, was captivating and fairy-like in her beauty. The following morning a swarm of young girls served and dressed Ma, treating him like royalty. The King congratulated Ma for his poetry and his marriage, and Ma was paraded before the King's subjects. Ma rode a magnificent sea horse. He was dressed in a bejeweled uniform and escorted by mounted guards, carrying not spears, but long-stemmed water lilies.

97

In the palace, Ma marveled at a glistening tree of jade, its wide trunk and translucent roots, its mighty stone arms and leaves of white jade coins. A flaxen yellow footbridge arched across the jade tree's meandering glass roots. Blossoms like bursting berries fell to the floor, creating tinkling music. An enormous bird with gold and green feathers descended upon a thick branch of the jade tree. The bird's long tail was iridescent, and its mournful song sparked memories of Ma's village and his parents. When Ma told his beautiful wife of his homesickness, she understood his longing. Insisting that Ma return to his home and his parents, his princess bride warned that he must never return to see her, but they would remain faithful to each other to their deaths. His new bride was with child. After three years, she promised that the child would be delivered to him. If the child was a boy they would name him Fuhai, meaning Happy Sea. If the child was a girl, her name would be Longgong, meaning Dragon Palace. His princess wife warned him that his mother would enter the "long night" after a year of his return home. A year later, his mother, already an old woman, died, and at the sight of the grave a ghostly young woman paid her respect. Three years after his return, on a visit to a southern island, Ma encountered two small children bobbing upon a wave in the sea. These were his children, Fuhai and Longong. Although Ma was never capable of returning to see his wife, Fuhai, his son, was allowed to make the voyage to meet with his mother when he was old enough. Longgong, being a girl, was not allowed to join her brother on the voyage, but she was soon to marry. Her dowry was a collection of exquisite items inherited from her mother; a tall coral tree, fragrant dragon amalgamate, large pearls, and boxes inlaid with precious metal and radiant gemstones.

....

The vivid story was like a lullaby sung to me at bedtime. I lay in the dark marveling at the contrast between the fairytale of the sea and our ocean excursion. I fell into a dream in which small gnomes, perched upon the gaffs, ropes and masts, taunted my family and forced us to strip bare. We were thrown into the sea and escorted by dolphins and seahorses to a pagoda of carved jade.   A smiling dolphin opened a wooden chest hidden beneath seaweed and coral.   Inside were garments constructed of abalone shells, pearls, and small coins webbed in fishing net.   We swam and played in the sea. Dolphins swam circles around us and seahorses performed flips and cartwheels. When we washed ashore the beach was a hard metallic gold – there was no sand.   The surface of the beach was wet and slippery and we were unable to stand up. No matter how hard we tried, we kept sliding back into the foaming waves of the sea.

Fourth Moon – Day 18: Birthday of Huato,
          Patron god of medicine.

STORM AT SEA

Days passed barely distinguishable from nights. I slept more. I listened to Zhe's stories. I missed whole days without adding anything to my journal. Bean porridge became the mainstay of our diet, although we noticed that this tasteless soup seemed more watered down with each new batch. We didn't see anymore of the sweetened pudding, but every third or fourth day a few extra hardtack would be lowered down into the hold. You could have paved a road with these biscuits and passed them off as white cobblestones.

The wind howled and then whistled, and a dampening mist formed droplets upon the grate. Droplets slowly swelled and loosened themselves from the metal bars, falling like gargantuan tears. Late in the evening a fierce rain drenched all of the shelves. The ship tossed and tilted like a toy bobbing in a jostled washtub. The vessel groaned and at times screamed in agony. Huge waves smashed upon the deck, pouring gutters of icy seawater through the grate. Inside the hold we were drenched and shivering cold. The muted yelling of sailors preceded the closing of the hatch doors. In the darkness we were thankful for the barricade against the cold seawater, but we now feared the suffocating shortage of air we would face. The Chinaman across from me mumbled about the foreign devils' neglect of our wellbeing. "They don't care if we are dry or wet, they are only afraid that seawater might sink the ship." This was one of the first times I heard the man speak.

By the time the sea had calmed, we were bruised and frozen. We were like skeletons in a vast catacomb. As the ship ceased tossing, the hatch was reopened and chilling fresh air spilled into our cavern. Many of us developed a high fever. I suffered a severe cold turned to influenza. My throat was swollen and aching, my head pounded and my bones seemed to wage war with my own flesh. I was young and quickly recovered, but many suffered for over a week. By the end of eight days, fifteen men had died of exposure, or the flu, perhaps of food poison. No diagnoses or investigation was called for. The bodies were pushed over the railing. It seemed apparent to us that the British were punishing us like prisoners of war. In the passing weeks food dwindled to a murky, lukewarm broth. Our weakness turned to delirium. At least three men in the hold lost all nutrition to the brain, and were transformed into babbling lunatics resulting from the ordeal.

I lost all interest in my journal. Even Zhe's storytelling sounded like an echoing voice heard from far, far away. I lost my ability to concentrate. After possibly ten days in a stupor, the quantity and quality of the food suddenly improved. Upon the second day of this phenomenon, Uncle explained that the improvement in meals was a sure sign that we were nearing our destination. The Chinaman across from me claimed that he had died and gone to heaven. At this Uncle and Zhe started laughing uncontrollably. Perhaps the sound of laughter was funnier than the joke, but the laughter was contagious and I too laughed hysterically.

Zhe's storytelling began to make sense again and time passed like a lazy dream. Two days passed, then three. We decided that Uncle was wrong about the food. "Maybe the old chef died, and a new one took charge," declared a voice from below me. Then a sailor could be heard hollering "Land ho!" and the crew stampeded the deck like galloping oxen. A great cheering and cries of celebration rang out, and a chattering and bustling consumed the hold while new cheering rang out overhead.

Our exchange bargain had grown a little lopsided. A page of my life for a page of her life was the intended tradeoff. Ms. Montez became so entranced by the story of my ocean voyage that she put off her own story for days. "A reader is moved by the misery of his fellow man," she insisted, proving the worth of my uncle's advice. "And furthermore," she claimed, "an actress is an artist of a craft entirely unlike that of writing." In the end we agreed that as soon as my ship had arrived in San Francisco, it would be her turn to continue telling her history.

LOLA MONTEZ IN PARIS
(more of Ms. Montez' autobiography)

After my scandalous outburst in Montrose, I was placed in the care of Sir Jasper Nicolls. Sir Jasper had a daughter my age named Fanny, a fun-loving, red-haired girl who traveled with Sir Jasper between London, Bath, and Paris. For all her quick wit and carefree disposition, Fanny was capable of subduing her spontaneous nature and posturing herself as a well disciplined and courteous lady. I learned from Fanny that due respect to etiquette and an eye for manners can help to roll out the red carpet in your favor. Sir Jasper was well aware of many of my redeeming qualities, so he did not view me entirely as a beast prone to ferocious outburst. After staying in London at Sir Jasper's house, I traveled with him to Paris to join Fanny in her studies. The cathedrals and great museums of Paris stood amid palaces, and castles. An air of inventiveness, of brisk adventure and romance mixed with a sturdy inclination to adhere to tradition. Bold spirits delighted in flaunting their rebellious mannerisms and breaking of rules. These new behaviors initiated a breakdown of staunch role-playing.

Fanny and I were chaperoned from one class to the next. The music and dance classes were taught by masters of their fields. We were constantly under the noses of our regular teachers, training us in the graces of the society, and instilling in us a deep regard and rich history of the arts. I grew up multilingual, and French was a delightful language that filled my imaginings with a great detail for insinuations, symbolism, innuendoes, and subtlety. The French are vivacious and yet understated, and the result was a charm that I intended to absorb.

Like my father, Sir Jasper moved in diplomatic and military circles. We took residence on the Rue de Rivoli. Like the Rue Castiglione, the Rue de Rivoli was a bustling social circle for Anglo-Indian girls in boarding schools. The schooling was a discipline both extensive and intensive.

By the mid 1840's my second and more formal arrival in Paris paved my reputation as a Paris socialite. I have been called a courtesan, and to this day I refuse to scoff at this. I came to know Litszt, the famous composer. I drew the attention of Alexander Dumas, the novelist who wrote *The Man in the Iron Mask* and *The Count of Monte Cristo.* I had performed at the Potsdam military review, and created a scene by ripping off my garters and tossing them into the audience. Alexander Dumas changed lovers like he changed overcoats. Alexander Henri Dujarier, the co-editor of La Presse, took me upon his arm into the literary circle of the scholarly party known as the Olympians.

After studying with Leon Pillet, a ballet master on the Rue Pelletier, I appeared at the Paris Opera on March 30, 1844. It was a disastrous night for me. Theophile Gautier was in the audience, always visible in his waistcoat of scarlet velvet. In his critique, he pointed out that the "only thing Andalusian about Mademoiselle Montez is a pair of magnificent eyes." I had offended my instructor as well as the audience by dancing without tights. The tights were called maillot. Amongst the applause, some of the audience took to hissing loudly. I restrained my anger, as only Fanny could have taught me, and with a beaming smile, I tossed my slippers into one of the boxes. This brought about a standing ovation, but not so much for my credibility as a dancer as for my stance as a free-thinker among the French elite.

Dujarier may have escorted me into the social literary circles of Paris, but truly he was a drab and morosely withdrawn character. It was through Listzt that I became acquainted with George Sand. Listzt lived together with Countess D'Agoult at the Hotel de France in Paris in quarters just below George Sand. She would listen to Listzt's music through her open window. It seems that George Sand stole my habit of wearing black outfits that served nicely for pinning a vibrant colored flower. I stole from her the habit of smoking cigars. As was the trend of that era in Paris, what I admired most in George Sand was her inclination to freedom of thought.

FIRST DAY IN SAN FRANCISCO

My pulse pounded with excitement at the thought of climbing out of the hatch. The rope ladder dropped from heaven as we prepared to escape the dark underworld of the ship's hold. In my mind's eye I was a grey squirrel scampering up a Chinese elm, but my legs and arms were so weakened by the ordeal of the journey that I felt lightheaded and out of breath as I stepped onto the crowded deck. My shelf bunk was so close to the hatch opening that I dared not mention how weak I felt. After all, I didn't want to be compared to an old man – I had barely outgrown boyhood.

At the bottom of the gangway, Uncle Ān Lè, Mochou, Zhe, and I waited among the crowd for Doctor Youzong to join us. His bunk had been deeper into the hold. I noticed that the land beneath my feet seemed to sway and breathe as if I were still out at sea. Mochou explained that it would take a while to get my "land legs," that the motion of the sea had altered my sense of balance. The pier was crowded with such a diverse array of characters and costumes that Chinese Opera seemed like a narrow scope in comparison. Uncle and I listened to the small voice of a Chinese man behind us describing how unrecognizable San Francisco had become in merely three years. "You would not have recognized the squalid town back then, where moored ships served as hotels. There were so many seagoing vessels simultaneously arrived that the ships were crowded five and six deep out into the bay at every possible shoreline beach. Passengers without paddle boats jumped overboard and swam ashore, impatient to start gathering golden nuggets. I remember a large passenger ship called the Apollo had successfully made passage around Cape Horn of South America. Beached like a whale in San Francisco, the Apollo was transformed into a saloon there on the shore where it had moored. The huge ships, after having been run ashore, became silted in. The hulk of the brig Euphemia was transformed into a new prison, and the Niantic became a bunkhouse, like many other ships that anchored nearby. The shoreline became a chaotic disaster area of makeshift tents and lean-tos that cluttered the hillsides like a garbage heap."

Uncle had posted a lithograph in his office back home in Kowloon that showed a windblown village of four or five hundred residents. The sketch displayed a roomy town called Yerba Buena Cove, with tiny tilting sailboats in the foreground and barren hills behind the sleepy settlement upon Mexican soil. The illustration was a gift from a merchant who had explained to Uncle that Yerba Buena soon after was renamed San Francisco. He also claimed that Yerba Buena was a Spanish name for a mint plant that grew abundantly in the area.

I could place the three pictures in order in my mind. The lithograph of Yerba Buena was followed by the chaotic onslaught of ships in 1849, and finally the picture that I then stood within on the pier that day. I felt an electric excitement in the atmosphere as my ears were bombarded with the languages of a modern day Tower of Babel. Many of us were anxious rookies, half expected to stoop down and scoop up fist-sized golden nuggets, over-stuffing our pockets, and crossing an invisible threshold into a wealthy, refined, and respectable life. I, too, was guilty as the next man in my greedy, selfish vision. I pictured a more worldly and distinguished version of myself, returning to my farming village in Guangzhou. My new rank would drive friends and neighbors to my door, asking my advice, seeking my favor.

In reality, we were met for days with a pent-up despondency that only grew as we awaited transport to our actual gold panning sites. After such a tortuous journey, our dreams were carelessly pushed yet further from our fingertips. Awaiting the tedious arrangements of being assigned a work team, and then being delegated to a specific destination in the Mother Lode, the drawn out delay made me feel like a tea kettle on the verge of boiling over. I reminded myself again and again that months had already passed in our journey to Gum San, the Golden Mountain. Surely I would survive a few more days of delay.

We were all worn out as cross-country mules, each with a dangling carrot before out hungry eyes. We could smell it – we could taste this world renowned *gold*. Ancient pasts of our respective cultures lived on in each one of our visible mannerisms, our countenances, our beliefs, superstitions, and behaviors. As we merged from corners of the earth, the ways of our old countries remained engrained in our very bones. I was slapped in the face with this clash of cultures upon meeting a Northern Mongolian man whom everyone called Jim-Jim. His dialect was unintelligible to me, but he was able to mimic my Cantonese tongue, explaining that the white demons would see my braided queue as an emblem of my foreign status. Initiation into the foreign devil's way of life would most likely be enacted with the quick severing of my queue at the nape of my neck with a bowie knife. Frequently a thick scar on the back of a Chinaman's neck was a sign of this savage ritual.

For a Chinaman, the loss of his queue meant ill fate for plans of returning home. When the Manchu had conquered China in the 1600's, they had imposed upon all Chinese men the wearing of the queue. According to Manchu degree, any man not wearing a queue would be considered a criminal. The dangerous crossing of the Pacific Ocean was rarely intended as escape from China. We intended to return with new found wealth to share with our families, and the loss of our queue only endangered our safety, therefore smashing our dream.

Jim-Jim warned me, "You might resort to the cowardly trick of coiling the long braid on top of your head and hiding it beneath a slouch hat. This might help you in befriending a foreign-tongued prospector. It might save you from the hands of rowdy drunkards. I however, choose to be proud of who I am, and unwilling to bow to the white devils in this respect." Jim-Jim had an impressively angular face, lined in rows by the wind and sun and hard work. He smiled only briefly, revealing his crooked, dull brown teeth. Within his stern and gentle gaze, he recognized my young innocence, and I welcomed his fatherly advice.

Before the journey, back in Kowloon, Uncle had been advised by various sea merchants about safeguarding his hard-earned money. In San Francisco, they warned, the Chinese tael, a unit of silver roughly 38 grams in weight, would be worth very little. Paper bank notes would be useless because Californians only trusted metal coins. Silk would be valuable and Chinese tea could be sold at a decent profit. As a result, Uncle shipped two crates of silk, and one of tea. There was a three crate limit per passenger, and the shipment fee was outrageous. Uncle had given Mochou money to ship an additional three crates. I was employed by Uncle to do likewise. Doctor Yaozong had already arranged for the shipping of medicinal herbs and doctor's supplies, including acupuncture needles and equipment not traditionally found in European medical practices. Zhe, the philosopher sage, insisted that he had no use for the burden of shipping crates. "I have faith that my needs will be met, as I have learned to need very little."

After locating Doctor Yaozong, we proceeded to claim our shipments where cargo was being unloaded. Huge trunks and barrels were lifted by ropes and pulleys, and lowered somewhat carelessly onto the sandy beach. We had to hire a dray to be drawn by a horse, so we sat upon the crates, bouncing and jarred by the ruts and huge holes in the road. The driver was familiar with a joss house within a settlement of Chinamen. Uncle had corresponded with a fellow Cantonese from Kowloon who lived next to the joss house. We did not, of course, call the sanctuary a joss house, this was rather a word taken from Pigeon English. Joss was a mispronunciation of the Portuguese word Deos, meaning God.

Uncle's friend was named Li Bo. Li Bo had a small cottage-sized home near the joss house. There were small cypress trees and cherry saplings, recently planted in the narrow yard behind a tall, unpainted picket fence. Li Bo had long since given up on panning gold, and started a laundry service for the cramped neighborhood. He was energetic and friendly, inviting Uncle to sleep in the kitchen. Two small children, perhaps three and four years old, peered from within the doorway of a tiny bedroom next to the kitchen. "These are my children, Mai Ling and Quan Cai." We bowed and the children lowered their chins to their chests, their hands folded politely. A basket of laundry appeared through a square hole in the ceiling, and was lowered by rope to the floor. A small woman in pastel green climbed down the ladder from the ceiling. She stopped midway to nod her head at us. "This is my wife, Yue Bing." We bowed and giggled – *yuè bǐng* means mooncake.

The tiny house had a small back porch where Mochou ended up sleeping, and Zhe chose the flat roof beneath the laundry lines and the starry sky as his sleeping area. It was expected that I would sleep in the kitchen, joining my uncle, but I chose to sleep up on the roof, leaving room for Doctor Yaozong in the kitchen. Yue Bing gave me a candle and a small plate for collecting the drippings. "Be careful to blow out candle before you lie down to sleep. No fires, please," she smiled and I knew that she trusted me like a son. The first night I wrote a letter to my family on Guangzhou. "I arrived today on the Gold Mountain. The journey across the ocean was long and unpleasant. I am thankful to walk on the still earth again. Uncle is healthy. I am healthy, also. I look forward to collecting large rocks of gold so our family will be wealthy. Hope Brother's arm is healed and everyone is healthy and prosperous. Uncle and I will return home as soon as possible." I placed the letter in an envelope and carefully addressed it with the appropriate Chinese symbols. Uncle had been warned that letters should be mailed from the Asia Pacific Sea Merchants' office, as most English speakers would be unable to decipher the Chinese address and the envelope would more than likely end up in the trash. I blew out the candle as Yue Bing had requested.

As for sleeping arrangements, the roof turned out to be the best choice, because Zhe told me stories as we gazed up into the night sky.

THE KITCHEN GOD

"I noticed in Yue Bing's kitchen a porcelain jar shaped like a happy and well-fed god, the Kitchen God," said Zhe the first night after I blew out the candle. I had noticed the smiling Kitchen God jar also, and recalled a similar illustration that my mother kept hanging near the oven. "The story of the Kitchen God goes back to a Taoist priest named Li Shao-chün. The Kitchen God had bestowed upon Li Shao-chün a life without growing old and without the necessity of eating. Upon visiting the Emperor Hsiao Wu-ti of the Han dynasty, Li Shao-chün proposed that the emperor patronize the Taoist religion and encourage its practice among the people. It was through this acquaintance that Emperor Huang Ti learned of alchemy, and this "magic" enabled him to make gold. The priest was asked to introduce his divine patron to the Emperor, but instead the Emperor was tricked. In a dream one night, Tsao Chün appeared amidst ingots of gold that were promised as a gift to the Emperor. The Emperor became obsessed with seeking the pill of immortality, one of the promises made in the dream, but upon realizing his mistake, humbly made a sacrifice to the God of the Kitchen. Never before had a sacrifice been formally offered to this new deity."

"The Emperor learned to mistrust Li Shao-chün, so the priest devised a plan of writing phrases of coercive advice upon pieces of silk that were mixed with the feed of an ox. The ox, of course, swallowed the silk pieces without notice, and Li Shao-chün announced to the people that a mystic message would be discovered inside the stomach of the ox. The ox was slaughtered, and the message was found, but the Emperor recognized Li's handwriting. The Emperor had the priest put to death. The public proceeded to worship the Kitchen God all the more, until the image soon appeared in every home, always near the stove."

We gazed in silence as shreds of clouds drifted past a crescent moon. I said, "I thought the Kitchen God had granted Li Shao-chün immortality. How then could the Emperor put him to death?" "This is a clever observation on your part," responded Zhe. "The Kitchen God granted him immunity to old age and immunity to the need for food. This was not truly immortality, for Li Shao-chün was out of luck against the punishment of death."

SPIRIT

THE KUNLUN-CHUNGNAN MOUNTAINS

It occurred to me the second evening we spent upon the flat roof beneath the clotheslines, that Zhe had told us many Chinese folks tales and legends, but I had learned nothing about Zhe himself. "Why do they call you a sage and a philosopher?"

"I am an ordinary man who chose an unusual path. I am not unique or alone in venturing upon the path into the mountains. The Kunlun-Chungnan range of mountains is part of early legends from China's oldest religion. This religion bridged the dark river between life and death by envisioning immortality as the waning and waxing of the moon. The moon goddess lived high in the cloud shrouded peaks of the Kunlun-Chungnan range. A few of the devoted followers of the religion gained access to the moon's divinity. They were said to have magic powers. These people walked the Walk of Yu, dragging one foot like a wounded animal. They did this to evoke the pity of the mountain spirits. They were shamans, like Yu the Great who originated the Walk of Yu. As shamans, these individuals had learned to master a blissful state of religious experience. In this rapturous trance, the shaman leaves his body, traverses through a sequence of various heavens, communicating with numerous celestial spirits, gathering and acquiring knowledge for the benefit of his people. He protects his community from dark forces by linking himself to the spiritual realm. He returns with knowledge that he acquires there, but he lives separately from the society he is helping."

"The highest of celestial spirits is in the capital of Ti, a city on earth surrounded by the magical peaks in the Kunglun-Changnan range. The goddess of the moon lives in the capital of Ti. The goddess, His-wang-mu, possesses the elixir of immortality and distributes the elixir as she see fit. The shamans also collect ingredients for their own elixirs as they ascend

111

through the heavens. Those who die young in these realms may have already lived eight hundred years. In this celestial world the sun and moon sleep, in fact, anything is possible. The celestial spirits delight in their every whim and wish. Strange beast and miraculous creatures live here. These creatures have been described by shamans, but earthbound people consider them so unusual that they refuse to believe in them."

"One such creature is a magical beast of ancient China called the *Shanhaiching,* a giant owl with a man's face and a stupendous wingspan of scarlet red wings. I suspect that a sorcerer stirred the pot of yin and yang, mixing the spirits of the four directions. For each direction in ancient China, there was delegated a unique spirit. Blue Dragon was the Spirit of the East. Black Turtlesnake was the Spirit of the North. The Spirit of the West was White Tiger, and the Spirit of the South was Red Bird."

"I have ascended the Kunlun-Chungnan range, where I learned to leave my body, by releasing my spirit. You, too, have this ability within you, clever boy. I recognized that the Kunlun-Chaungnan mountain range was the backbone of China, like the dividing line between yin and yang. All the rivers north of this range gathered their waters in the mountains and flowed in northerly directions. All the rivers heading south were born in the brooks and streams south of the ridge and gathered into mighty rivers flowing to the south. The north and south are, however, as inseparable as yin and yang. Notice that within yin there is the eye of yang, and within yang there lies the seed of yin."

GRASS VALLEY HOME OF LOLA MONTEZ

(1854)

Ms. Montez was so occupied with socializing, gardening, decorating, and other creative projects that she devoted very little time to writing. As a result, I decided to add to my journal by describing in my own words her Grass Valley House.

Lola Montez's House in Grass Valley stood at 248 Mill Street on the corner of Walsh and Mill Streets. (A young protégé, Lotta Crabtree, lived three doors away at 238 Mill Street.) Newspaper articles and clippings, carefully pasted into a scrapbook, supplied me with brisk sweeps of Ms. Montez's history. These articles served as general introductions for the societies of New York and San Francisco. "Lola Montez, Countess of Landsfeld (a title bestowed on her by Ludwig I of Bavaria) was in actuality an Irish girl. After a series of scandals, each to the benefit of the Countess of Landsfeld, she came west to act and dance in New York and San Francisco theaters. She impersonated herself in *Lola Montez in Bavaria* and performed her famous Spider Dance, a cross between the Polish Mazurka, the Bohemian Polka, the Viennese Waltz, and an Irish jig. One critic called the dance a contrivance for showing off cancan kicks and waving her petticoats about immodestly. By the age of thirty-six, when she arrived in Grass Valley, she had been married five times. Shortly after her acquaintance of Ludwig I she discarded her first husband, Thomas James. Ludwig I of Bavaria was to be driven from the throne. Ludwig's dignitaries perceived that marrying this high society courtesan would be an embarrassing threat to the welfare of Bavaria. She was exiled from the country. Her third husband, a French journalist named Dujarier, was killed in a duel. George Heald, her fourth husband, managed to maintain discretion about his involvement with her and the consequent demise. Patrick Hull, a San Francisco editor, married her and was soon divorced after their arrival in Grass Valley. Johnny Southwick, a local mine official, helped arrange

113

her residence in the cottage on Mill Street. Southwick flipped the bill for furnishing the cottage in grandeur. It was reported to have cost him several thousand dollars. An Oriental bathtub was imported, panels of window glass sliding upon rails were installed, and an Austrian marble fireplace was erected, to name a few of the luxuries. Roaming the yard, roped to an elm tree, she kept a bear cub as one of her pets.

Several doors down the street, Mary Ann Crabtree was unlike the harshly judgmental women of Grass Valley. Mary Ann was not dismayed that the Countess of Landsfeld smoked cigars in public; that she created a stir when she horsewhipped a local newspaper editor, or that she catered all-night soirées, dancing for her guests and performing on the harpsichord. The miners named a nearby peak Mount Lola in appreciation of her charms and eccentricities.

Lola took a liking to Mary Ann's daughter Lotta, and the pair were frequently seen horseback riding. Lola gave the child high-spirited classes in performing and dancing, which included the Spanish fandango and the Highland fling.

Lola's house was no castle, but the furniture and décor was elaborate. The parlor was a showcase of china, snuff boxes, scent boxes, glass decanters, a brass bird cage and opera lorgnettes, displayed within opulent cadenzas, chiffoniers, corner cupboards, and mantelpieces. A massive Turkish rug was anchored on one end by an eighteenth century Spanish carved-walnut coffer positioned beneath a stained glass depicting ballet dancers. The drawn chiffon draperies created for the dancers the curtains of the stage. At the other end of the Turkish rug stood the leather and sealskin traveling box that I had seen when I first saw her at the train station. In the center of the room stood a low, Regency circular drum table with a sugar maple engraved upon its tabletop. A single scarlet iris stood regally in a turquoise Lutz glass jug upon a salmon fringed satin napkin centered on the table. Directly above the iris, a twelve light ormolu chandelier dominated the room, giving off an amber glow. A gothic style horseman's armour stood propped upon a coat rack in one corner of the room and a Flemish harpsichord painted with lavender and saffron grapevines held court at the opposite corner near a grape-velvet Belgian loveseat. Beside it a Louis XVI credenza displayed a "frogger" grease lamp used by miners, an assay kit with small glass stopper jars of chemicals, a blowpipe, an alcohol lamp, three legged magnifiers, and a high quality scale. An early eighteenth century yew wood corner cabinet stood beside a closed window-display of long white candles that had dripped impressive mounds of wax tears upon their crystal candleholders. Within the glazed doors of the yew wood cabinet were a collection of goblets, decanters, a brass sundial, a Victorian chromatic stereoscope, a metronome in an oak case, and two long-barreled dueling pistols by Wogdon of London. A delightful George III black and gold lacquered long-case grandfather clock gave off a hypnotic tick-tock and chiming that blended with the chattering of lovebirds in a brass birdcage shaped like an arboretum. Beside it, a framed lithograph on the wall featured the Crystal Palace in London, soon to be imitated at the World's Fair in New York. The lovebirds' brass birdcage seemed to resemble a skeleton of the Crystal Palace in miniature. A Regency-period gilt convex mirror gave a warped spherical view of the whole room and all the guests therein. There was a blurred, paint-splattered depiction of a horse-drawn carriage entering a thick forest, and another strange painting of a curved path through singed birch trees upon which a lone satin shoe was filled with fire. There was a charming collection of unusual toys; a tall paperweight containing a castle with a musical automaton choir of singers, a delicate model of a Portuguese galleon, a Spanish dancer doll, and a tiny penny farthing cycle.

Very few of these articles originated in California, but similarly, very few of her guests originated from North America. A starkly clever contrast was drawn by stepping from this collage of European finery out into the light of day and her yard of wide banana leaves, tall ferns, and bizarre cacti. She had collected the magic of the world to surround her, and she made me feel as if I were part of this magic.

GOLD PANNING ON HORNITOS CREEK

Mouchou, the silent giant, and my Uncle Ān Lè were sent as fellow members of my first group of miners on a pack train of donkeys to a small settlement on Hornitos Creek. In comparison to Mouchou, the donkeys looked liked small dogs. The donkeys would stir and honk in Mouchou's presence, and Mouchou seemed equally uncomfortable around them. Seeing that no donkey would allow Mouchou on its back, Uncle hired a palomino mare for Mouchou – it was either that or the pack train's owner would have refused to send Mouchou with us. My small frame made me a likely fit on a donkey's back, so I was taught to guide a donkey pulling a cart. The donkey's name was Blisters, and it didn't take me but one day to learn the meaning of this new English word. The donkeys were loaded with provisions and miners' tools and we stopped to unload at various general stores along the journey until we arrived at our destination. Our final destination was a settlement called Hornitos, a Spanish word meaning "little ovens." Three Dutch bakers had located there, making a successful profit from baking and selling bread to the miners. The Dutch bakers' mud ovens were shaped like domes. During my stay, I encountered a gruesome coincidence – the Mexican burial mounds built above ground resembled the mud ovens that the Dutch used for baking.

The original town of Hornitos was recognizable as a small Mexican town built around a plaza. An abundance of pepper trees and sturdy cottonwoods surrounded the plaza, creating shaded walkways along the rows of adobe shops. Yellow corn lilies and red monkeyflowers planted in rounded clay pots were placed beside doorways and along support beams of wooden railings. The Mexican people wore colorful clothing. Some wore large straw hats that resembled the Chinaman's bell shaped hat of woven reeds. The Mexican hats were more flexible and curled up around the brims.

We passed a general store with wooden tables heaped high with serapes, boots, tall towers of stacked hats, and plenty of miners' pans, bowie knives, rifles, water pouches, and rock candy. Inside the high windows stood rows of tequila bottles, whiskey flasks, and jugs of rum and hard cider. Downstairs there was a fandango hall with a wrought iron gate secured with a heavy chain and an oversized padlock. The gate was opened and relocked when a rowdy drunk needed a night to cool off his heels in the dungeon below.

Cantina de Sancho was a small bar made of orange bricks and roof tiles of red clay. We could hear yelling mixed with barking, growling dogs out back of the bar and decided to take a peek for ourselves. As we passed along a row of dead weeds lined up against the side of the bar, a loud roar excited even more vigorous yelling and barking. A half circle of miners blocked our vision of the spectacle, but I noticed a slender elm tree nearby that I climbed up for a bird's eye view. What I witnessed from the elm tree was a morbid and barbaric battle staged within a wire mesh cage. Six large dogs had been set loose inside the cage to battle a black bear that had been chained to a sturdy tree. Mouchou was tall enough to see over the crowd. When he turned and spotted me in the tree, he could see by the stunned look on my face that I was alarmed and dismayed. In his long stride he approached the tree and reached up to pull me down from my perch. "This game I see before, call Bear Baiting," he said. "Poor animal rip each other apart. Miner drink, think fun." I said nothing as Mouchou set me back on the ground. I thought of all the wars and feuds between men. I would have thought that men could be satisfied with their own man-to-man conflicts without instigating, in the name of amusement, gory tooth-and-claw battles to the death between animals.

Half of our group was employed to quarry large blocks of stone from the hills that slanted gently upward from the town. These men were referred to as "Chinese coolies" by the townsfolk. Their job was to load the stone blocks on their backs and carry them into the edge of town where a new town jail was about to be built. The wild scrambling for wealth triggered an overwhelming number of robberies and murders. At least half of the miners carried a thick coil of rope on their belts, and not one day or two would pass without a throng of men gathering around the hideous old hang tree, exercising their impromptu justice for lack of deputy sheriff or any organized police force.

There was a committee of miners, but they were always too late to respond. When a Chinaman attempted to scare off a mischievous gang of young rascals by firing a bullet at the opposite side of the ravine, the bullet ricocheted, grazing the leg of one of the youngsters. The unlucky man was called China John, and a squad of miners hauled him off to jail, accusing him of shooting an American boy. That night a mob gathered around the tiny jail window with its iron bars. Someone managed to coax China John to reach out the window for some whisky or opium, giving the crowd a chance to seize his arms. A noose was thrown over his neck and China John was strangled against the bars of the miniature window from within the jail.

Mouchou, Uncle Ān Lè, and I lived in the Hornitos Chinatown, a small maze of cabins, tents, sheds, shacks, and lean-tos. Residences were added upon rooftops and sleeping space was crafted within tunnels below some of the cabins. Amid the chaos and disarray stood a three-story pagoda, a joss house painted red and black, decorated with brilliant colored paper and gilt.

Mouchou, the giant, my Uncle and I were sent with a small team of miners to pan gold on Hornitos Creek. We were spared from the hard labor in the quarry because Uncle had paid half of our roundtrip fares for the voyage across the Pacific. The Chinamen in deeper debt were chosen to haul the heavy stone blocks for building the new town jail.

A miner named Dustpan Sam taught me how to pan for gold. The miners said that Dustpan would never be rich, because he would yahoo and yippee every time he uncovered the slightest bit of gold dust. Ol' Smokey assured me that Dustpan Sam knew how to handle the pan as good as any nincompoop in all of Hornitos. Dustpan wore knee-high boots and when he saw my teeth chattering from standing in the icy creek, he pulled at the tops of his boots and crossed his arms to convey "Keep warm." (Uncle bought me some knee-high boots the next morning in town.) Dustpan Sam taught me to fill the pan three-fourths full of sand and rocks, and then lower the pan into the water to fill it. Next I was taught to set the full pan on a level rock or the creek bank so I could squeeze the sand in my hand and break up any loose clods and mud. This allowed any gold to sink to the bottom of the pan. Dustpan Sam had me pulling out any rocks or large objects, inspecting them, and then tossing them aside. He taught me to give the pan a few shakes back and forth and then from side to side, helping more of the heavier substances to settle to the bottom.

Putting the pan just below the surface of the water, as he showed me, I tilted it slightly away from myself, and made circular motions from side to side. Loose sand began to spill over the edge of the pan. Every now and then, Dustpan instructed, I would have to level the pan while shaking it back and forth. This was the best time to check for nuggets. I continued the whole process until only black sand and the heaviest concentrated material remained. This mixture was stored in a box to be inspected later.

The process doesn't sound very tedious, but repeating it over and over became more complicated than a rookie might imagine. If my focus upon the gold panning distracted me from keeping a sturdy stance, the push of the creek water on my shoes might cause me to slip, leaving me splashing in the creek water. The first day I fell in three times. The first time the pan got away from me, and the old timers hooted and hollered until my face flushed red. A few hours later, my third fall wasn't so detrimental. By that time of the afternoon, the sun was getting hot and the cold bath was almost a relief. I was fortunate to learn gold panning in the Hornitos Creek. Panning in a river requires more skill because it's more dangerous. Another trick to master was being able to catch something shiny spilling out of the pan without spilling all the remaining debris. An ongoing challenge was figuring out how not to crook my stiff neck, and ways to keep my arms from cramping up from the endless repetition of cradling and dipping the pan. Dustpan Sam taught me to pan standing up, then sitting down, or to take a smoke break, or to cup my hands for a drink of water, and then wash my face – anything to break up the panning process.

It wasn't until later that fellow Chinamen taught me to have the patience to collect and compile the gold dust. This was something few other miners had the patience for, but most

Chinamen already knew that some good things take the discipline of much time spent doing a tedious task.

Later the first night, Mouchou started scratching his wrists and arms until purple welts rose up on his skin. He scratched at the dark rashes 'til they bled, and a miner named Panama Pete told Mouchou it was poison oak. Panama Pete tore off one of Mouchou's shirtsleeves to make strips of bandages that he soaked in cool water. He tied the wet bandages around Mouchou's wrists and arms and gave him a piece of black soap to wash his hands and scrub his fingernails.

The next morning on the trail back to the creek, Panama Pete pointed out the small sprouting leaves at the base of oak trees and in small patches nearby. "When you see three leaves together like this, stay away and don't touch." It was turning out that the Golden Mountain had its share of curses. This was my third week here and I wondered if I would even see one single golden nugget. The trail was beautiful, though, passing thru steep hills covered with orange poppies and purple lupine mixed with small patches of buttercups and red paintbrush. Tall grass tilted away from the trail, crossed by the meandering roots of huge oak trees. I would lose myself on these short treks to the creek, forgetting that I am Chinese. I was a young man on a mountainside trail. The trail would turn upon new vistas, giving me time to forget my apprehensions and my sense of uneasiness around so many strange new foreigners.

compliant

THE MINER'S TEN COMMANDMENTS

A claim for mining purposes within this district shall not exceed one hundred square feet to each man...

No man within the bounds of this district shall hold more than one claim...

Each and every man holding a claim within the bounds of this district shall work one day out of every three, or employ a substitute, otherwise such claims shall be forfeited...

Each and every man holding a claim within the bounds of this district, shall designate such claims by erecting good and substantial stakes at each corner of their claims, or dig a ditch around said claim...

When any dispute arises concerning claims, and either party shall refuse to refer such dispute to a committee of five, two to be chosen by each party and the fifth to be chosen by the other four, the party so refusing shall forfeit all right to such claim in dispute...

A standing committee of ten (shall) be appointed, to whom complaints shall be made in all mining disputes, and it shall be their especial duty to see (the above article) enforced, and that said committee (shall) be empowered to summon a posse at any time when necessary to assist them in the discharge of their duty...

(It is) Resolved, that (these laws) be published in the Sonora Herald, and that 500 copies be printed in handbills.

We staked out a rectangular shaped area on both banks of the creek, signaling to other prospectors that this section of the creek was our claim. Small groups of prospectors and occasional lone miners would pass by our claim, continuing along the trail that headed further up-creek. Once a day, or perhaps every other day, someone would recognize Dustpan Sam or Panama Pete and stop to inquire if we were having any luck. Dustpan Sam wore striped pants held up with suspenders over a faded pair of long johns. He tucked his baggy pants into his knee-high boots, and wore a battered looking felt hat shaped like a cowboy hat. If somebody asked Dustpan if we were having any luck, he'd say, "Oh sure, we're so bloody rich that we're still standing here in the mud."

Dustpan had an Irish wolfhound named Buckaroo. Buckaroo was copper brown with grayish black hues streaked throughout his coat. Buckaroo followed dustpan around like a shadow. When Dustpan waded into the creek to pan for gold, Buckaroo would circle around busily, sniffing, inspecting, and lifting his leg to wet down a tree trunk or tall grass blades. He'd eventually sit down panting and smiling at Dustpan, and then take long naps on the creek bank, guarding the area surrounding Dustpan. Buckaroo would rouse and growl, then stand up barking, always first to detect any approaching strangers or wildlife. Dustpan would slip Buckaroo scraps of food now and then, and if the chow was plentiful, Buckaroo might get a slab of meat or a hambone. We all learned to stay clear of Buckaroo if he was feasting on animal flesh. Mouchou walked too near the wolfhound as the dog was gnawing on a porkchop, and Buckaroo let out a deep-throated growl and bared his long pointed teeth. Mouchou held up his hands and backed away gingerly. We all laughed at the sight of the giant man terrified out of his wits.

Panama Pete had a darker complexion and kinky black hair that sprouted out below his little straw hat. A yellow and blue striped ribbon encircled the base of his hat, and Panama wore matching suspenders. His canary yellow jacket was dirty and wrinkled, but he wore it with poise and a debonair manner. He occasionally smoked a corncob pipe and stuffed it with sweet smelling tobacco, the smoke of which smelled like burning cinnamon. His pale blue shirt had ruffles at the cuffs and down the front, which might have seemed feminine on a lesser man, but gave him a gentleman's flair. He was muscular and lean, a man accustomed to walking, perhaps horseback riding. His pants were made of shiny black leather and he wore black cowboy boots. If somebody on the trail recognized Panama Pete, the enthusiasm was obvious and a lively conversation sprang up. Panama's English had regal British intonations smothered in a thick accent that all but disguised his dialogues from most of us. Gestures and poses, pantomimes and facial expressions embellished his words with theatrics. Coins and knives and who-knows-what were juggled and exchanged. Ol' Smokey called Panama a "wheeler dealer." I made an educated guess that "wheeler dealer" meant a gambler.

Ol' Smokey resembled a grizzly bear – dirty and hairy. Brown and black were his predominant colors. These colors seemed to ooze from his grouchy personality. He was pessimistic, irritable, easily angered, and quick to be discouraged or depressed. Even the foul smelling cigar that hung from the side of his lip failed to cover the acidic odor of his sweat stained clothing. From a distance Ol' Smokey looked like a steaming clod of mud. Smokey's hair rose up from his forehead in a shocked crown like a lion's mane. He always looked like he was walking into a strong wind, and the mangy tangle surrounding his face gave him a surprised look, like an unexpected blast of gunpowder. Most of us avoided encounters with Smoky, but he would occasionally amaze us with small gestures of kindness – returning a jacket left behind on the creek bank, or sharpening someone's bowie knife on the grindstone that he kept inside one of his hobnail boots. You could get Smoky to laugh, but it was usually at the misfortune of another miner.

The other six in our group were Chinese; Mouchou, Uncle Ān Lè, myself and three other Chinamen, Ch'ang, Hsiáng, and Wu. We Chinamen were all new arrivals from the dreadful voyage on the *Seringapatam*. Smokey, Panama, and Dustpan were like our new world overseers. They initiated us into California mining life, communicated with English speaking encounters, warned us of dangerous situations, and eased us into new and bewildering cultural practices.

I must have been lucky to apprentice with Dustpan Sam. He was enough of a simpleton to put up with my lack of English skill. Uncle Ān Lì and Wu helped Panama Pete to build a rocker. Dustpan said that a rocker was a contraption that was 'pose to increase our profits. Smokey pointed out that an increase from nuthun' wasn't bound to 'mount to much. Uncle and Wu smiled and laughed at much of Panama's directions, but they were both in the dark when it came to understanding his instructions in English, or whatever you might call Panama's tongue. Panama's new motto became, "Do what I do, jus' do what I do." Mouchou overheard this and changed the motto to "Monkey see, monkey do." Panama got a kick out of this and started prancing about like a chimpanzee saying, "Oo-ooo, ee-eee, ooo-oo, eee-ee." Panama would hammer pieces of two-by-fours to form the rockers outer frame as he chanted "Oo-ooo, ee-eee, ooo-oo, eee-ee," scratching his sides beneath his arms and hopping about like a chimpanzee. Wu would pick up the hammer and boards and join in, "Oo-ooo, ee-eee, ooo-oo, eee-ee."

Sixth Moon – Day 13: Birthday of Lu Ban, patron deity
of builders and carpenters.

THE ROCKER

The contraption that Panama Pete taught them to build resembled a baby's cradle. Ol' Smokey called it a cradle while Dustpan Sam called it a dolly, but most miners called it a rocker. From the outside it looked like a simple wooden box, although some rockers that I saw later were much longer than others. Rounded half moons of wood on the bottom enabled the box to rock, and a handle on top enabled a man to maintain its motion. Wu designed a handle made from a sawed-off broomstick. The upper end of the box held a removable tray called a hopper. The hopper was square with sides the length of a small man's arm and as deep as a fist. On the bottom of the hopper was an iron plate with perforated holes about as wide as fingers. Panama Pete placed the hopper on top of an inclining frame inside the box that sloped from the middle of the box down to the top end. Uncle Ān Lè had stretched a piece of burlap over the frame and secured the cloth with small nails. The burlap, or apron, was meant to trap gold that fell through the holes in the bottom of the hopper. Beneath the hopper, at the bottom end of the box, were three or four slats of wood that Panama called riffles. "The riffles trap any gold pebbles or dust that has escaped the apron," said Panama. The process relied on the heavier weight of the gold. Water was ladled into the hopper with a dipper. The water washed debris through the holes, and the sag of the apron caught the heavier debris (hopefully gold) while the lighter rocks and sand washed down the incline to the bottom of the rocker. The rocker itself was set on the incline of the creek bed.

Panama Pete assigned assistants to their duties. "Ān Lè, you shovel the gravel. Wu, I want you to rock the cradle and ladle water into the hopper." Panama demonstrated rocking the box while dipping into the creek for water to gently pour into the hopper. "Pour the water gently, a sudden gush of water might wash away the finer gold dust." Wu made his monkey sounds and imitated Panama's movements. Uncle was shown how to shovel gravel into the hopper, and then after a thorough washing, to dump the hopper full of gravel into the puddling box.

Mouchou was put in charge of raking the gravel inside the puddling box. His long arms were good for long strokes of the rake. The box was filled with water to dilute the mud and clay. The puddling box was as large as a double bed and over a foot deep. So many of the rocks and pebbles were encrusted in mud or clay, it was necessary to break up the clay and dry-cemented mud to inspect the rocks hidden inside. Mouchou worked intently in the puddling box, but nearly everyone took a shift at sifting through the box looking for any sparkles or glimmers of gold. The puddling box had plugs underneath for draining the mucky liquid, exposing the raked over rocks inside the box.

I had taken a break from gold panning, and took a turn at inspecting the gravel in the puddling box. Panama Pete meandered by, stood beside me, and picked up a few rocks out of the box. I asked him, "How you idea make wocker." Panama was used to a Chinaman having difficulty pronouncing the letter R. "The rocker wasn't my idea," he said, "I got the idea from a Chinaman in Hangtown." We looked up at each other and smiled.

Eighth Moon – Day 16: Birthday of Sun Wukong, the Monkey King, Great Sage Equal to Heaven. The mischievous Monkey King appears in the novel *Journey to the West*. The Monkey King is a trickster of immeasurable talent and cunning wit.

TOOTHLESS ABE AND EVIL-EYE ZACHERY

Sometimes we'd load the two rockers we had built onto small wagons that could be towed behind us on the trail for hauling back into town after a days work. We created leather harnesses for attaching two ropes around the shoulders of the unlucky fellow whose turn it was to pull the wagon like a beast of burden upon the uneven trail.   If the weather was decent, three of us would camp out at the claim, guarding our rockers, the puddling box and the tools as we slept under the stars. Sleeping outside was risky business because outlaws would take advantage of campers in the darkness, not to mention bears and bobcats that wandered the hills looking for food. If Dustpan Sam camped out with a couple of us, we had Buckaroo to wake us before anything or anyone approached us. Unfortunately, every time that Buckaroo woke us with his growling and barking, poor Dustpan couldn't get the dog to quiet down. If an outlaw with a gun were to stumble upon us, the barking would be a dead giveaway of our location.

Luckily, weeks passed without a serious incident involving our own clan of miners, but we weren't finding any substantial amount of gold. The little bit of gold dust and tiny pebbles that accumulated in a month's time were not paying off our dept to the Asia-Pacific Sea Merchants and keeping us fed well enough to keep the same claim for much longer.   I overheard Uncle and Panama Pete discussing whether to give the creek another week or two before moving elsewhere.

One fall morning, we headed out from Hornitos on our way to the trail. We passed the central plaza with its pepper trees full of hanging limbs of foliage like weeping willows.

There was a cool mist in the air creating a fog that erased trees and businesses into clouds of gray. Buildings and horse-drawn wagons appeared like ghosts as we neared them. It was a mysterious, dreamlike morning as we ambled along the trail that led to the creek. I could hear the voices of Dustpan and Panama ahead of me, and the Chinese comments behind from Ch'ang and Hsiáng. By the time we reached our claim, the morning light had burned off the mist, and the creek shone like the polished silver of a Samurai's sword. Mourning doves called out gently, and tiny black birds darted through the air like arrows released from crossbows.

It was one of those mornings when work seemed like a blessing instead of drudgery. The thought crossed my mind that we might actually find a whole nugget today. I remember how naively optimistic I had been about collecting bulging pockets full of weighty gold nuggets. After two months on the Golden Mountain, I managed to diminish my disappointment by remembering that this was an adventure unlike anything imaginable back in Guangdong. This morning Ch'ang and Mouchou helped Panama Pete with one rocker while Hsiáng and I helped Ol' Smokey with the other rocker. Uncle Ān Lè was raking gravel in the puddling box, and Dustpan was out panning in the creek. Buckaroo started growling then barking, and sure enough, within minutes, we heard horse hooves on the trail. Two hats appeared on the top of the south hill, and then the faces and bodies of two men on horseback as they approached our camp. Buckaroo barked wildly.

One of the men yelled out, "Panama Pete," and Panama yelled out, "Top of the morning, Evil Eye." Dustpan stepped out of the creek to attempt to calm down Buckaroo. "This is my business partner, Toothless Abe," called out Evil Eye. Evil Eye wore a patch over one eye, a black leather hat upon his head full of long greasy hair. His black horse had a white diamond shaped spot on its forehead. Toothless Abe was a scrawny man in a ten-gallon hat, propped up on a tawny colored mare. Evil Eye and Panama started yelling words at each other. Even if I had understood English better, I probably would have missed the nature of the conversation because Buckaroo was barking as if a wildcat was ready to attack. "Shut up your damn mongrel, Panama," yelled Evil Eye. "It's not my dog," called back Panama.

Evil Eye pulled out his long barreled pistol so fast, that not one of us could have reacted in time. Straightening his long arm, Evil Eye fired the gun at Buckaroo. I heard a high pitch yelp from the poor dog, and Buckaroo fell upon the ground. We all gazed at Buckaroo in astonishment as a dark pool of red blood soaked into the dry dirt. Buckaroo panted rapidly as he whimpered weakly. Dustpan Sam yelled out, "Buckaroo!" in anguish and pulled out a pistol from his belt. He fired in the direction of Evil Eye and Toothless Abe, but the two had already hightailed back down the path. All I saw when I looked up was two hats as they bounced out of sight over the hill.

Dustpan kneeled down by Buckaroo. The dog's panting had ceased and his tongue hung motionless from his parted mouth. We could see that the bullet had pierced the dog's chest and the gushing blood had drained the life right out of him. The dog lay motionless. Dustpan laid his face on Buckaroo's neck, weeping silently. When Dustpan lifted his face, his cheeks were streaked with tears. I don't think there was one of us that felt shame to see a grown man cry. The rest of us were holding back our own tears. Dustpan looked up at the sky as if some answer or voice would sound from the splintered sun overhead. Then he kneeled down to pick up Buckaroo with both arms and asked me to grab the shovel. It was not something that I felt the heart to do – digging a hole for poor Buckaroo, but Dustpan was his best friend and I knew it had to be done.

After the task had been completed, with help from the others, Panama Pete positioned two sturdy birch limbs tied together to form a cross. He drove the cross in the ground above the grave and Dustpan said a few words starting with God and ending with Amen. After a moment of silence Dustpan added, "I will find this scum, Evil Eye, and I will pay him back." We all turned away from the grave, knowing that a good day's work had come to an early and treacherous end.

The boisterous saloons and taverns of gold rush
California made booming business day and night, whether to
celebrate new wealth, new friends, new deals, or carouse for a
woman. Every sort of loss, be it money, a leg or an arm, the loss
of a co-worker, or loss at the gambling table – every misery was
worth drowning in a cheap bottle of whiskey or countless mugs
of foaming draft beer.

Panama took his crew of miners straight to the
Grizzly's Saloon, a stone's throw from the central plaza. At the
back of the bar was a buffalo's head mounted on a wooden
plaque, and above the rows of bottles behind the bartender was a
ferocious black bear's head with a wide open mouthful of long,
pointed yellow teeth. As we positioned ourselves at an empty
round table, my eyes adjusted to the darkness and I looked up in
awe at the huge span of antlers on the moose head above the
doorway. Four men at a nearby table were playing Black Jack
while smoking pipes and cigars. Ruffians sat upon high stools at
the bar, but most men stood and slammed their glasses on the
counter. Yelling and bantering across the room lent the air a
threatening festivity on the verge of recklessness. Among the
loud and animated, I noted several threatening characters with
expressionless faces of stone.

Panama ordered a jug of hard cider and nine glasses
for the table. Smokey and Dustpan downed their first glassfuls
like travelers in a desert who had found an oasis. Panama took
hearty swigs of the thick brew, but the six Chinamen (of whom I
was one) sipped the harsh smelling liquid with caution. The
sweet liquid had a brazen heat in my mouth, and I spewed the
first mouthful out onto the floor. Panama laughed and slapped
me on the back, but my fellow countrymen looked at me in
horror as if I had committed an unforgivable display of
disrespect. Uncle demonstrated the art of downing a small swig
of the devil's drink, bypassing the mouth and literally tossing the
brew down the throat. I took a few breaths, looked into the wide
mouthed glass at the golden cider, and threw a hefty swig down
my throat. Swallowing hard, the men round the table cheered. I
slammed my glass upon the table and grabbed my throat. A
fierce fire unfurled into my chest. Attempting to cough, my

throat tightened. It was too late. The burning blaze was within me, and I gasped for air. Everyone seemed to be laughing as if death by asphyxiation was a lighthearted topic. By the time Smokey ordered a tall glass of water, the warmth had spread to my stomach and my throat had gone numb. I swallowed the full glass of water and wiped tears from my eyes.

Loud cheers rose up from a table of gamblers, and drinks were being downed, bottoms-up fashion at the bar. The men seemed to relish slamming their empty glasses upon the worn counter. A tipsy cowboy yelled out something harsh at the bartender, who sauntered over with a deadpan expression to pick up the drunken cowboy's glass. The cowboy wasn't the only drunk in Grizzly's Saloon, but he seemed to be the most volatile character of the moment. The bartender calmly placed a large mug on the counter and reached for a bottle of whiskey. The cowboy swayed and wobbled, on the verge of falling down. The bartender stepped back abruptly, and a trap door opened beneath the feet of the rowdy cowboy, who fell through the floor screaming. The bartender quickly leaned forward and the trap door shut as he picked up the large mug.

I asked Panama, "What happen?" and Panama explained that the bartender had a lever he could pull from behind the bar. "The big-shot cowboy just got 'shanghaied'." (My companions laughed at this.) "Below the trapdoor is a large box with a mattress in it, and a couple of ruffians ready to take his gun and knives before he knows what hit him. They'll probably tie him up 'til he cools off or falls asleep. They might give him a few doses of laudanum to keep him knocked out for a day or two. By the time the cowboy wakes up, he'll be on a whalin' boat far out at sea. Grizzly's Saloon must make a killing sellin' hard-heads to the whalin' boats. You can't round up a good crew for whaling these days with every jackass in sight runnin' off to pan for gold."

Dustpan seemed indifferent to his surroundings. He had already refilled his glass and took a second gulp of cider that emptied half the glass. It occurred to me after a few drinks that the barroom full of exuberant and raucous men was not so threatening as before, that the gathering of miners had merely set beside their drudgery and woes to celebrate a lighter side of life. This lighter side was carefree and easy going. I felt

131

companionship to all these beaten down animals of burden. Who could deny them this exuberant feeling, this weight lifted from their shoulders? I too wanted my spirit lifted, this flight from the heaviness and fatigue. Somehow, though, the remainder of the evening erased itself from my memory like a page torn from a book and thrown into the fireplace.

I awoke in an acute state of suffering. Was I dying of the black plague? My brain felt as if an ice pick had been driven through its middle. I lay on the floor in a pool of vomit that matted my hair and stuck to my shirt. I tried to rise up from the floor, but the ice pick's sting was even more excruciating in my skull. My stomach was queasy and I began heaving up green bile. It was Ol' Smokey who ended up changing my shirt and washing my face and hair in cold water. He forced me to drink a full glass of water and led me to my bunk to recuperate. It was later the next day that Mouchou and Hsiáng were piecing together bits of Panama's drunken storytelling. He had reminisced about loading crates of bananas onto the cargo ships in Costa Rica. His hard work had failed to make him a rich man, and when the landlady of his hotel room had fallen deathly ill, he had nursed the poor woman upon her deathbed. During evenings of tending to her and feeding her spoons of medicine and tea, he had discovered an envelope inside her nightstand that contained a large sum of money.

He pocketed the envelope and continued to nurse the ailing woman. Discovering her dead one early morning, he fled Costa Rica with her stash and on to Panama where the floods of migrating wealth-seekers were crossing land to shorten their journey to the gold rush of California. In Panama, he acquired his new name and a reputation as a trader of imports of rare or useful items. He soon succumbed to the gold fever and joined the river of humanity headed for San Francisco. Both Mouchou and Hsiáng were uncertain of the nature of the argument between Evil Eye and Panama. They agreed, however, that Evil Eye was not angry at the barking dog, but at Panama Pete himself. The dead dog was just a warning of some wrongdoing left unresolved. When revenge is piled upon revenge a loosened rock can snowball into an avalanche. This was not the type of battle that Chinamen in California wanted to participate in. The laws were laid against us and the lynch mob would surely hang each and every one of us. I could picture my Uncle and Mouchou swaying limply from ropes that had snapped their necks. I would be one of the bodies, alongside Wu, Hsiáng and Ch'ang. The elation of the hard cider was a short-lived enticement that had turned on me, poisoning my body and revealing this dreadful vision. I vowed to never drink again.

MINING THE GOLD MINERS

"Where is all the gold?" asked Ms. Montez. "You traveled and suffered and went into debt to purchase your way across the ocean, and now you have nothing to show for it but your lovely smile and your talent for documenting your story. It seems to me that you are beating your head against a rock, and the rock contains no gold. When I moved to Grass Valley, I heard a story repeated several times about a miner who had one evening returned home to share dinner with his wife. The miner sat down at the kitchen table, tucked a napkin under his chin, and his wife approached the table with a large iron skillet with a copper lid. The woman placed the skillet upon a quilted pan holder upon the table. The miner leaned forward to inspect the dinner as his wife lifted the copper lid. There in the skillet was a fist-sized gold nugget that the miner's wife had discovered in the flower box."

"This story occurred nearly four years ago when the surrounding area of the Sierra Nevada Mountains was plentiful in gold. Nowadays a miner would be lucky to walk away with a thimble half-full of gold dust collected in a year's time. The successful people in California are now the bankers, the building constructors, the tailors, the shoemakers, the ranch owners and farmers, the restaurant and hotel owners, the jewelers, and the furniture makers. What do all these miners need? They need clothing and food, homes, and entertainment. The pot of gold is no longer the gold itself, but what the gold miners are willing to pay for. In San Francisco, the Chinese laundries and restaurants are making more money than the Chinese gold miners. Somehow, I envision you doing something more profitable than cleaning and pressing shirts. The question is – what is your pot of gold in California?"

I looked directly into Ms. Montez's flashing eyes. She had such intensity in her gaze that she could have melted me down to a puddle of candle wax. My English was improving. I had not graspped each word and phrase of her proposition, but I had to agree with the gist of her reasoning. These very thoughts

134

had occurred to me as I traveled from mining town to mining town, observing the successful characters, each finding a booming business of supplying the miners and newly arrived foreigners with services and goods other than gold itself. The uncanny thing about her little speech was that Ms. Montez had put into words the very thoughts that had accumulated in my own mind over the passing months. It was dumbfounding to hear my Chinese thoughts put into English words.

MOVING ON

Fortunately, during our pack train journey by donkey to Hornitos, we had stopped at various mining towns to drop off supplies. We had passed through Stockton following the Calaveras River to Angels Camp where we then headed south to Sonora, Chinese Camp, Carson City, Jackass Hill, and Dogtown. Uncle and Hsiáng decided we should relocate to Chinese Camp so as to lose track of any further encounters with Evil Eye and Toothless Abe. A Chinaman was worth no more than an animal in this strange land. If a dog's life was ended as a warning, then a Chinaman could be shot without a second thought. And so we left Panama Pete, Ol' Smokey and Dustpan Sam in Hornitos. Uncle hired a horse drawn wagon that would hold the six of us and our belongings. The roads were dirt and gravel, and the holes and bumps were numerous. Narrow passages that were passable by donkey were not easily traversed by wagon. Nearly every hour or two, the six of us would be forced to jump down off the wagon, unload our possessions, and push or lift the heavy wagon over obstacles in the road. If the road was a steep enough incline uphill we would all have to walk behind the wagon or push until the road leveled off enough for the horse to again be able to pull. The heat of summer had subsided, and the coming of autumn made for agreeable travel weather.

As we traveled, Ch'ang took to singing a sacred folksong called *Wóu Liang* which told of the spiritual lessons and experiences of Buddha.

Wóu liang a a Fó
Yào tch'ōū kīa ya,
Nai híng e híng k'ou a
Kīn a tāo a louèn fa,
Tch'éng teng tsèng na kóuei
Hóua jéng tà fã:
Ā mí t'ouo Fó

Blest eternal Buddha,
Abandoned wife and child,
He journeyed to a place of suffering,
With golden sword He cut His hair,
Transformed then to holiness,
His great profound law:
Ā mí t'ouo Fó.

English © 1966 by Charles Haywood

Ch'ang sang with a high pitched piercing voice, a sharp edged Chinese opera voice that created a ripping cry through the calm mountainous air. The birds in the trees were silenced and the breeze answered like whistling ghosts. A chill found its way to my bones at the realization that this song carried the spirits of the Middle Kingdom, releasing them upon this Golden Mountain. The hills appeared as yet unchanged by the melody, but a yearning and intuition rose up within me that the hearts and minds of Chinese people were set free to sail upon the winds of the Sierra Nevada Range. California was upon the verge of transformation.

On our journey we passed the famous hang tree. The wide trunk grew at an exaggerated tilt as if the weight of hundreds of dead spirits were pulling it over. A sturdy horizontal branch reached out horizontally far above the ground. If one man were to stand on another man's shoulders the branch would have been hard to reach, but a long rope with a noose could easily be thrown over the branch. The noose would be lowered to the shoulder height of a man seated on a horse, usually without saddle. The man's hands were always bound behind his back. It was a simple form of execution – placing the noose around the criminal's neck; the horse would be smacked on the rear. The horse would gallop off leaving the criminal swinging from the rope. I had the misfortune to witness this several times as a teenager.

Upon arrival in Chinese Camp we encountered an adobe building with a small opening with metal bars. The opening was high upon the back wall of the building. Young barefoot boys had leaned long elm branches against the tiny barred opening to enable them to climb like chimpanzees up to the small hole and peer into the building. We were guessing that they were spying on a house of prostitution, but were informed that the adobe building was an opium den. This was an embarrassing and disheartening reminder of the growing addiction problem back home in China. The barred opening in the opium den was designed for the escape of putrid fumes that filled the crowded room. What the boys witnessed was tiers of bunks along the wall, much like the living arrangements upon our tortuous ocean journey. Stacked like underground catacombs, the bodies lied sleeping in stacks. The emaciated faces of disillusioned miners and homesick Celestials had closed their eyes upon the world and their bitter failures. *Celestials* was a common term used by Californians in reference to Chinamen, presumably because our lunar calendar and our horoscope of the stars.

Laurel trees were plentiful in Chinese Camp and the fumes of their purple blossoms were notorious for causing severe headaches. Ground squirrels scurried and busied themselves with the numerous acorns that fell like stones from the giant white oaks. The squiggly branches of corkscrew willows meandered like veins in an old man's hands, and the long leaves curled and twisted as if they were undecided of their destination. Shrubs of juniper with small purple berries sprang up everywhere and low crawling vines of jimson weed netted the ground and offered up ominous white blossoms tinged in purple. I heard a local miner refer to the jimson weed as a thorn apple.

We encountered a Chinaman named Shòu Yì who had befriended a young Mexican named Diego. They knew of an abandoned cabin outside of Chinese Camp, and negotiated with Uncle and Hsiáng a trial agreement for staying there a few days. Shòu Yì and Diego led us through fields of dry snakeweed and crumbling stones. Shòu Yì walked with disciplined posture, always looking straight ahead, but Diego liked to kick the loose stones or jump up to grasp tree branches or to swat low hanging leaves. Diego would turn his head as if checking to see that we were still following. He must have noticed that I was the youngest of my group. Sometimes Diego would walk backwards with his hands behind his neck. Several times we met eyes. We seemed to be scrutinizing each other.

Hostile looking Indian thistle huddled in ravines and flowering spikeweed gave off wafts of a sweet, honey scent. We finally neared the abandoned cabin. It looked dilapidated – the small porch had caved in. At the east end of the cabin a crab tree stood near a window that held jagged shards of broken glass. Inside, the window was curtained with a mud-stained green blanket. At the west end of the cabin, a small white oak held out its few massive leaves like a multi-handed Shiva goddess. The window panes of the west end window were still intact, but painted over with dark gray paint from the inside. As if etched by a child, someone had scratched one of the panes with a nail, leaving stick figures of a man walking a dog. The orange light of sunset made the stick figures glow, whereas in the mornings they shone white. In our comings and goings the stick figures repeatedly reminded me of Dustpan Sam and his murdered dog Buckaroo.

After our three day trial period, we were invited to stay longer and negotiated a weekly payoff to our hosts. Diego gradually became a friend of mine. I think it began on an evening that several of us were gathered around the fireplace, warming ourselves and drinking hot cocoa. Hsiáng asked me if I knew a Chinese folk tale that I could tell. Knowing that I was unaccustomed to joining in group conversations, I think Hsiáng considered this a way to include me in the group. I remembered the story that Zhe had told about the River God's Wife. Shòu Yì translated my Chinese sentences to Spanish as I told the story. Diego nodded and smiled and awaited each new sentence that Shòu Yì carefully spilled out like dry beans into a bowl. By the end of the story, Diego was excited and spoke rapidly as his thoughts rolled off of his tongue in Spanish. Shòu Yì held up an open hand, pushing down the air, a gesture meaning "slow down, calm down." Shòu Yì explained to us that Diego had a story about a woman and a river that he wanted to share. The woman in the story he told was known as *La Llorona.*

LA LLORONA (THE WEEPING WOMAN)

In a small village lived an exceptionally pretty girl named Maria. People claimed that she was the most beautiful woman in the world. Hearing this, Maria thought she was better than everyone else. With each year her beauty increased and her pride grew stronger. She claimed that the men of her village were not good enough for her. "I will marry the most handsome man in the world," she said with her chin held high. Her pride continued to grow. One day, a very handsome man rode into town on a fast galloping horse. The son of a wealthy ranchero, he rode his horse like a Comanche. He gave away his tame horses, so that he could rope a wild horse from the open plains. The man believed that it was unmanly to ride a horse that was not half wild.

Maria noticed that the man was unusually handsome. He played guitar impressively and sang with a rich deep voice. Maria knew exactly how to coerce the ranchero and win his heart. Whenever she crossed his path, she ignored him as he spoke to her. If he came to her house to serenade her with his guitar, she refused to appear on the balcony. She turned down extravagant gifts that he attempted to give her. As a result, the young ranchero was so drawn to Maria that he declared, "I will marry this girl."

This was exactly as Maria had planned, and soon the two were engaged and soon after a huge wedding was followed by a wedding celebration to be long remembered. The first years together they had two children and lived a contented family life. Gradually as more years passed, the ranchero longed for his wild life of the open prairies. He began disappearing for months at a time. When he returned home he only seemed interested in his children. Feeling ignored, Maria become enraged and when her husband was gone for long periods, she would treat her children cruelly because they had replaced her as the center of her husband's attention.

One afternoon, as she was walking along a riverside path with her two children, a carriage approached. On the cushioned seat of the carriage sat the ranchero beside a young woman with large plumes in her hat. The carriage stopped, and the ranchero spoke to his children, but he completely ignored

Maria. With a snap of the whip the carriage pulled away abruptly. Maria, filled with fierce rage, turned upon her children. She grabbed the two of them firmly by the arms and threw them into the river. The current swiftly carried the children down stream, and Maria panicked at the realization of what she had just done. She ran screaming and flailing her arms, reaching out for her children, who were swept away – out of her reach.

The following day a traveler discovered the dead body of a beautiful woman alongside the river. Word spread to the village, and it was decided to bury Maria where she was found lying beside the river. The very first night after Maria's burial, the villagers heard the sound of crying. The weeping sound came from the river, but it was not the wind, it was La Llorona crying, "Where are my children?" Various people witnessed a woman walking up and down the river, her long white gown blown by the breeze. It was the gown that Maria wore when she was placed in her grave. La Llorona was seen many evenings since, walking solemnly along the river and crying for her children. She was never again referred to by her name Maria. Instead, the villagers called her La Llorona. Mothers frequently warned their own children to never go out in the dark. If they did, the mothers said, La Llorona might capture them, never to let them go.

DROWNING

It took me by surprise and from behind. A large hand had cupped my head and pushed me face first into the river. I held my pan tightly until it was pulled away from me. I expected to jump up and hear the laughter of the co-workers, but the hand continued to hold me under. I panicked as it occurred to me that somebody wanted me to drown, so I attempted to fight back. The man was much larger and stronger than me and he grasped my arm with a death grip. Suddenly his grip loosened and I was able to surface. I gasped for air, coughing up water that I had swallowed. The man fell forward into the water, slapping the surface like a fish thrown overboard. There were three sturdy wooden rods piercing his back, and the water downstream from his body began to flow in red and purple clouds. Somebody had shot him with a crossbow and saved my life.

As my coughing subsided I noticed a dispersal of galloping horses along with the scattering of members of my mining crew into the riverside shrubbery. Several shots rang out from behind me and ahead of me as all of the horsemen disappeared into the thick foliage of beech trees and laurel. Diego emerged from a shrub of flowering aster, signaling for me to follow him. I crawled upon the dusty river bank. My clothes and hair were sopping and weighed me down. I stood up, feeling lightheaded, almost dizzy. Diego was signaling frantically as if our lives depended on quick retreat. He saw the danger clearly; I was out in the open – a sitting duck. I breathed deeply and pushed myself to run despite my disoriented sensation of shock. I caught up with Diego as he began running, waving me on. I jogged behind him; crushing small pinecones, cracking loose twigs and dry pine needles as my boots skimmed the ground. We tore through an open space of goldenrod grown as high as our knees. A small flock of golden-crowned kinglets scattered as we continued running. As the goldenrod thinned, cunning lizards the color of the blanched dirt darted across our path.

143

We entered a dense forest of ponderosa pines, hemlock, and juniper trees. The air was clean and damp with a mossy, turpentine aroma. We had slowed to a walk, which allowed me to catch my breath. I thought about Uncle. "Return to find Uncle," I called out to Diego. He stopped and turned toward me, shaking his head as he said, "No. It's too dangerous to go back." I looked back over my shoulder, wondering if Uncle had been injured. "Maybe need help," I argued. "Uncle Ān Lè ran into the forest," Diego insisted. "He's running away just like us," he said. Pulling on my arm, Diego led me as I looked back, hoping to see Uncle appear from the thick foliage. I resisted, but not for long. Maybe Diego was right. If we all returned looking for the others, me might all end up murdered.

Gradually, Diego gained distance ahead of me, but I continued on behind him. The soil was no longer dry and clear prints of Diego's boots were left behind him in dampened molds of dark sod. The canopy of tall trees created a cool, shady retreat. The raspy calls of ravens could be heard high above our heads. We heard the rapid-fire pounding of a woodpecker – the woodblock clatter resounding around us.

Diego slowed our pace and shifted to stepping lightly and carefully, avoiding the crackle of twigs or the scraping of rocks. He signaled for me to hush by holding up his open hand and lowering it slowly as he walked with exaggerated care. He was warning me that we were approaching something or someone. He didn't want to alarm them. I thought, or rather, I guessed that Diego might be bringing me to his family's home. Diego had explained to me, although his verbal communication with me was difficult, that his father had voiced a strong distrust for Chinese men. Apparently, his father, named Alonzo, distrusted white people, native Americans, black people; for that matter, anyone who was not Mexican blood. Diego told his father that the Chinese were hard workers who kept to themselves – they were reliable and peaceful and, at times, proved to be ingenious. Diego's assessment threw his father into a rage. Alonzo told Diego not to be charmed by poisonous snakes. Diego pointed out that there were plenty of poisonous snakes among his own people. This was crossing a line that Diego's father would not tolerate. Alonzo grabbed Diego by the arm and pulled him out to the barn. Pulling a shoulder bag from a nail on the wall, Alonzo scolded his son, "If you think so much of those good-for-nothing Chinese, then you go and live with them!" With a jerk of Diego's arm, Alonzo shoved the shoulder bag's strap over his son's head and pushed Diego to the ground. "Get up, ungrateful son, and leave my house. You are no longer my son."

The words had stabbed Diego in the chest, but Diego was equally infuriated that his father could be so intolerant. Diego had walked a half mile from his home, where he stopped to sit at the side of the road beneath a giant oak tree. After more that half an hour of tossing stones and chewing on dry grass, Diego returned home briefly, but secretly. Sneaking noiselessly in through a small window, Diego gathered a few of his own belongings, stuffed them into the leather shoulder bag, and disappeared into the darkness.

Two days later he was taken in by a Mexican family in Big Oak Flat. The mother fed him spicy pinto beans and hand pressed corn tortillas. It was this woman who managed to extract the truth of Diego's exile. Her name was Maria and her husband's name was Augustine. After hearing the story of Diego's disagreement with his father, Maria and Augustine sided with Diego. They both agreed with Diego's assessment of Chinese people. *"Pero, todavía es el padre tuyo, y debes regresar,"* Maria pointed out. (But he is still your father, and you should return.) Diego explained that it was his own father who had asked him to leave. After pondering this, Augustine and Maria promised to introduce Diego to a Chinese friend that they knew and admired, a man named Shòu Yì, the very man who was with Diego the day we encountered them on our arrival in Chinese Camp.

Ms. Montez was fascinated by the two stories, *The River God's Wife* and *La Llorona*. She said that in all of her travels there were rivers that inspired ghost stories and mysterious feelings of ominous treachery and dark deeds. Murder victims were frequently dragged down to the river where their bodies could be hidden among dense foliage, or sunk below the surface with ropes and large stones. Rivers were often the homes for hermits and outcasts, for insane and crippled individuals incapable of surviving comfortably among the rules and expectations of ordinary citizens. The caves and gullies and abundance of branches and hollowed trunks were ready-made shelters for the down-and-out.

I asked Ms. Montez if she had ever heard of Lady Godiva. "Of course," she said as she pulled the cork from a slender green bottle. "Where did you hear of Lady Godiva?" she asked.

"The miner many time say, 'California need more lady.' One day Dustpan Sam say he wish Lady Godiva ride horse to creek. Panama Pete and Ol' Smokey laughing and happy. I not understand. I write Lady Godiva in journal."

Ms. Montez smiled as she poured a milky pale green liquid from the green bottle into a crystal glass shaped like a fountain on a pedestal. The glass contained chunks of cracked ice that chilled the substance. Upon a perforated spoon shaped like a spade, she placed a cube of sparkling white sugar. From a decanter, she poured droplets of water over the sugar cube, which gradually dissolved and leaked through the holes of the spoon into the milky liquor, which seemed to swirl and lighten in color. It looked like liquid opal. She placed the rim of the glass to her painted lips and breathed in the fragrance of the liquor. She looked up toward the ceiling and released a sigh of soothing relief. I had seen this ecstatic look on my mother's face as she lowered her feet into a hot bath of rose water. Ms. Montez took a delicate sip of the sinister looking elixir, placed the small crystal goblet on the marble surface of the table, and began to describe Lady Godiva.

"In a land not far from my birthplace, but long before my birth, a prominent man named Leonfric, the Earl of Mercia, placed such burdensome taxes on his people that they were starving and desperately poor. Leonfric's wife, Lady Godiva, had a good conscience, and begged Leonfric to annul the taxes. Leonfric decided to settle the disagreement by challenging his wife. If she would ride naked through the town, he would abolish the taxes. Of course, Leonfric expected Lady Godiva to refuse, thus settling the argument. Lady Godiva caught him by surprise and agreed to the challenge. She ordered that all the townspeople remain indoors and that all the windows be covered at noon. Upon her white stallion, she rode through town completely naked except for her long hair, which for the sake of decency, covered much of her body. Leonfric showed mercy upon the townsfolk and Lady Godiva became a local heroine and legend."

"Many people today who know of this story do not know this additional bit of trivia. During Lady Godiva's ride, there was one man who disregarded her orders and dared to gaze at her bare flesh. This man became known as Peeping Tom, and it is said that he was struck blind. I have heard many lady folks declare that any man who spies on a woman should be struck blind, and Peeping Tom deserved it. I, for one, don't like being spied upon, but I would hardly blame a man for his natural desires."

"You tell good story," I commented.

Ms. Montez looked up at me with a dreamy expression as she gingerly took a sip of the strange concoction. "I feel strong empathy for Lady Godiva. She and I have something in common. We both have experienced passing through the streets naked."

The comment embarrassed me. "You're blushing," she laughed. "Your face is a red as an apple." She pushed a small goblet toward me and poured a miniscule amount of the golden green fluid. I may recall mistakenly, but I thought I saw a spiral of green vapor ascend above the liquid's teetering surface. I shook my head no, and she smirked. "This is a popular cocktail I learned to enjoy in Paris. They call it *Extrait d' Absinthe.* She repeated the ritual of cracked ice, and placed a new sugar cube upon the pointed spoon with holes. She allowed the water droplets to dilute the elixir to a paler shade of green amber than the mixture in her own goblet, before pushing the mysterious concoction even close to me.

I imitated her ritual of smelling the brew, and was greeted with a soft sweet smell. "Smell like candy," I said. She picked up her glass with an exaggerated lift above the head, and extended her arm toward me. "Pick up your glass, and let your glass touch mine." I held my goblet out, and she tapped her glass against mine. A small ringing sound like a small bell pierced the air, and she drank down a large gulp of her *extrait d' absinthe.* I followed suit, and took a small gulp. The taste was sweet but quickly turned bitter to the tongue. When she saw my sour face, she quickly poured a glass of water from the decanter. I drank the water quickly, remembering how sick I was the day after our rounds of drinks when Buckaroo was shot. I proceeded with caution. Fortunately, a woman's manner of slowly sipping a drink was much less devastating. After several careful sips a soothing, dreamy feeling washed over me. My brain felt liberated from its usual restraints, and my imagination found unusual correlations between naked women in the street, a female ghost of the river, and the underwater wives of the River God. I could see, in the determined spirit of the woman who sat across the marble table, a bold and adventurous desire to break loose of the limited corners that a woman can be pushed into. This was a woman who ran screaming and naked from a house of rules and regulations. This was a woman who rode horses freely with a young female companion. This woman had traveled from country to country, crossed oceans and mountains in her quest to live fully and to step outside of the ordinary and mundane. Like Lady Godiva, Ms. Montez was a heroine in my eyes. I was no longer looking with Chinese eyes.

The following morning I rose from my bunk without a headache or a wretched stomach. I had managed to drink only one solitary little goblet of absinthe without carelessly downing glass after glass after glass, a practice that was customary among miners. I felt disappointed that I was unable to recall the train of thought that had so inspired me the previous evening as I had sipped the murky liquid.

After a small breakfast of white rice and strong black tea, I gradually recaptured the lost revelations. I dug out my journal, brush, and ink and documented my correlations between the female legends of the river and the bold spirit of my friend Ms. Montez. I noted coincidentally that Queen Victoria reigned over the British Empire while the Empress Dowager Tz'u-hsi was the absolute power over the Middle Kingdom. I lived within a turning point concerning the prominence of women in society.

After carefully storing away my journal, paintbrushes and ink, I stepped outside into the bright morning for a short stroll through Chinese Camp. The sky was a deep shade of powder blue. Brilliant white clouds piled like huge bubbles were circumscribed with golden rays of the sun. The sunlight fanned through crevices of the cumulus clouds like palm fronds. The morning seemed enchanted and peaceful. Birds chattered and yellow butterflies flitted from flower to bush. Upon a post office bulletin board a large poster had been tacked up. It was titled *The Miner's Ten Commandments* and within the wide border around the typewritten document were eleven detailed illustrations, the largest of which, directly above the title, depicted a large elephant raising its trunk above a document of the commandments posted upon a cabin. The elephant had become a mascot for California miners who frequently spoke of having "seen the elephant." The phrase referred to the unknown and adventure that gold seekers associated with California. Many of the miners, once skeptical of the wealth to be found, had at some point in time made the decision to venture to California in search of gold. These skeptics and reluctant individuals had supposedly envisioned or dreamt a prophetic vision that changed their minds. Perhaps they had merely heard the repeated rumors until doubt had shifted and they were newly persuaded. They had "seen the elephant."

I began to read the document, skipping down to number one: *Thou shalt have no other claim than one.* My eyes shifted to the right. Commandment number six, in the center column of the document, stated (at points comically): *Thou shalt not kill thy body by working in the rain, even though thou shalt make enough to buy physic and attendance with. Neither shall thou kill thy neighbor's body in a duel; for, by "keeping cool," thou canst save his life and thy conscience. Neither shall thou destroy thyself by getting "tight," nor "stewed,' nor "high," nor "corned," nor "half-seas-over," nor "three sheets in the wind,' by drinking smoothly down – "brandy-slings," "gin-cocktails," "whiskey-punches," rum-toddies," nor "eggnogs." Neither shalt thou suck "mint-julips," nor "sherry-cobblers," through a straw, nor gargle from a bottle the "raw material," nor "take it neat" from a decanter, for, while thou art swallowing down thy purse, and thy coat from off thy back, thou art burning the coat from off thy stomach: and, if thou couldst see the houses and lands, and gold dust, and home comforts already living there-* " *a huge pile" – thou shouldst feel a choking in thy throat; and when to that thou addest thy crooked walkings and hiccupping talkings, of lodgings in the gutter, of broilings in the sun, of prospect holes half full of water, and of shafts and ditches, from which thou has emerged like a drowning rat thou wilt feel disgusted with thyself, and inquire, "Is thy servant a dog, that he doeth these things?" verily I will say, Farewell, old bottle, I will kiss thy gurgling lips no more. And thou, slings, cocktails, punches, smashes, cobblers, nogs, toddies, sangarees, and juleps, forever farewell. Thy remembrance shames me, henceforth, I "cut thy acquaintance," and headaches, tremblings, heart burnings, blue-devils, and all the unholy catalog of evils that follow in thy train. My wife's smiles and my children's merry-hearted laugh shall charm and reward me for having the manly firmness and courage to say NO. I wish thee an eternal farewell."**

Amazingly enough, I recognized many of the terminologies for drunkenness and the endless array of spirits and mixtures that a miner has pounded his fist upon a bar demanding.   I, too, had pondered how a man could venture across a continent, or sailed around two, just to roll in the mud and disgustingness of drunkenness and never accumulate the desired wealth to return and share with his family. (Years later I would look back on this bright morning, with my rosy cheeked outlook and that spark of absinthe in my blood, and thank my ancestors, the stars that spelled out my fate, and any amount of luck that might have steered me clear of further encounters with the devil's drink.)

* "The Miner's Ten Commandments," copyrighted in 1853 by James M. Hutchings, Placerville, El Dorado County, California, HEH

THE NISHENAN VILLAGE

As the path began to ascend a series of hills, Diego stopped and cupped his hands with bent thumbs. Placing his thumbs against his lips, he was able to create a deep-toned whistle. With a slight flapping of his elbows, the cup would open and close, allowing the tone to warble, like the sound of a mourning dove or a loon. After repeating the bird call several times, the call was answered by a similar mournful sound. I wondered if Diego had learned the magic of communicating with birds. This would be an extraordinary story I would feel obliged to share with Uncle and Zhe, the philosopher – sage.

After several exchanges of the strange whistling, an unusual wild man appeared from the trees at the base of the hill. This man appeared about the size of Zhe, a small framed, dark-skinned man with straight black hair much like mine. His mouth formed a gentle smile, an indication that Diego was his friend. There was a piercing animal glaze to his eyes as he inspected me, as if half-alarmed by my presence. Except for his dark skin and odd looking attire, he resembled, in features, my older brother, Ching Hah. Upon his head he wore a folded cap of suede or deer skin. Braced within the fold of the cap was an arrow with a braided tassel hanging beside his face. The hat looked at once silly and ominous, giving the jolting impression that he had an arrow stuck through his skull. There was a dark band at the base of the cap with a series of decorations. He wore a deer skin shirt with a low collar. He held a quiver of arrows wrapped in animal furs.

The man placed his right hand on Diego's shoulder, and Diego placed his right hand on the man's shoulder. They both said *"Ahnah"*. Diego turned to me, placing his right hand on my shoulder, *"Ahnah."* The man then placed his hand on my shoulder. I followed Diego's example, placing my hand on the man's shoulder. The man repeated the word, *"Ahnah,"* and I repeated the new word after him. "His name is Poahee," said Diego, "and this is Yaozu." We looked at each other directly in the eye. He looked very determined and strong willed. There was a slight sadness in his face. He said a short series of words to Diego, and turned to lead us up the hill.

The Nishenan village created a circle upon the hilltop. Circular huts formed a smaller circle near the center of the village. We approached the village after sunset. The village was a dark silhouette against the deep blue of the falling curtain of night. An owl was calling out gently, "Hoo-hoo, hoo-hoo." The air was cool and we were happy to be ushered into one of the circular houses. A woman in a blanket came to greet Poahee. She carried a small naked child upon her hip. She smiled at the sight of Diego and looked at me as Poahee explained our presence. The floor of the house had been dug out several feet deeper than ground level. A large central pole supported the roof and the walls were a framework of wood covered with mud. There were no separations of rooms inside. The house created a decent-sized room for several people. The woman, named Moahnee, placed blankets and soft leather pillows in an open space near the wall. We had bedding and she offered us decorated gourds containing a pale milky liquid. Diego accepted the gourds, pressing one to his lips as he handed me the other. I nodded to Moahnee in appreciation. The liquid tasted slightly bitter and smelled like mint and pine. The late night drink had a calming effect upon us both. As we lay in the darkness in the guest bedding, I marveled at my strange luck to experience such an unusual guesthouse.

FIRST DAY – MAKING ACORN MUSH

The dry heat of summer had long gone. Days were cooler and cooler. Gentle breezes rustled the oak leaves and swayed the tall grasses. My first morning among the Maidu people, Diego and I helped the children to gather acorns that we found abundantly strewn about on the nearby grounds. We were given hand-made pouches with shoulder straps. Some of the smaller children carried small baskets and we all returned several times with full containers of acorns. Some of the children were mischievous or distracted, but there were enough of us to collect plenty of acorns. Diego seemed to know the names of most of them and called out sternly to the ones who starting throwing acorns or chasing after each other. After a while he gave up and let the children make their own choices.

Several young women cracked the acorns open, holding fist size rocks that they pounded upon rows of acorns lined up on a flat rock surface. The particles of the inner nut were rinsed in water and then placed into a hollowed stone and mashed with an oblong stone. The mashed nutmeat was inedible because of the acidity of its tannins. The accumulated mush had to be leached of the tannins, a process left to the older women.

The older women had prepared a wide hole. The bottom of the hole was covered with a thick layer of sand, and pine needles were arranged over the sand. Upon the bed of pine needles the nutmeat mush was spread evenly. Cedar and fir branches were arranged on top of the mealy mush until completely covered. Pots of water heated in a fire next to the pit were gently poured over the branches. The process took the better part of the morning and early afternoon. Most of the small children wandered around and played games of riding long branches as if they were horses. Diego took me for a short walk and when we returned the older women were still pouring hot water into the pit.

Finally, the cedar and fir boughs were pulled off and the steaming mush was allowed to dry. Once dried, the acorn meal could be stored in baskets and baked later in a large cooking basket that was tightly woven and water tight. Water was added to the meal and stones from the fire would be rinsed and then dropped into the basket of mush until the mixture started to boil. The water that had been poured earlier over the cedar and fir branches had not only leached the tannins, but added a distinct flavoring from the cedar and fir branches. Other ground seeds could be cooked in this manner, and the women also collected roots called camas and wild carrots that came from the Queen Anne's lace plant.

The Nishenan lived in the Bear Valley area where Diego and I stayed for nearly two weeks. These southern Maidu originated from northern territory and believed that all life came from the volcano, Mount Lassen, to the north. A Great Man's desire had molded life forms and all things were originated from the molten mass that had spewed from the Great Volcano. As the mass began to cool, the Great Man desired a partner and created Woman. As the Maidu spread throughout northern California, many of their people settled in the Sacramento Valley. The Maidu also passed down a tale of another significant event of their people's history. During their many years in the Sacramento Valley, a season of overwhelming disaster brought a great body of water that washed over the entire Great Central Valley creating an ocean that wiped out all of the people. Only two survived the disaster, and these two became the new father and mother to all Maidu people.

Diego told me that his Chinaman friend, Shòu Yì, had an unusual talent for communicating with the native tribes of California. While panning for gold on the Kings River, he came to know a small group of Yokuts, a tribe of natives who had also inhabited the Great Central Valley of California. A Yokuts shaman taught him a song that Shòu Yì eventually translated: *My words are tied in one with the great mountains, with the great rocks, with the great trees, in one with my body and my heart. You all help me with supernatural power, and you, day, and you, night! All of you see me, one with this world.* Diego said that to live among these people was a privilege because the Maidu have been here for many centuries. His own people from the south are a mixture of the native Aztecs with the European blood of Spain because the Spaniards had taken over the land. I told Diego that Chinese people had begun to experience such a humiliation as Great Britain had taken the significant trading port of Hong Kong, an island near my uncle's home in Kowloon.

Diego knelt down to pick up an arrowhead. He pierced his fingertip with the sharp point of the sharpened stone. Holding up his bloodied finger, he handed the arrowhead to me.

With a nod of his head I realized that he was expecting me to do the same. I pricked my own finger with the pointed stone. Diego held his moist red fingertip toward me and gestured for me to move closer. We each placed our finger against the other, Mexican blood mixing with Chinese. The blood of two widely separated lands conjoined. Diego said proudly in his own tongue, "*Hermanos.*" I repeated the Spanish word with a strange fascination at the thought of a new family here on the Golden Mountain.

THE LEGEND OF COYOTE

In the late afternoon a group of men returned from a fishing trip. Several of the men had strings of two or three trout of varying sizes. As the cool air of evening moved into the settlement, a large fire was built not far from the acorn pit. Two of the men used sharpened stones to slit the trout along the bottom fin from chin to tail. The fish were gutted, and then placed upon large, scalding hot rocks in the fire. The simmering sound of the fish and the smoky, fishy smell spread throughout the settlement and some of the children wandered out from their roundhouses to watch the cooking of the fish on the fire.

The blackened trout were pulled out of the fire with long branches and piled upon a large stone slab. The whole village, some forty to fifty people – including children, circled the fire and an elderly man with long feathers in his necklace sang a short song. Diego explained that the man was a shaman and the song was an offering of gratitude to the Creator for supplying this meal of plenty for his people.

I felt ashamed to have done women's work all day while the men were fishing. When a piece of fish was offered to me I started to refuse, but Diego interrupted me and took the fish to share with me. He explained that to refuse their hospitality would be an insult, and they wanted me to feel at home in their village. The trout was delicious and came apart easily from the bone. Even the burned skin tasted wonderful.

After the meal the whole gathering moved into a large roundhouse where everyone managed to sit within a circle two and three deep. A man located near the central pole told a story and two other men danced within the circle. Diego explained to me later that night that the dancers were acting out the story that the speaker was telling. One of the dancers wore a coyote head as a helmet. The fur and legs and tail hung down his back. The other dancer wore a great fan of feathers behind his head that spread as wide as he could spread his arms. The story was about an argument that Coyote had initiated with the Creator.

The Creator had said there would be life and great happiness, but Coyote had argued that there will be sadness and crying, followed by death. The Creator announced that there would be only one language so that all beings and creatures will understand each other. Coyote called back that there will be many languages, and the beings and creatures will be unable to understand each other. All the birds and animals will have their own language. When the Creator realized that Coyote had won the argument by creating ugliness, death, and misery, Creator decided that Coyote would be punished, and from then on Coyote became a lowly scavenger.

Boys and girls played in the leopard-spot shadows of white oak leaves. Morning breezes swayed the branches and the shadows danced across the dry dirt clearing where the children had gathered. At opposite sides of the clearing, large rocks had been placed in two parallel lines. Two competing players were each assigned separate goal lines. The competitors raced back and forth, gathering one rock at a time, to create a completed pile of the entire string of rocks across the goal line. The first player to successfully pile every rock from his side within the goal area was the winner of the race. Running swiftly and maintaining stamina were not the only skills needed to win the race. Being able to change direction without slipping, missing the rock, or falling while stooping to pick up and drop off the rock might prove a weakness or a skill, depending on the contestant.

The spectators jumped up and down as they cheered and yelled out the names of the players. I sat on the ground among the exposed roots of a large oak three. With the naïve boldness of a toddler, a small, barefoot girl named Eisha came to kneel beside me. She looked up at my face with astonishment and reached behind me, placing my long braided queue into her small hand. She seemed content to marvel at my design, reminding me that I was indeed a foreigner from far away. As she touched and inspected the fabric of my clothing, I became absorbed in the fast paced race between two slender boys. When I turned toward her, she had wandered off. By the end of the next race between two girls, Eisha was kneeling again beside me. She seemed to leave and reappear without a sound. I looked down at her small round face and noticed a miniature basket that held purple and white lupine blossoms. As I smiled at Eisha, she lifted the small basket toward me. I leaned forward to smell the flowers and she started giggling. I smiled again and she placed the basket in my lap. Clearly, she was offering me a gift. I touched her shoulder as a gesture of thanks, and she looked at my fingers as if she had never seen a human hand. She gazed up at my face with an expression in her eyes that I have seen in small puppies. Abruptly, she jumped up and ran away. In spite of her short, pudgy legs, she ran away with amazing swiftness.

160

The back-and-forth racing continued, but a few of the boys had started a contest of throwing consecutively larger and larger rocks. Diego emerged from the doorway of the roundhouse where he had been sleeping. When he noticed me at the base of the oak tree he came to join me. Immediately he noticed the small basket of lupine flowers, and pointed to them with an inquisitive look on his face. When I explained that Eisha had given the basket to me, he began to tease me, "Yaozu has a new girlfriend, Yaozu has a new girlfriend." I told Diego to stop teasing. "Eisha is barely more than a baby girl, a small child." Diego took advantage of my discomfort. In a singsong voice he repeated, "Eisha loves Yaozu, Eisha loves Yaozu." I stood up and walked angrily away from Diego, who continued chanting behind my back.

A LAND OF PLENTY

In two weeks time I witnessed a society of people that lived simply, but with an acquired knowledge of their surroundings. The Maidu had the insight to store much of their acorn meal in tightly woven baskets. Holes were dug in the banks or slopes of the hill and then lined with pine needles to help keep the lid-sealed baskets dry. Once the baskets were stored in the cache, the hole was filled with cedar bark and dirt, and marked with a tall pole. In the winter months the poles helped to locate the cache buried below deep snow drifts.

The vegetation that surrounded the Maidu was rich in fruit and roots and the Maidu practiced the use of herbal remedies and knew which plants to avoid. When salmon and steelhead trout returned from the ocean, the rivers were plentiful. Beaver could be found along the river, and Eastern fur traders had discovered rabbits, beavers, fox, and raccoons long before the gold rush. The Maidu knew how to cure meat with smoke, and stored strips of dry deer meat for long winters.

I could not understand their language and much of what I learned of these people was accumulated in passing years, not only during the two weeks that I lived among them. In that short time, I did, however, experience their kindness and generosity.

friend

FROM THE JAGGED ROCK

Jagged rocks barely outside of the settlement formed a perfect lookout point. Diego squatted upon the topmost ledge of the angled granite. With his arms upon his knees he kept balance as he gazed out at the mountain crest. Among the sugar pines and ponderosas, deer roamed the ridges of the mountains. I sat on a lower ledge with my legs dangling over its edge. It was late afternoon and the sky was a washed out gray. Low flying fog moved in from the west. The colors of the forest had deepened and the smell of mist and sweet moss blanketed us.

I alternated between scanning the surroundings and looking up at Diego, who shredded bits of leaves like holly that he had torn from the squaw carpet that spread like ivy and strawberry vines. His dark brown eyes shone with intensity as he watched the mountain ridge. He was absent-mindedly shredding the strands of leaves, and ripping the small shavings between his teeth. As he pulled the strands through his clenched bite the bitter taste would spray his tongue, causing him to spit out curled shreds of leaf veins. Repeating this mindless routine seemed to focus his attention, to calm him. It seemed to be his Zen meditation, giving him staying power and stillness.

This morning Eisha had given me a bracelet of tiny smooth pebbles. The colors varied from rusty brown, avocado, moss, and a sandy shade of pine wood. There were three sand colored pebbles veined with red. She had tied the bracelet upon my wrist, but shortly afterward I had slipped it into my pocket before Diego would notice it. As I looked out at the misty mountainside it occurred to me that I enjoyed the admiration of this little girl. I considered the possibility of giving Eisha a gift; something Chinese in character and nature. What could I possibly give a child – one barely more than a toddler? It seemed that the only belonging that I carried that was truly Chinese was my paint brush and ink.

Diego spit out a round ball of the chewed squaw carpet. He pushed himself upward to a standing position upon the lopsided peak of jutting rocks. As he stretched his arms and rose upon his toes, he rocked his head back and forth, loosening tension. From where I sat just below him, he looked as if he would fly into the silvery sky. As if the Great Spirit agreed with me, a flock of raven soared up from behind him. Seeing the spectacle I was witnessing, Diego held his arms wide like raven wings. I feared he would jump, so I grabbed hold of his shins. He looked down at me and flapped his featherless wings. "Let me out of my cage! Let me go, master!" His cry rang out into the open air. His choice of words puzzled me.

THE CUTTING BLOCK

The morning drizzle of the following day had thickened to pelting rain. The roundhouses were surrounded by mud and the chill in the air made venturing outside undesirable. The children were not so easily dissuaded by the phenomenon of weather. Splashing and laughing, the more agile ones had taken running starts and competed by sliding through the slickness of the sludge, splattering each other without care or worry. One ingenious boy had found that a sheath of bark served as a small boat beneath his feet. Gaining momentum before jumping onto the sheath, the children took turns at riding the board of tree bark, creating a long track of flattened mud worn smooth by their unrelenting energy.

I had stood in the doorway of the roundhouse with the heat of the circular room at my back. The heat emanated from a mud oven built along the curved wall of the room. Heavy rain soaked the children, washing off the better part of mud caked upon them. An inventive boy found that by wobbling the board as he rode, great pellets of spewed mud would splatter the onlookers with new streaks of the dark compacted clay. I didn't feel inclined to encrust myself in such mess, and restless from watching, I pulled out my journal, my brush and ink. A flat-topped stump of wood rested on the ground near the oven. The stump served as a cutting block and a table top, worn smooth by use. Breakfast had long since been cleared away, so I set up my ink and brush and began documenting my days with the Maidu people. Shortly after painting only three columns of characters, Eisha appeared in the doorway, holding a blanket over her head for protection against the downpour. She stepped inside, folded the wet blanket in her best grownup mannerism, and then joined me beside the cutting block to observe

165

my Chinese calligraphy. She watched intently, her large brown eyes taking in the swift strokes of the paintbrush and the splashes of the brush in the inkwell. After I completed a new column of the text, she pointed to the scrawled shapes upon the paper. She spoke words I had heard within these walls, but as of yet, I failed to correlate any meaning to these sounds. There was an inquiring tone in her small voice.

I turned the page and painted the Chinese character for mountain, saying the Cantonese word as an explanation. Eisha looked all the more puzzled, only reminding me that my language was reciprocally without meaning to her. I painted an illustration of a mountain, but she looked at the image with a blank expression.

Three boys stood in the doorway. Water dripped in streamlets from their blue-black hair. The boys seemed curious about our small project upon the chopping stump. One boy was small like Eisha, but the other two were older. When we turned to look at them, they hastily ran off.

I had a better idea for Eisha. Turning the page, I painted an illustration of a horse and I imitated the sound of neighing. Eisha giggled and pointed to the horse, saying, *"Cah-wah-yuh."* I had never heard this word, but trusted that she understood. On the following page I illustrated the horse again, saying, *"Cah-wah-yuh,"* and then illustrated a progression of horse characters that arrived finally at the contemporary character that the Chinese now use for horse. I repeated the word, *"Cah-wah-yuh,"* and pointed to the contemporary character. Eisha made a sour grimace, letting me know that in the last character the image of a horse was lost. I had to agree with her. Except for the four unattached hooves, and the strange squiggle that barely resembled a horse, an untrained eye would see no animal at all. (Much later, a Mexican acquaintance explained to me that the first horses brought to this country were from Spain. The Spanish word for horse being *caballo,* the Maidu people adapted this word into their own language as *cah-wah-yah.*)

I pointed inside the oven, saying the Chinese word for fire. I wiggled my fingers and let my hands rise as I repeated the word fire, and then pointed to the flames in the oven. Eisah jumped up and down, saying, *"Shiow, shiow."* I painted flames on the next page, and then painted the character for fire. I pointed to the character and repeated her word, "Shiow." She smiled eagerly saying, "Shiow."

The three dripping boys reappeared in the doorway. As I turned to look, two ran off, except for one taller, slender boy who entered the roundhouse. He pushed his dripping hair back from his face, and cautiously sauntered over to observe Eisha's lesson. Eisha pushed the boy gently to avoid drops of water that fell from the tip of his angular nose. By the end of the lesson, I had given Eisha several pages of paintings, including the characters for horse, man, woman, and fire. The slender boy's name was Woaku. He was equally intrigued by the paintwork, so I gave him a painting of a tiger with its equivalent Chinese character and another painting of a boat with its Chinese character.

Eisha folded the papers carefully and tucked them inside her smock to protect them from the rain. Woaku held the papers as extensions of both hands like wings and swirled in two small circles before stopping to nod to me in thanks. I felt like a schoolmaster at the time. Later that night, as I wrapped myself in a rough, warm blanket to go to sleep, it occurred to me that without planning it I had returned Eisha's favor of gift giving.

The men of the Maidu tribe were planning a hunting expedition. The days were cooler and the nights were chilly. Paohee, the father of the roundhouse where we lived, stood at the doorway with Diego. Their slender shapes were outlined in morning light. Diego returned to fold up his bedding. He sat down to pull on his leather boots. When he noticed that I was awake, he said, "Paohee says that the snowbirds have returned. He says this is a sign that the first frost will arrive any day now."

Soon the caches of food would be the only food for the winter. Smoked deer meat or a goose or wild turkey would be a welcome change from a diet of acorn mush and camas. The camas, a bulb of a tall, blue flowering plant, were mashed and cooked in a pit for nearly two days. The cooked camas was sweet and was used as many people would use molasses or honey to sweeten bland food.

For several days now, Diego and I had been left with the children and women. We were not seen as immature so much as we were viewed inexperienced with Maidu practices. The men were rarely called upon to fight battles. Before the great influx of Westerners, Southern Hispanics, and now even the arrival of Chinese and Hawaiian Asians, the Maidu had survived peaceably without much need to defend themselves from neighboring tribes. Hunting wild animals, nonetheless, was considered the advanced skill of an adult male. Diego and I had not learned or developed any semblance of Maidu hunting techniques. Diego knew how to fire a pistol, and I had gone fishing with my father and older brother.

The initiation of a boy into manhood within the southern Maidu tribe involved the ingestion of momoy, as the Chumash natives referred to it. Diego was familiar with the umbrella shaped flower as *toloache*, its Spanish name. Miners frequently referred to this repulsive smelling white flower as jimson weed or thorn apple. The white flower looked like a partially unfolded parasol and the pointed edges were tinged in violet. To the Maidu, and many California natives, the plant was the most sacred of plants.

Maidu medicine men used the root to treat asthma. Because of its anesthetic ability, broken bones were set in a damp mush of momoy root. The ingestion of momoy could induce hallucinations and sacred dreams. Because of this desired effect, momoy root was used to initiate boys into religious rites. The initiation was a challenge to the boys, and not every youngster who ingested the toxic plant would live through the ordeal.

It was decided that Diego and I would be initiated. Four adult males and an elderly sage escorted Diego and me outside the marked perimeter of their settlement. As we passed through ponderosa and sugar pines under the pale moonlight, the men began singing. The melody was at once peculiar and yet soothing. The words to my ears were strange utterances. The elderly sage, or medicine man, held two painted sticks decorated with shells. In a syncopated rhythm that kept pace with the men's low voices, the elder shook the painted sticks, creating a menacing rattle.

In a small clearing of the forest, we all knelt upon the grassy ground beneath the glow of a crescent moon. From a beaded pouch that hung from a leather strand, the elderly sage extracted two colorless slices of dried momoy. In the moonlight the dried root looked like the wrinkled skin of the neck of the old man. With an unseen tool, the medicine man made a small incision upon his thumb. He pressed the blood of his thumb upon Diego's forehead and then upon mine. He then pressed his thumb upon his own forehead, and closing his eyes chanted a string of words sung in monotone. The old man was flanked on each side by two Maidu men, who joined him in the chant. The gentle sound seemed to drift upon the breeze. The elderly sage cupped his hands, offering the dried roots to Diego and then to me. We both held the wrinkled flesh in cupped hands, as if the ugly slabs of dried plant were delicately carved jade. The old man gently pushed our cupped hands up to our mouths and we placed the momoy upon our tongues. The flavor was harsh and slightly astringent. I swallowed my piece whole. Diego attempted to chew his and nearly gagged before swallowing.

Two of the four Maidu men turned back to the settlement, escorting the medicine man safely back to the roundhouses. The other two men lead us through the forest. In the dim moonlight I could make out a narrow trail that we were following. Within a few minutes a mild queasiness came over me. I felt nervous, not so much at the thought of walking in the darkness, but I wondered if I would soon die of poisoning. The slight uneasiness of my stomach and nerves heightened my awareness and quickened my pulse. As the gentle incline of the path became steeper I felt exhilarated to realize that I was not tiring or loosing my breath. Cresting the ridge of a hunchback mountain, a wide vista opened before us.

A wide valley stretched before us and the sky was an immense panorama of spreading moonlit clouds upon a dark void strewn with pierces of light. I told Diego that the clouds looked like the long white hair of an ancient woman floating upon a pool of darkness. Diego translated my description to the Maidu men. One of the men responded and Diego said it was the long hair of Momoy, a woman who had been instructed by the Creator to create the Momoy plant long ago. Amidst the white hair in the sky I saw a woman's face emerge. Her eyes sparkled and her smile was peaceful.

From this high vista, the two men turned back while Diego and I were beckoned to wander across the valley below. The dark silhouettes of the men's heads and shoulders sank as they descended the path behind us. A fear gripped me. We would be attacked by a bear or pounced upon by a mountain lion. We could freeze in the cold or lose our way and starve. I knew that I needn't voice these fears. These were the fears of a boy. To return with the men was to remain a boy under men's protection. The ridge where we stood was our threshold, a moon gate. We stood at a door that led to manhood. Ahead of us lay our initiation into Maidu adulthood.

We began our descent into the valley. The queasiness was subsiding. My heightened fear was my new source of energy. The first steps down the hill were like a flight into freedom. I unchained myself from the grips of my father and uncle, from the Emperor of China, from the Asian-Pacific Sea Merchants and The Miners' Ten Commandments. I left behind the invisible strings that pulled upon my puppet arms and

170

legs. *I* was so much more than the claims laid upon me by various people. I belonged to this beautiful night and this glorious sky. This mighty valley held me in godly arms. I belonged here as much as the tall pines and the whispering streams. I watched the graceful stride of Diego as he descended the slope ahead of me. He was a cat, a jaguar. His enthusiasm and joy shone in the quickening of his pace. We were connected to this sacred place, and the calm face of the old woman above looked down on us knowingly. Her white hair swayed. Diego and I ran sure footed and with night clarity I had never known. We leapt over fallen logs and jumped moon-sparkled creeks.

A hoot owl lured us to slow our pace as we approached a tall wide-based tree. We stopped to look up at the towering giant. "Sequoia," said Diego with reverence. "This tree is very, very old." I looked up in amazement. I spread my arms and pressed my body against the trunk. It would have taken many men, hand-in-hand, to surround this monumental sequoia tree. The hoot owl called again. We turned our heads toward the lovely sound and spotted the sentinel bird fringed in the silvery light of the moon that outlined the shelf of branch where the owl was perched. I stood still, owl-like, as the great bird gazed at me, and I at him. He spread his massive wings and slid into the air, swooping low over our heads as if a mutual trust had been exchanged.

We continued on, this time walking. We took in everything, in our breath, in our ears, our eyes, our faces exposed to the night air, our feet sensing the terrain beneath us. As the valley passed behind us, a new incline graduated to a steep upgrade. We were climbing again, and the fringes of the skyline were gaining the early light that announced the coming of sunrise. A songbird answered the distant call of another. Two birds quibbled and then four sang out. A grand momentum was gathering, a quintet of chattering became a symphony of bird calls that cascaded and swelled like rolling tides of fluttered messages. I recalled the painted sticks of the Maidu shaman covered with shells. I could hear the rattle among the songbirds.

The horizon turned to crimson-rose and golden-white while wandering strings of glinting water shone far below us like braided reflections of polished knives. Huge trees near us breathed in and out. Even the monolith cliffs, visible through the

171

columns of trees, swelled and exhaled. Everything was alive and untamable. The order and laws of man seemed fraudulent and ridiculous. The universe unrolled its carpet and a great clamoring accompanied glimpses of sunlight radiance. Taken aback by the magnificence of the sunrise, Diego and I sat upon low branches to behold the blossoming of day. Diego had crouched upon his ankles, his forearms holding his knees and his cat eyes gleaming in the new splinters of dawning light. He was a strange and marvelous bird upon the branch. Our human forms were so amorphous; lizard and cat, bird and insect. We were the makings of magic.

Through a rustling of leaves appeared a wolf. He bared his teeth and gave out a low hideous growl. The irises of his eyes were like unfurled Japanese fans. I saw in the wolf's posture his fear of our attacking. We sat unnerved and motionless, gazing calmly at his show of defensiveness. The great beast lowered its head and peered up at us as if our illusiveness had struck a chord of passivity. Maybe we looked like painted branches. Unexplainably, he turned and gingerly pranced back into the foliage.

Had we learned a secret of power over hostility? We had done nothing really. We had not shown fear. Was that the secret? I couldn't say. It was an unexpected and odd encounter.

As the wide golden glow of sun peeked over the eastern cliffs, the incredulous shapes of wild flowers and scurry of wildlife took on unfathomable hues. Messages of the ages were imprinted in the sprouting of a spiked seed pod that dangled among the arabesques of perfectly veined oak leaves. Trees reached miraculously outward and upward, worshippers of the expansive heavens and the dance of wind, the blessing of rain. Steep cliffs rose up like monuments to unworldly gods. We had entered a deep haven, a hidden sanctuary of nature. Time stood still and yet we walked endlessly, lost in rapture at the immensity of the high mountain walls that enveloped us. We walked with heads tilted back as spills of water from a higher world fell endlessly as if drained from the moon.

The cliffs on both sides narrowed before they widened. Long slanting shadows meandered beneath cliff tops, peaks, and a thin cascade of water – all in the bright spotlight of new light. If the Four Kings of Heaven reside on Mount Sumera in the Middle Kingdom, these cliffs were the Golden Mountain's steps to the Great Creator.

We came upon a stream where we knelt to drink. A bobcat walked along the opposite bank, pretending to ignore us. When we finally reached a wide meadow it was midday, the sun riding high in the sky. The meadow was green with new grass, and the ground was soft and muddy. A huge dome of rock loomed far above the meadow. It looked like a boulder that had been chiseled in half, leaving bare a perpendicular flat face of rock mounted high in the air. There were several free falling waterfalls, the fall so long that water descended in slow motion. The place was hypnotic – a fortress of cliffs and falls with a secluded meadow far from the greedy hands of the blood-thirsty miners with their spades and picks.

We thought of the Maidu scouts who had escorted us to the first dark ridge overlooking the wide valley beneath the stars. They must have known that we would arrive at this unworldly, sacred place. It was gift like no other I could imagine. These wise people had given us the gift of knowing that we are part of the earth, the wide sky, the sailing wind, and the vastness of water. We would return to their roundhouses and campfires. Gazing into the dancing flames we would possess peace of heart, knowing this great truth.

We headed back at a slower pace. We took in the richness of the unusual land. We breathed in the fresh air, drank again from the stream. We stopped at the edge of the meadow to lie on our backs and gaze up at the sky. The clouds drifted and performed their flying magic. A nearby ash rustled in the breeze, asking the world to hush and listen. A green insect fluttered and lighted upon Diego's sleeve. The creature remained frozen as I sat up and realized that it was no insect. I pinched the delicate wing between my thumb and finger, inspecting the labyrinth of veins. It was a samara carrying the seed of the ash tree. The flight of the seed to the earth where it sprouted and grew for decades into a sturdy tree that would offer up new winged seeds; this spiraling circle of life and rebirth was the perpetuation of all things, myself included. A clear image in my mind's eye of the Katsura tree in my family's garden reminded me of the dragonfly seedpods that hypnotized me in childhood. The tree had caught my attention as I prepared for Uncle's visit from Kowloon. I had no knowledge that he would invite my brother to the Golden Mountain, nor that I would be shuffled to take my brother's place. The moongate within the courtyard wall flashed before me, its circular view of the curving path through low spreading ferns and flowering foliage. I stood now within the outside world that as a child was a mere porthole through the wall. The top of the wall had formed gently curving waves. Enraptured in the visions of this day and those in my mind, I felt my spirit soar. I was a samara in the wind.

We knew it would be dark by the time we returned to the settlement. It was in fact dark when we reached the ridge overlooking the valley, where the Maidu men had left us to wander into our manhood. What a wonderful vision of manhood the Maidu gave to their sons. This was not a lesson in strength or power; it was a lesson in reverence for all things.

Upon the ridge, we filled a narrow gulley with pine needles and collected cedar boughs to create a covering. Beneath the camouflage of the cedar boughs, we had intended to rest for a short time before continuing on our trek back to the Maidu settlement. We fell, instead, into a deep sleep filled with dreams of fantasy and flight. I dreamed that a mountain of water had rolled over the land, washing over me. I swam like a fish until I washed over a high cliff and fell endlessly in a curtain of water to a calm lake that seemed miles below the cliff. When I rose to the surface I continued to rise upon the air like a bird. The feeling of flight was breathlessly joyful. I flew above the towering cliff with its great waterfall. I ascended above the clouds and crossed the immense face of the sun, a giant disc of blazing light that dominated the sky. A huge owl with scarlet wings and the face of a man crossed my path. The bird told me that I was not a boy, nor was I merely a man. "You are all things and all life is sacred," said the bird. I awoke to the soft cooing of mourning doves and splinters of sunlight that spilled through the cedar boughs. "Daylight," I said to Diego, who woke with a calm expression and propped himself up on his elbows.

"I met *Shanhaiching* in dream! He have message." I explained to Diego that *Shanhaiching* is an ancient magical creature from Chinese legends. Diego opened his eyes wide with surprise and grasped my shoulders. "Yaozu, you are a lucky man," he said with a smile.

THE END OF OUR INITIATION

From the ridge where we had slept, the trail led downhill to the settlement. The air was cool and still, the sky held high wisps of clouds like strokes of paint by a giant hand. We were eager to see Paohee and his wife Moahnee and their small child whom they called Meke. We expected first to encounter trails of smoke from the roundhouse ovens drifting at slants above the tall pines around the settlement. Our ears awaited the yelling and cheering of native children playing out in the open.

We spotted the domed shapes of roundhouses. No smoke poured forth that morning. The children had all been hushed. Perhaps there was a communal prayer or the preparations of a slain buck had captured their undistracted attention. As we neared the settlement I made out what appeared to be a pile of deer, their carcasses stacked like firewood. We stopped in our tracks the instant that we could clearly see that the bodies were not deer or elk or any hunter's prized game. The stack of bodies was a pile of Maidu women, their clothing half torn from their bodies. Half naked and slaughtered with swords and hatchets, their mutilated bodies lay lifeless and bloodied in broad daylight. Where were all the children and men? As if reading my thoughts, Diego said, "The men must have gone hunting." We approached the doorway of a roundhouse with caution. The attackers might be holding the children inside as they awaited the return of the men.

Diego grabbed my arm and pulled me to the right of the door, where he pointed to stones on the ground. We quietly collected two or three each, and then pitched the stones over the roundhouse, creating a small barrage of noise. Seeing that nobody stepped outside the doorway to investigate the noise, we carefully rounded the entrance to the circular room. First to catch my sight was a tall boy tied to a pole that supported the roof. The boy's head lay forward on his chest and blood covered his stomach. His throat had been slit. On a similar pole across

175

the room a tall girl had been bound and axed with a hatchet. The small girl named Meke lay flat on her back with a bullet hole in her forehead. In each roundhouse the grim scene was much the same.

In one roundhouse, an old man lay on the ground, his tongue cut out and his ears sliced off. The handle of a bowie knife stood between his ribs as he lay on the blood drenched ground. A tall, thin boy must have put up a courageous fight – his skull had been split open and his brain spilled upon the dirt. A pudgy girl with a round face held a cluster of folded papers. Her throat had been cut so quickly that a spray of blood had splattered her papers. Her large round eyes stared blankly up at nothing. I knelt down beside her and whispered, "Eisha, little Eisha." Turning my head to avoid her empty gaze, I could see that the boy with the split skull was Woaku, the same boy who had joined our little Chinese lesson.

I found Diego outside. He was holding a boy half his size in his arms. Tears poured down Diego's cheeks. Two bullets had passed through the child's body that now hung lifeless in Diego's arms.

There were no words that we could say to each other. We were silenced. For the remainder of the afternoon we sat half-stunned or paced back and forth, awaiting the return of the men's hunting party. By sunset, the men returned, finding us both slouched back-to-back upon the ground. We looked desperately worn out, dirty, and blood stained. Paohee and another hunter ran to see if we were injured. We pointed grimly to the pile of butchered women. A loud wailing filled the evening accompanied by angry shrill cries that sounded like calls to war. Bodies were dragged from the roundhouses and some men clutched their lifeless children or their slaughtered wives to their bodies, as if the love that raged within them could bring back the dead. Paohee came to stand near me. He held his hands over his chest. He appeared as if he would explode if not collapse. He stared out at the sunset. It seemed odd that the heavens continued unfolding. How could the sky be so lovely, knowing that all these lives had ended violently? Where were the souls of Moahnee and her small child now? Where were the freed spirits of Eisha and Woaku? Were they all sailing into the sky – following the sun's descent over the horizon? The paradise and magic of yesterday were now torn apart and my soul felt shredded and battered. Diego's eyes were veined in red and dark shadows formed grieving half moons beneath his listless gaze. Our glorious initiation into manhood had taken a terrifying turn.

AFTERMATH OF THE DEVASTATION

After dark we moved outside the settlement, returning to the jagged rock lookout. Three or four of us would take our turns upon the moonlit lookout. We would poke each other with small branches, making sure that those of us on guard kept from dozing off. At the base of the slanted formation the remainder of the men rested. I could not have chosen between the agony of exhaustion and the torment of the hideous nightmares. We slept but little when others relieved us of guarding. Lying upon the ground barely relieved the aching and tension. At rare intervals, gazing up at the sky, I could see the thinning of clouds and the icy, cold pinpoints of stars. Those silvery jewels were Maidu spirits looking down upon us. The charcoal clouds would wash back over them, removing them from the sky.

The following morning, before the sun's first rays, we returned to the camp, gathering long leafy branches that we piled into several large beds for the deceased. The grim bodies of small children and half-grown youth were placed beside their mothers and grandmothers. There were only three elderly men who were placed near each other. One of the old men was placed on the end beside his wife, their daughter, and two grandchildren.

Diego explained that a funeral ceremony was usually quite lengthy, but this mass exodus of spirits would be honored by a shortened ritual owing to the impending danger of the location. A rigorous prayer was followed by communal chanting that ended abruptly. A pronounced silence spread around us, filling the universe with stillness. Each of us chose a sturdy branch to serve as a torch. We surrounded the large tangled beds, the funeral pyres of these beloved people, and together we lit the edges of the foliage. Kneeling briefly, we placed our burning torches upon the beds, closed our eyes as the smoke began to rise, and rising together we turned away from the incineration of flesh and bones. Few of the men's faces were wet with tears as we left behind the settlement and hiked into the forest.

I managed in my despairing state of mind to gather my journal and warm clothing. I pulled the bracelet of colored pebbles from my coat pocket and Diego helped tie it onto my wrist. Months passed before I would open the journal or write entries. Rage and despair boiled within me the first week after the mass slaughter. Exhaustion finally caught up with me. I slept for days on end. The cold and the snow came. The wind howled in night like an injured dog. Despondency took hold of my soul and a beast-like animal nature emerged in my core and manifested in my mannerisms. I forgot to talk to people. I forgot to think in Chinese. I gave up learning English. I lost track of my old mutilated dream. I quit thinking about gold and wealth. I survived in a savage way without remembering how to take care of myself. I don't remember saying goodbye to Diego or separating from the Maidu men, but I wandered alone in the forest. I would sit against a frozen tree that stood in a gully between two ridges, protected from the worst of harsh winds. I would see from the side of my eye a barefoot girl in the snow, but when I turned my head she would disappear and I would yell, "Eisha, Eisha," my own cry, howling along with the tireless wind. Life staggered onward. The weather was cruel and uncaring. The great ancestors of my people became indifferent strangers. The Great Creator moved elsewhere, leaving behind an icy, blistering cold. *Xiaoxue*, the Small Snow passed and *Daxue*, the Great Snow arrived. I turned into a sleep walker. I lived in amnesia with my eyes open. I stumbled upon a collapsed and rotting cabin buried in the snow. I slept inside the dark collapsed roof for warmth. One morning Uncle woke me, insisting that I wake up to go to work on our claim. I sat up, excited to see him alive, only to see a large gray owl fly out of the triangular crawlspace of the caved-in cabin. Uncle was no where to be found, only another cruel trick or my muddled mind. I grew tired of looking for anyone or anything. I forgot what cliff I had fallen off. I wanted to sleep endlessly. Why did I bother to keep waking up? I chewed on snow. I found particles of dry food in my pocket linings. I gnawed on frozen twigs. I slept and slept, trying to disappear.

Second Moon – Day 2 Birthday of the Lord of the Earth,
Tudigong, depicted as an old gentleman
with a long flowing beard. The Lord of
the Earth resides on every street or
neighborhood to keep the peace and
ensure general prosperity.

CENTRAL PACIFIC STATION, MARIPOSA, CALIFORNIA

A cathedral-sized big-leaf maple formed a spectacular awning that nodded above the grand arched entry to the train station. I sat at the maple tree's base, wedged between exposed octopus tentacle roots. A gray squirrel nibbled nervously near my feet. His belly was white as a napkin stuffed under his chin. His long, bushy tail stood poised, but only briefly. A violet green swallow swooped low beneath the canopy of maple leaves, sending the gray squirrel scurrying and scraping up the rough-barked trunk.

A round-faced toddler in a frilly bonnet waved a plump hand at me. Her mother, dressed in a long drab gown and a similar bunched bonnet guided the unsure-footed infant across the yard toward the yawning entrance of the station. Nobody seemed to take notice of me. The street and walkway were jammed with carriages and buggies. Horses flicked their tails and bobbed their heads. Mules stood deadpan while boys and men unloaded bags, crates, trunks and luggage.

Among the faces of the world, the rich and poor, an image of my father appeared over my shoulder. His eyes were stern and penetrating. His mouth was drawn into a sneer. Whether he was ready to scowl or ready to grin, I could never predict. As if through a crystal ball, I saw through my father's eyes. He would feel shamed to see me, my queue shorn off, and my remaining hair matted with mud and grass. My hands were filthy, nearly black with grease. My lightweight Cantonese clothes had long since disappeared. He would have seen me in a floppy old hat and a fancy topcoat, now worn at the elbows. He would see my thick wool shirt, stained kneebreeches, and hobnail boots too big

180

for my boy-sized feet. He'd watch me then, sauntering through the arched doorway of the train station, my hands in my pockets. He'd look on as I hid behind a thick support beam. "Hiding like a rat, like a scared animal," he would criticize. His tight-lipped sneer would have been unmistakable, and shaking his head he would turn away.

It was not really my father's image, but my own conscience (inherited from him) sitting on my shoulder, anticipating what I was about to do. The trip across the Pacific Ocean seemed on that day a hundred years ago, and my life in China had been left far behind, a thousand years gone. I was truly a scared rat caught in a treacherous trap. There was a tightness clutching at my throat. Tears seemed long forgotten, and any form of comfort in my life had become long lost. I brushed caked grass off the shoulder of my jacket. My survival demanded action.

The station was bustling and raucous. There were beggars and farmers and merchants, and, no doubt, gamblers down-on-their-luck. The well-to-do were also mixed into the crowd. That's who I focused on, the wealthy ones. Apparently, even royalty wanted to find gold and become yet wealthier. I heard dialects and tongues from all corners of the globe, all babbling and gurgling in that mammoth room like a gargantuan soup pot.

A group of Chinese men had gathered in a far corner of the room. They appeared to be Manchurians from the north. I carefully avoided them.

The high arched windows of the room welcomed slanting sunbeams into the station. Like spotlights, the sunbeams singled out foppish dandies in the snaking mass of humanity. Three gentlemen had offered their assistance to a stately lady who twirled a fringed parasol above her head. She apparently cared less that an open umbrella was bad luck indoors. Two of the dandies shared the burden of her brass-handled cedar chest, while the other, eager-looking gentleman balanced two suitcases, a hat box, and a large handbag. The men's high boots were shined to perfection, their coattails were long, and their top hats were well kept with black silk ribbons.

All heads turned to take in the splendor of the elegant woman twirling her white satin parasol, its black fringe in flight. She wore a massive hat of emerald batiste. An outsized bow on the hat matched her parasol. Her vermillion dress spread to the floor as if covering a Chinese funeral bell. A black netted shawl draped her shoulders and arms. A white gloved hand braced the parasol, while the other hand steadied a tiny booklet. Her face, through a veil, looked whimsical, even coquettish. Turning to double check on the gentlemen guarding her luggage, her dress whisked the wood floor like a shushing whisper.

As if eavesdropping, the crowd hushed. The dandy with too many bags arranged them neatly behind the lady on the floor, and ran off on an errand. As if this were the end of act one, the crowd resumed their various conversations in their varied tongues. I noticed that everyone was pretending to ignore the grand lady, with her tiny book and twirling parasol. Occasional quick side glances from spectators indicated that she had not truly lost center stage.

From my position, behind the wide support beam, I saw that the wide arched entryway was no longer blocked by the entering crowd. I took in one long breath and dashed across the room toward the magnificent lady, intently studying her tiny booklet. I snatched up the large handbag. Immediately, the stouter of the two remaining dandies bellowed out, "Hey, you!" The other gentlemen in his top hat cried out, "Thief, thief!"

As I flew through the doorway, I heard a woman's shrill scream. Turning left outside the arched entrance, I crashed headlong into a sturdy market woman. She whacked me in the head with a loaf of bread that felt like a brick. I kept running. I heard the chorus of "Hey you" and "Thief, thief."

AND THERE I MET YOU

Ms. Montez looked at me, and proceeded to reread the description of the scrawny street urchin who had long since snatched her carpetbag. "You've been through so much, and your story is brimming with the harsh ways of men and the dreams of innocence."

From the kitchen came a startling crash of heavy chinaware and shattering glass. Ms. Montez raised her eyebrows and screwed up her face in a comical expression of worry and disgrace. Handing the journal to me, she stood with a rustling of her dress cloths. With a screech, followed by a jumble of chattering, her red-vested monkey tore through the hallway. "Mahalakshmi!" she scolded as she scuttled like a geisha into the drawing room where Mahalakshmi had hidden. "Mahalakshmi, come out at once," she demanded, "you naughty little scoundrel." As she kneeled on the floor to look under an elegantly contoured loveseat, Mahalakshmi screeched and scampered over the loveseat, across the room and back out the door. I had to laugh at the sight of a small red-vested monkey getting the better of Ms. Montez.

She threw her hands up in resignation. "Let's go survey the disaster area." We stood in the doorway to the kitchen, amazed to see the strewn shards of several large porcelain platters and the sparkling claws of shattered crystal. She tip-toed through the room, opened a narrow door, and pulled out a broom with curled and worn wisps of straw. Clearing a path to the window, we looked through white lace and violet bougainvillea out into her back yard. Tethered to a magnolia tree, Lady Macbeth, her pet bear, lay sleeping with her head resting upon crossed paws. I spotted the red vest upon Mahalakshmi on a branch of the loquat tree. "There," I pointed. "Clever little weasel, isn't he?" she said.

She swept the broken dishes into a pile where she left them. She placed the broom against the wall and led me back to the parlor where we had been discussing my journal. "Youzu, relax here a moment as I prepare some tea and visit the powder

183

room," she said as she bustled out of the room. After about six seconds of sitting in the cushioned armchair, I realized that relaxing was easier said than done. I stood up, and crossed the parlor to examine a collection of books that Ms. Montez kept on a cherry wood bookstand. There were a variety of unique titles to choose from: *Undine,* by De La Motte Fouque. Elegant cursive manuscript inside the inner sleeve of the cover read;

> *Dearest Countess,*
> *This delightful tale translated from German is*
> *a romantic fantasy set in an enchanted forest. I*
> *relished the water spirits in the story and thought*
> *immediately of you.*
> > *Yours truly and everlasting,*
> > *Count Verlaine DuBois*

There was *Frankenstein* by Marry Shelley, *Pickwick Papers* by Charles Dickens, *Indiana* by George Sand, *Tales of the Grotesque and Arabesque* by Edgar Allen Poe, *The Scarlet Letter* by Nathaniel Hawthorn, and a small oxblood colored booklet that I recognized immediately: *Gemmologist's Pocket Compendium* by Robert Webster, F.G.A. I pulled the tiny booklet from the shelf and leafed through the advertisements... "Diamonds – All shapes, sizes, qualities": "Pearl and Bead stringing", "Specialty: - Rough Lapiz Lazuli", "The Mounting of Gems, Jade, Zircons, Turquoise, Tourmaline, Sapphires, Rubies, Coral, Lapis – The Jade Dragon Ltd".

Ms. Montez entered the room with a silver tray, porcelain teacups and an urn of steaming hot black tea. "Ah, you have rediscovered the Gemmologist's reference guide that you returned to me. May I show you a couple of interesting aspects of this little book?" She carefully placed the silver tray upon the marble top table and held out an open hand. I placed the leatherette booklet in her palm and she opened it randomly to page 15. "This is a glossary of names and terms used by jewelers and jewelry dealers. Here is an unusual term," She pointed to the entry **Crocidolite; name used for pseudomorphs of quartz after oxydised blue crocidolite asbestos, properly called "Tiger's–eye." See *Quartz.* We repositioned ourselves in our seats and she poured out two cups of citrus aroma black tea. She turned to a later page in the booklet: Tables of Useful Data - Physical Properties. Midway down the page she pointed to a list titled Scales of Hardness. Above the title, hardness was defined as the power a substance possesses to resist abrasion (scratching) when a pointed fragment of another substance is drawn across it. The list read as such:

	Mohhs's	Brinell's
Talc 1		3
Gypsum.........................2		12
Calcite 3		53
Fluorspar.......................4		64
Apatitie.........................5		137
Felspar.........................6		147
Quartz.........................7		178
Topaz.........................8		304
Corundum......................9		667
Diamond......................10		

Mohs's Scale	
Finger nail	about 2 ½
Copper coin	3
Window glass	5 ½
Knife blade	6
Steel file	6 ½

"A dear friend from San Francisco gave me this booklet. He now has a jewelry shop here in Grass Valley, which, by the way, gives me a splendid idea. I would like you to meet him. His name is Charles Guthrie, and he is looking for an apprentice. I'm not going to tell you more; I don't want to give you any preconceptions or taint your meeting him with any prejudice."

Of course, I didn't understand half of what she had just said, but I caught the drift about wanting to introduce me to a friend.

A chiming and tinkling of glass tonalities announced the arrival of a guest. Ms. Montez had an ingenious device that was activated by pulling a wooden handle on a rope beside the front door. The rope traversed over a pulley near the top of the door and a hole in the wall allowed the rope to pull upon a brass ring inside the door. The brass ring ascended until it collided with chimes of glass and brass, creating a pleasant tinkling and ringing that alerted Ms. Montez that somebody outside the door had just arrived.

"One moment, Yaozu," said Ms. Montez as she lifted her grand bell of skirts and glided out of the parlor. I could hear as she opened the door that Lotta Crabtree had arrived and the young girl's exuberant tones bounced down the hallway like a bright balloon as Ms. Montez escorted the small protégé into the parlor. Lotta wore a baby blue satin dress with a huge blue bow pinned askew to the top of her head of tawny red hair. Her long white boots laced up to her knees, and the girl had a commanding presence and a bright shiny smile.

"Yaozu, you remember Lotta?" she said. It was more of a statement than a question. "It is time for her rehearsals, but if you would return tomorrow around two p.m., we could have lunch together with my friend, Charles Guthrie. He is a sweetheart of a man, and I feel certain that you could benefit from his acquaintance."

I agreed to return for lunch. I bowed and pardoned myself as I departed, wishing them happy rehearsal. They both giggled and saw me to the door. They waved goodbye dutifully and playfully from the doorway as I opened and closed the gate in the fence.

MR. GUTHRIE'S WORKSHOP

Lunch the next day was served on a long table with a lace tablecloth, embroidered serviettes, painted chinaware, and finely embossed silver. Mr. Guthrie was a small, portly man with wavy white hair and spectacles. He invited me after lunch to visit his workshop on Vista del Monte Boulevard. The boulevard was lined with colorful shops and flourishing businesses: McGregor's Tools, Purveyors of Unique & Extraordinary Décor, Bentley's Rifle Emporium, Saddle Sally's Saloon and Guthrie's Jewels, to name a few. From the boulevard, Guthrie's Jewels was merely a shiny black door with bold, red and gold circus-style lettering. Ted's Barber's Shop and the Sweeny's Candy Store shouldered the jeweler's black door to the left and right, giving the appearance that the black door gave access to a narrow alley or a delivery entrance. Once opened, the doorway revealed a rose-vine carpeted hallway. At the far end of the hallway, a man sat smoking a pipe, his wooden chair tilted back against the wainscot along the peach colored wall. As we neared the man with a pipe, I noticed his reading glasses balanced on the end of his nose, his striped suspenders, and a copy of the Grass Valley Gazette in his tight grasp. With his heavy accent, perhaps Russian or French (European accents confused me more than English itself), the gruff man stood with bent back to greet Mr. Guthrie while shuffling the newspaper behind his back and onto the chair. I noticed him pulling a large key ring from his belt as Mr. Guthrie introduced me to him – the old man's name was Mizhousser or some such enigmatic name. Mizhousser unlocked a door cage. Behind the cage a heavy oak door opened upon a stairway that led to yet another door upstairs. Mr. Guthrie had his own key for this second floor door, and once inside we were directly above Sweeny's Candy Store. We stepped inside a very dim and chaotic looking repair shop. Mr. Guthrie lit an oil lamp and adjusted the flame with a twist of his wrist. Table tops were covered with canvases and the walls had an expansive grid of holes that held a myriad of hooks from which dangled wrenches, hammers, torches, rolls of wire, and an

187

endless assortment of peculiar looking devices with handles and pincers.

A drawn curtain in the corner of the room resembled a dressing room. Mr. Guthrie yanked open the curtain, unveiling door number four. This door was forest green. It was double bolted with a keyhole above the doorknob. After unlocking this door, Mr. Guthrie asked me to carry the oil lamp inside. Once inside, Mr. Guthrie mounted a step ladder in order to pull open the blinds on three small, high windows that bordered the ceiling. The light of day spilled gently into the room, revealing display cases of finely crafted jewelry. First I was drawn to the damascene art of inlaid gold and silver against the contrasting black background of steel. The ornamentation of two earrings resembled the geometric medallions seen on Arabic mosques, and an octagonal jewelry box combined the motifs of ancient Arabic characters with floral designs. There was a striking sword letter opener of black steel inlaid with decorative flourishes of gold. There were pill boxes, brooches, bracelets, tiepins, thimbles, and ornamental plates. Mr. Guthrie stood beside me as he said, "I would like to show you later how I carefully wield gold thread with my left hand as I use a steel punch to hammer the thread into the metal base with my right hand. This is how gold filament is inlaid onto steel." He unlocked the door behind the glass case and carefully extracted a small candy dish. The dish was black ringed in a gold outline. The delicate pattern of tiny flowers and a fern leaf stood out boldly against the stark blackness of the small plate.

"Pure gold," he said, "is too malleable for making jewelry." He looked at my bewildered expression. "Pure gold is almost mushy compared to steel. If you touch pure gold with a knife or a screwdriver, it is easy to leave a mark. A pure gold ring would loose its shape too easily. A customer would be very unhappy after purchasing an expensive ring, to later discover that accidentally stepping on the ring could easily bend it out of shape. Pure gold is like this; too malleable, too mushy or soft. We make gold more durable by combining it with copper, or silver, or palladium. These strengthening metals are called alloys when they are combined with gold. The choice of alloy will give the gold different hues; yellow, green, or white."

"You may already know this, Yaozu, but pure gold is said to be one thousand fine. Another manner of saying one thousand fine is twenty four karats. Eighteen karat gold is eighteen parts pure gold, and six parts alloy. The fineness or purity can also be expressed in parts per thousand. Eighteen karat gold contains 750 parts pure gold and 250 parts alloy."

"I hear Uncle talk carrot of gold," I said, "but, I never see gold shape like carrot or onion or potato." Mr. Guthrie laughed like a cackling hen. "I understand what you say," I said, "One thousand equal pure gold."

"That's a good start," he said.

And so it began. Mr. Guthrie asked me to become his apprentice. I didn't ask him why Ms. Montez would have referred a Chinese foreigner who had once stolen her carpet bag. I soon learned that Ms. Montez had also made mention of my Uncle Ān Lè to Mr. Guthrie. It was not essential that I be a promising assistant in the labor of jewel making as long as I became a valuable link to my uncle's prestigious trade expertise and numerous contacts. Unfortunately, I had lost track of my uncle's whereabouts the day that somebody tried to drown me in the river and bandits shot bullets at our team of miners. I had thought of writing my parents in China to see if they had received a letter from Uncle. I had failed to mention it in my letters so far, because I felt irresponsible and guilty for losing track of him, and I didn't want to alarm them if they had heard nothing. It seemed that now there might be pressure from Mr. Guthrie to seek out Uncle's whereabouts. I decided that it was time to inform my parents of the disappointing loss of contact. I also felt embarrassed that my older brother would surely point out that I was incompetent, and Uncle would have done better to take him with a broken arm than to take me when I was obviously too young.

In the meantime, Mr. Guthrie paid me a better salary than I had pulled in working the gold mines. He seemed to enjoy my company and was unimaginably patient with my meager English skills.

He gradually, over a period of weeks that turned into months, showed me the basics of melting, annealing, pickling, refining, and then graduating to the numerous techniques of rolling shapes, drawing wire, incising, forging, and soldering. As I became more and more proficient at these, he slowly eased me into the more advanced techniques of linkages, closures, and rings.

Mr. Guthrie also displayed a separate collection of imported jewelry in his showroom. He had several fine Mongol pieces. A Manchu hairpin resembled a frilly butterfly lit upon a flower stalk. A circular silver amulet box depicted an ancient Chinese legend of three Taoist disciples. The three disciples had performed miraculous feats in gathering peaches from a dangerously positioned tree suspended over a cliff's edge. A dazzling headdress consisting of a scalloped, oval silver plate that was worn over the forehead, embedded with twisted rings of corals and turquoises, while the surrounding headdress was lined with tiny silver beads, corals, and malachite beads. A single, weighty earring hung like an immense tiger's tooth of pearly jade surrounded by dangling stylized butterflies. A bracelet of coiled silver latched together at the meeting of two dragons' heads, both of their jaws clutching at a single jewel of jade.

A WINDY DAY IN SAN FRANCISCO (1857)

I may have been at work that day. I didn't see the passengers crowding the pier with their Saratoga chests, carpetbags, and duffle bags packed tight with changes of clothing and souvenirs. Later that month, newspaper articles described a windy day that set sail to several hats. The gentlemen had to grab hold of their stovetop hats, and the ladies' hoop skirts were tossed about comically. Famous couples climbed the gangway to the deck of the *Sonora,* a steamer headed south to Panama. Adeline Mills Easton was small and lively, the sister of Darius Ogden Mills, one of the richest men in California who would later found the Bank of California. Her husband, Ansel Easton, built a fortune in California selling furniture to the steamship lines. A readily recognized face in San Francisco, Billy Birch was seen setting foot aboard the *Sonora* with his new wife Virginia, who carried a parakeet in a cage. Billy Birch was a favorite of the San Francisco Minstrels. He was known for singing *"The Grapevine Twist"* and *"I'm Fatter Than I Wish to Be."*

It was not uncommon for famous people to be seen boarding steamships in San Francisco. What was uncommon about the steamship *Sonora* was that a consigned shipment of gold amounting to $1,595,497.13 was being delivered to New York via Panama. It took the *Sonora* fourteen days to reach port in Panama, where the passengers, numbering about five hundred, were transferred to new open-air railcars to cross forty-eight miles to arrive in Aspinwall, a port city on the Caribbean. In Aspinwall, the passengers boarded the side-wheel steamer SS Central America, bound for New York, with one overnight port in Havana. There was no public knowledge of the twenty-one tons of gold en route, but the consigned shipment was soon to become very famous.

A Massachusetts' newspaper ran a dramatically illustrated depiction of the disaster. The ship was all but sunk in huge waves in which debris and swimming passengers were scattered overboard, while silhouettes of men dangling from loose cables and a small crowd could still be seen upon the deck of the exposed stern jutting from the surrounding waves. The caption read: WRECK OF THE STEAMSHIP CENTRAL AMERICA. APPALLING DISASTER. On Saturday, September 12th, 1857, Capt. Herndon, bound to New York, From California, with the Pacific Mails, Passengers and Crew, to the number of 592, and treasure to the amount of over $2,000,000, foundered in a hurricane, off Cape Hatteras. Number saved, 166.

Mr. Guthrie put on his long woolen overcoat and emerald green stovetop hat. "Come along with me, Yaozu," he said as he buttoned the overcoat's whalebone buttons. He locked up shop and we descended the stairs, passing Mister Mizhousser whose chair was once again tipped back against the wall as he read. We exited the lacquered black door onto the street, and proceeded several blocks down Vista del Monte Boulevard. High overhead, stringy wisps of clouds curled at the ends like dust swept from a porch. The day was cool and bright. Ladies in bonnets carried covered baskets and bid Mr. Guthrie, "Good day," and men with walking sticks would nod their heads and tip their hats.

We arrived at a small shop with a wooden sign suspended from a rusty chain. The sign read *Smith and Samson's Metallurgy.* A thick burnt odor of metallic smoke hung in the air and the workers wore thick glass shields over their faces. "Most of the gold in my shop is melted in this shop," explained Mr. Guthrie. "The most commonly used alloy in crafting jewelry is 18-karat gold, which is 750 fine. Metal can be alloyed in different types of ovens. Eighteen-karat yellow gold is usually alloyed with a mixture of half copper / half silver. White gold is the result of adding palladium, silver, and nickel. After the melted metals are mixed, they are cooled inside a mold. The molded gold is called an ingot."

Mr. Guthrie collected four ingots of yellow gold and three ingots of white gold from Mr. Samson. He asked me to pick up one ingot. It was much heavier than it looked. I carried the three ingots of white gold in a drawstring bag as Mr. Guthrie toted the four others. We returned to Mr. Guthrie's shop above Sweeny's Candy Store. Today the sweet smell of salt water taffy rose up from the candy store, filling the jewelry shop with a cheerful scent. My first lesson as an apprentice in his shop was learning how to clean the metal and keep it from oxidizing. "The most commonly used cleaner," said Mr. Guthrie, "is borax, which strips away surface oxidation. Potassium nitrate, also known as saltpeter, works well, as does sodium nitrate and common table salt."

There was a knocking at the door at the top of the steps. It was Mr. Mizhousser. "Three fine looking ladies have arrived to inspect jewelry," he called out through the closed door. His raspy voice sounded like a wheezy old dog's harmless barking. Mr. Guthrie unlatched the door and went downstairs to greet the lady visitors. I waited in the workshop as the four of them bustled up the narrow stairway. The first two ladies to enter the door were older, dressed in navy blue and ecru. They both wore gloves and held their faces in stony expressions, resembling military inspectors more than ladies of charm. The stouter of the two had the jowls of a bulldog, while the bonier one had a pointed nose like a Doberman pinscher. They both pretended to ignore me with a disapproving air.

Entering the door behind them, a much younger woman in a violet gown with strawberry blond hair piled upon her head stepped into the shop wearing a delicate grin on her face. Her skin was creamy white with a pink flush. She noticed me immediately, and her large eyes shone icy blue like a bright winter sky. Mr. Guthrie entered last and stepped forward to introduce us. "Mrs. Beasley and Mrs. Oxford, this is my young assistant, Yaozu." I bowed to the older ladies who nodded their heads, both maintaining their severe demeanors. "This is Miss Gwendolyn Oxford, Mrs. Oxford's niece." The younger woman with the sky blue eyes smiled gently, "Hello, Yaozu. I am pleased to meet you." "I am please to meet you, Miss Gwendolyn," I said stiffly with a bow.

I had met a few miners with blue eyes. I had tended to imagine that some kind of malnutrition or anemia had drained the color from their irises, but the men had tended to be either quite tan or very dirty, and their bright blue eyes looked startling to me. Miss Gwendolyn looked very soft and pale, and her coloring seemed to be more a gentle strength than a deficiency. The foreign devils frequently referred to Chinamen as celestials, but this woman in a violet gown looked as if she had just recently descended from a visit to the heavens with her eyes shot through with visions of celestial paradise.

"Miss Oxford is engaged to marry this summer, and her aunts have graciously invited the bride-to-be to shop for a necklace to be worn with her wedding gown," reported Mr. Guthrie as he unlocked the display room. I expected to stay behind in the workshop, but Mr. Guthrie signaled for me to tag along with a side dip of his head. I grabbed the oil lamp, and he ushered me into the display room ahead of the women so as to light up the dark room. I placed the lamp on a drapery covered display table and located the step ladder. Without asking Mr. Guthrie, I went ahead and opened the blinds of the three high windows as the ladies sauntered into the display room. Mr. Guthrie pantomimed the theatrical moves of a street magician, pulling the draperies from the display cases with quick flamboyant jerks. Holding the draperies like a matador, he turned gracefully to gingerly fold the velvet cloths with expert showmanship. Instinctively, the women held their gloved hands to their throats as they cooed their soft ohs and ahs.

The older women inspected the displays consecutively, as if touring a museum. The stouter bull dog woman pointed occasionally, her forefinger poised upon the glass as the leaner Doberman pinscher lady slowly nodded with a tight-lipped grimace. Mr. Guthrie talked to Gwendolyn, inquiring into the nature of her personal tastes in adornments. He cleverly asked her if she had a favorite animal, if she preferred bodies of water, high mountains, or open fields. Gwendolyn was fond of butterflies and loved mountain streams. She also loved a night sky full of stars and a crescent moon. As she mentioned the crescent moon, her face lit up and she wondered if Mr. Guthrie had ever seen an eclipse.

"Ah – hah!" said Mr. Guthrie. "I think we have hit upon something." He guided Miss Gwendolyn to a display case opposite the backs of the older women. With a miniature key that he pulled from a small pocket on his shirt, he opened the lock on the display, lifted the glass and extracted a chain necklace suspending a delicate gold medallion. "Oh, my," said Miss Gwendolyn. She signaled to me to step nearer.

The gold medallion resembled a golden sun with curling tentacle rays of light. Resembling the dark yin tear of a yin-yang symbol, a dark crescent moon of blue onyx fell across the right portion of the medallion. "It's an eclipse!" exclaimed Gwendolyn. Her discovery was filled with a gleeful radiance.

Her words rang like the sound of water spilling from a fountain. And so I learned a new word: eclipse.

Her aunts inspected the cleverly fashioned necklace. One wagged a pointed finger as the other clucked like a hen. "It's rather gaudy, don't you think, dear?" said Mrs. Beasley. "Entirely inappropriate for a wedding," added Mrs. Oxford. "It's perfect," said Gwendolyn as if mystified by the eclipsed sun medallion. The two aunts tugged at Miss Gwendolyn, pulling the bride-to-be across the small room to a display case beneath the center window. Mr. Guthrie dutifully unlocked the case with his tiny key, and the aunts pointed out several gold crosses, two of which were embedded with small diamonds. I had many a time seen these gold crosses suspended on the necklaces of miners, even a few of the women. I knew that it was a symbol of a means of torture and the death sentence dealt to a historical religious leader of many of the foreign devils. Diego, my dear friend who had led me to the enchanted village of the Maidu people, wore a gold cross on a gold necklace. Evidently, many people held a great significance to this symbol, but I had yet to learn of its deeper significance.

"They are beautiful," Miss Gwendolyn assured her aunts, "but I have chosen the eclipsed sun." The aunts shook their heads in dismay. In the end, the aunts selected a simple gold cross and Gwendolyn chose the necklace with the eclipsed sun. "I will wear them both on the day of my wedding," decided Miss Gwendolyn. Not only did her preference impress me, but her diplomacy was commendable as well. The ladies departed shortly after their purchases, but the image of Miss Gwendolyn and her stiff aunts has remained with me over the years. Years later I witnessed an eclipse of the sun and thought again of the lovely Miss Gwendolyn. Of course, the eclipse looked more like a dark bite taken from a glowing pie. The medallion was very stylized in comparison, but the design was impressive.

Many times during our labor or jewelry making, our tasks would be interrupted by men shopping for jewels to impress the ladies, or women looking for trinkets that caught their eyes. There would be special occasions: dinner parties, nights at the opera, gallant proposals of marriage, weddings, going away presents, anniversaries, and such. Frequently a man who discovered a gold vein or a hit pay dirt would venture in to make an investment in "fancy jewelry." Mr. Guthrie taught me to look for tendencies and trends. "If the public wants gold crosses, we must supply them. Diamond studded rings are always in demand. Our own personal visions of beauty may lead us well in our craft, but if nobody is purchasing our own creations, we are failing as a business. Watch the customer. Get to know him personally and understand his taste and his intentions. If you know your customer you will sell jewelry. You are a bright young man, Yaozu, quick to learn and very alert. You have the makings of a fine jeweler. Watch and learn, son, watch and learn."

I had yet to locate my uncle, so Mr. Guthrie's original intentions were left unanswered. He was gaining faith in me. I gained faith in myself. This is a great gift and I remain grateful to Mr. Guthrie for investing in me.

Mr. Guthrie enjoyed smoking a pipe. He said his tobacco was shipped from Virginia. He also loved coffee or hot black tea. Occasionally, he would purchase peppermint candy from Sweeny's Candy Store, or butterscotch hard candy. I never once saw him drink an alcohol beverage, but he may have enjoyed a cognac or whiskey drink in the privacy of his home. He never invited me to his house. This was no concern of mine, as our relationship was that of employer – employee, and he was a very kind and generous employer. Mr. Guthrie showed me far more respect than I was accustomed to under the employ of the foreign devils in gold mining endeavors.

Today's lesson was annealing and pickling. "When working with metal the gold alloy may become very hard," said Mr. Guthrie. "The ingot may be pounded flat, forged, or rolled, but as it reaches three fourths of its original thickness it may start cracking or splitting. The temperature for annealing different alloys varies from metal to metal. Pure silver can be annealed at a lower temperature than platinum, for example. Watch the color of this yellow gold as I heat it over a block of charcoal."

Placing the flattened gold slab over the block of charcoal, we watched for several minutes. We had to step away from the oven to cool off, and Mr. Guthrie offered me a peppermint from a small glass bowl. He pointed to three different projects that he was working on. After several more minutes we returned to the oven and the gold slab had taken on a dark reddish glow. "It takes practice to recognize that each particular metal has its own temperature and time for annealing. This dark red color is the annealing taking place in the gold alloy. Pure gold is not likely to crack or split apart, so pure gold does not require annealing. As I said before, pure gold bends too easily, so we prefer to use gold alloys. This yellow gold has an alloy of copper and silver. This makes for durable jewelry, but working the metal into shape may cause cracking, so we must anneal the gold alloy. This particular heat, which is recognized when the gold alloy is dark red, must be maintained for several seconds, before allowing it to cool."

"The annealing, however, creates surface oxidation. Pickling is the method we use for stripping off the surface oxidation. Pickling can only be done after the metal has cooled, and we have to be careful not to cool the metal too quickly, because the abrupt change of temperature can cause the metal to warp. After cooling an annealed piece of metal, a layer of oxide forms on the surface. This oxide is the reaction of copper to oxygen. There may also be flux, or scraps of soldering liquid or borax used in the alloying. To strip off the oxide and flux, we use a solution called pickling acid. The common solution is one part sulfuric acid to warm water. This ratio is best for pickling gold or silver. The solution is heated up because it works faster than cold water."

Mr. Guthrie taught me that I should never add the water to the sulfuric acid, but instead add the acid to cold water, and then heat up the solution. If the water is already heated when the acid is added a dangerous reaction occurs. The vapors from the sulfuric acid are poisonous, so we mixed the solution beside the open door at the top of the steps. Mr. Guthrie gave me thick gloves and mask and apron so as to not splatter myself with the acid solution. "This solution will burn your clothes and your skin. Take your time and take care." After removing the gold slab from the acid solution, we rinsed it in a light solution of baking soda. Acid trapped inside hollow spaces or unusual shapes was thereby neutralized by the salts of the baking soda.

CONTAMINATED GOLD

Mr. Guthrie pulled open a drawer from the underside of the worktable. He pulled out a flat shingle of gold that looked charred and splintered with fissures. "This is contaminated gold. If the gold comes in contact with lead or tin, it will crack apart as it is rolled out. We call the gold contaminated, and this makes the metal impossible to work with." He dropped the shingle of gold onto the tabletop. "Did you hear the ringing sound of the metal hitting the table? Listen again." He picked up the contaminated gold and dropped it again. There was a low pitched, dull sound. He found a similar shaped gold shingle that looked smooth and clean. He dropped this piece of gold onto the tabletop and a higher pitch ringing sound was emitted. "That deeper, duller sound is one way to determine if the gold is contaminated."

"There is a process for extracting the lead or tin from the contaminated gold. This process is called refining. Just like pickling, refining involves a type of acid mixed with water that creates a poisonous vapor, so once again we put on the mask and thick gloves and cover our clothes with a good apron. This acid is called nitric acid and we mix an equal amount of nitric acid and water to form a refining bath. First, the contaminated gold must be alloyed with copper. The process calls for four parts copper to one part gold. I used to alloy gold with metals, but these days I take my contaminated gold back to Smith and Samson's Metallurgy, and I have them alloy the gold in their larger ovens. They only charge me for the copper, and they keep one fifth of my contaminated gold. If my profits are high enough, I'll go ahead and pay them to alloy the gold, but I'm not sure it's worth the price they charge."

"I like the bracelet you are wearing," commented Mr. Guthrie. He touched the rounded beads of stone, rolling them on the flesh of my wrist. "This is gift – little girl to me," I commented. I looked at the tiny stones, my memento of each individual tied together in a bond of family and the nightmarish morning that we found them savagely murdered. I had chosen to wear it as a reminder that jewelry can hold significance beyond its simple appearance.

SHAPING THE INGOT OF GOLD

The actual process of jewelry making began with reshaping the ingot of gold. The ingot looked like a very shiny brick. The easiest shapes to form were sheets, wires, and tubes. Once the jeweler had molded any of these desired shapes, he could begin sawing, soldering, or forging to form different designs. The pressure involved for shaping the ingot was intense enough to deform and even change the makeup of the internal structure of the metal. If the metal was not annealed regularly, the metal might lose its malleability and would crack or even break. Each time the shape was annealed it had to be pickled and then rinsed in running water with a little baking soda. Mr. Guthrie had three rolling mills. The crank on top of the mill could only be tightened about a half turn each time the metal was pressed through the mill. The mills pressed the ingot into flatter and flatter square bars, which could be repressed multiple times until the metal formed a sheet. The metal had to be annealed several times during the process to assure the malleability of the metal. Once the sheet was thin enough it could be pressed through a mill that created square rods of the metal. One end of the wire was then pressed into a point so that it would fit through a slightly smaller hole than the square rod. The rod was then pulled with tongs through consecutively smaller and smaller holes. This process was called drawing wire. The cross-section of a wire could end up being circular, square, half-circle, or rectangular, depending on the shape of the hole it was drawn through. After every fifth or sixth draw of the wire, Mr. Guthrie made sure to anneal the wire, pickle and rinse. "The wire will eventually break if you don't keep annealing it," he explained. The original square rod might have been as thick as a finger, but was pulled over and over until it became the desired thin wire.

Forming a tube was achieved with the use of a grooved forming block and a cross peen hammer, also called a jeweler's hammer or goldsmith's hammer. The edges of the hammer were rounded so that no marks were left on the tube. With the rounded surface of the cross peen hammer the sheet of metal was struck along the length, bending the sheet into a "U" shape. The tube was then closed up and drawn through two holes of a wire plate, just like pulling wire. The tube was then annealed and soldered. If the tube reopened during annealing, it could be closed by striking it on the outside with a hammer. After soldering, the seal was filed and the tube was drawn again through the wire drawing plate. Tubes could be used for forming a hinge or cut into the form of a ring. Various shapes were needed to assemble a mount for displaying a gemstone on a pendant, necklace, ring, or brooch.

Mr. Guthrie stepped outside onto the landing of the stairway to smoke a pipe. When he returned he praised me for my work and mentioned that he looked forward to the day that he might meet my Uncle Ān Lè. A look of doom must have consumed my facial features. I knew I owed Mr. Guthrie an explanation. "I sorry, I looking for my uncle, but I not know where to look." Mr. Guthrie looked at me sympathetically. "I write letter home – China, asking my father and mother."

"Maybe I could help you," said Mr. Guthrie. He explained that mail sent from Grass Valley was more likely to be delivered if the envelope was addressed in English. He also explained that there were special international rates of postage, and he would be glad to help me pay for extra postage to assure delivery of the letter. "Thank you," was all I could say. Mr. Guthrie wrote an English translation of the Chinese address on a new envelope, and I wrote the Chinese symbols below that, ensuring that the letter would find its way from Hong Kong to Guangzhou. The letter was registered, which meant that the deliverymen would obtain a signature from each post office the letter passed through, and a copy of that delivery would be returned to Mr. Guthrie, allowing him to know how far the letter had traveled thus far. It was an expensive but less risky manner of assuring the delivery. If my parents had heard from Uncle Ān Lè, they would be able to send back his latest address. Mr. Guthrie included a self-addressed envelope to his jewelry shop in

Grass Valley. He explained that my parents could address the upper part of the envelope to the Asian Pacific Sea Merchants in San Francisco, and the letter would be more reliably forwarded from there if the English address was legible.

All in all, the delivery and return seemed much more promising. However you looked at it, though, the Pacific Ocean was a wide, wide expanse, and there was no possibility of a truly rapid response. We would have to wait it out, and see if my parents had heard from Uncle.

FILING AND SANDING

The final appearance of the work of jewelry could be greatly enhanced by filing and sanding. These two tasks looked easy, or even self-explanatory, but the complexity of the shape and the desired result were better achieved with an experienced hand and a good variety of tools. Files usually came in three different teeth sizes: each size was referred to as the grade of the file. Larger teeth were more capable of cutting deeper, but were, unfortunately, more likely to leave deeper teeth marks on the surface. The deeper the teeth marks, the more time required for sanding with emery paper. The files cut only on the forward stroke. The reverse stroke served to sweep away the filings. As a result, the files had to be cleaned regularly to clear away any buildup of debris. In addition to three grades of teeth, the files were designed in a variety of shapes. A cross section of any particular file might have been circular, square, half moon, rectangular, or triangular. An expert jeweler easily had from fifteen to thirty different files. Practice and expertise with a variety of crevices, seams, and shapes determined the particular file that the jeweler reached for.

Mr. Guthrie had a generous selection of emery paper grades. The back sides of the papers each had a number along the bottom edge: 180, 320, 360, or 1200, for example. Final sanding tended to be done with the larger numbers, which stood for a finer grade of abrasive. Mr. Guthrie had glued a variety of sand papers to various shaped wooden rods. He taught me to start with the courser grades of paper and gradually work with finer and finer grades of paper until the piece was smooth and shining. Sanding in one direction, he said, would only result in deeper marks. The direction of the sanding should be constantly rotated and crisscrossed to eliminate the filing marks. He also owned an emery wheel with a handle that resembled the handle on Ms. Montez's coffee grinder. The emery wheel had an assortment of pins, or wheel bits, with sand paper coiled around the tip. As the handle was turned, the wheel bit spun, which created a very efficient sander.

Mr. Guthrie claimed that a jeweler's saw was one tool that truly depicted the craft of jewelry making. Stone saws were used in the ancient Neolithic Age, and Romans later designed a saw frame that resembled the jeweler's saw of today. By sawing holes or any other negative shape into the piece, the jeweler was capable of creating designs of the open spaces. Sawed openings were also used for fitting pieces together or adding hinges, latches, and gem settings. Saw blades, of course, varied in sizes and manufacturers marked the blades with identifying numbers. The thickness of the metal of the jewelry determined the selection of blade size.

"Specific jeweler skills can take weeks, months, or years to refine. Some jewelers seem to excel at a few or only several skills, while others manage to become wizards of the entire spectrum of processes. Teamwork can be indispensable for two or more co-workers who seem to specialize more in one skill than others. I have seen solitary old geezers who juggle the makings of up to twenty fine pieces of jewelry in a single day. Of course, each of the twenty pieces is a work of art in progress, perhaps months in the making. What these solitary old geezers like to do is switch from task to task, piece to piece in rapid succession, so as not to go insane from the endless, mindless task of repeating one particular task over and over all day long."

"Yaozu, you are a well disciplined young man, and I would not expect to hear you complaining aloud that your task has become tedious or monotonous, or that your neck is aching or your shoulders have become tense. You seem to understand that to some extent, working may become mildly tortuous and undesirable, and that is one reason we are paid for our work. We are paid to do something that many people might not be able to stomach the thought of doing, day in and day out. Face it, Yaozu, some of the tasks to which we commit ourselves are tedious, boring, and even strenuous at times. I have directed your apprentice so far. I have dictated the amount of time you spent pressing, sawing, soldering, forging, sanding, wire pulling, filing, annealing, and pickling. As you develop as a jeweler you will decide on your own that you have had enough of one task, set aside the piece and move onto another piece for a change of pace and some personal peace of mind. Some co-workers are very responsive when you ask them to take over a task. Other co-workers prefer not to be interrupted with your requests. If you abandon a piece of work halfway through process, another co-worker may be more inclined to pick up the task on their own accord because they see it sitting there unfinished. These self-motivators might be more inclined to choose their own moment to chip in and assist you with a task, and you might learn not to ask them. The solitary old geezer may have once worked with a large team of jewelers, and having found a particular style and personal success, arrives at the day that he plays the role of multiple assistants all by himself. He's bound to look like a mad professor, and his workshop may look like a chaotic disarray of rampant insanity. Some of these strange creatures are the most productive and creative jewelers of them all. On the other hand, some of the world's most renowned jewelers are insidiously tidy and their appearance is impeccable. God works in mysterious ways, and he never ceases to amaze me."

"I'm rambling, Yaozu, but more simply put, I recommend that you find your own pace, your own rhythm, so to speak, and listen to your own clock. Change tasks when you feel the need to change tasks, whether to relieve the monotony or to rest your tired hands. Learn to ask for help and learn who is easier to ask for help and who will resist it. I'm a happy-go-lucky guy, usually, and I am easy to approach for assistance. If I feel that I don't want to interrupt my immediate project, I will let you know without barking at you or holding it against you that you asked. (There are workers who bark back or hold it against you that you failed to persist, and we all learn how to work around these characters somehow.) I also don't mind finding a process half finished because the worker needed a break. I have jumped in to help or left other projects alone, either way, I trust that the work will take shape within a day or two of time elapsed. So I'm going to give you a little leeway and freedom to move about from task to task without my direction or timeframe held above you. Some people always prefer taking a single piece of work from start to finish without switching over to another project. If it is so ingrained in your nature to do so, then so be it. Most of us get frustrated at some point or other, and a stepping away from the project helps us. We return to it later with a fresh start."

Mr. Guthrie turned his back on me and began picking up scattered tools from the counter, returning the tools to their orderly arrangement of hooks on the rows of holes in the wall. "I also have a surprise for you," he said and then looking over his shoulder at me, "Tomorrow we are going to visit my jewelry store in San Francisco."

TRIP TO GUTHRIE'S JEWELRY EMPORIUM

Mr. Guthrie had hired a private carriage to Sacramento, where we boarded a "fire dragon" to San Francisco. Of course, only we Chinese referred to a steam engine locomotive as a "fire dragon," but this misnomer for the winding body and the fire breathing body held a powerful image for family members back home. Many Chinese were yet unfamiliar with these newfangled railroad trains. The journey was exhilarating and pleasurable. However noisy the engine and the echoing blast of the whistle, there was as compensation a subtle accelerating, rhythmic vibration that grew hypnotically soothing to the muscles and bone. Trees and hills and livestock flew by us as if we were flying low, a hungry hawk swooping in on its prey.

With only half an hour or less remaining before our arrival in San Francisco, we could see a huge tumbling gray cloud of dense fog that scrolled over the terrain like a monstrous lion's paw. We arrived in a dreamlike haze in which apparitions unveiled themselves only as they grew near. Women stepped out of the clouds before us dressed in fur-collared capes and attractive lace-up boots. Haloed glass lamps upon tall poles emerged while men wearing black gloves with their coat collars turned up and their top hats tilted upon their heads stepped like mirages from smoky mists. Tall pillars of marble like Greek Olympus faded in and faded away as rows of golden windows and business doorways drifted past like barges shrouded in sea mist. A street marker rose up like a ghost that read Grant Avenue at one angle and Clay Street at the other. Like a cluster of cottages stacked upon each other and side-by-side, the Saint Francis Hotel revealed itself in portions, a dark and beaconing gate of heaven hidden in the clouds.

Making a turn onto Clay Street we arrive within a block at the huge double doors embedded with beveled glasswork and curling S-shaped brass doorknobs. "This is Guthrie's Jewelry Emporium," boasted Mr. Guthrie. Stepping inside was like entering an arboretum. A high domed skeleton of gothic arches supported huge panes of glass forming a sparkling skylight. Potted banana palms and mammoth ferns adorned the circular expanse of floor and a bubbling fountain pedestal stood regally center stage. Finely dressed display clerks resembled museum tour guides more than clerks, and their shining display cases, nestled among the banana palms and arching ferns, rose like embankments of a exclusive fishing harbor.

Mr. Guthrie gave me a dazzling tour of jewels of the early years of Queen Victoria, my long-time enemy: a shoulder-knot of diamonds, pearls, rubies and emeralds made for the Queen of Spain purchased from the Crystal Palace, a corsage ornament fashioned in carbuncles and diamonds, earrings and brooches of fossil ammonites, snakestones mounted in gold and silver, and a hairpin starburst of cut jet, or black glass resembling a luminescent black carnation.

We moved on to another display of more historic jewelry: a tiara of gothic design in which tiny cathedrals of enamel and rubies stood in a tidy row along a diamond studded gold street fashioned as the headband, a bracelet of oval cameos carved upon lava medallions and set alternately among rungs of gold upon a beaded ladder, carved ivory crosses twined in delicately blossoming vines of the same carved ivory, a bulky bracelet of tortoiseshell, gold and enamel alongside a gold bracelet of molded grape leaves and twirling vines holding seed pearl bunches of dangling grapes.

Yet another display held unusually crafted ornaments, earrings and brooches of coral. Polished beads of coral in deep red and pale pink were crafted into elaborate necklaces and bracelets. One jewel clerk, a rosy cheeked woman of porcelain complexion with shining black hair wore an attractive red velvet gown. She explained that Italians like to wear coral to ward off *jettatura,* the evil eye. This bit of instruction struck me as serious business, not to be taken lightly.

Mr. Guthrie smiled at the rosy cheeked woman, and she flashed him a wink as she whispered, "Mr. Guthrie." Crowds of well dressed clientele circled from display to display, careful to avoid collision. Several couples were seen with well tailored children, like miniature adults guided by the hands of their mother, father, or grandparent. As I looked at the design of a branch coral brooch, I saw berries lodged in thorns, but then the illusion of a flock of human bodies seemed to fly in a circular path like a school of fish. The tapping of a finger on my shoulder interrupted my concentration, and a man said in perfect Cantonese, "Is this Yaozu, my friend, Yaozu." I turned with a start to meet the smiling face of Zhe, the philosophy sage. "Zhe, honorable friend and storyteller, Zhe," I said in amazement. "I never would have expected to see you in such a place." "And why not?" he inquired. "You always travel so light," I said, "and seem so satisfied with owning so little. I would not have imagined you shopping to purchase fine jewelry," I said.

"You know and remember me well, but I must say that to enjoy a thing of beauty does not necessarily inspire in everyone a desire to own. I love to look – I have, however, no need to purchase what I admire," he said in his standard tongue-in-cheek mannerism.

NEW PASSAGE: RETURNING HOME

There is a resplendent silvery daylight in the wake of a recent storm or thick fog that lightens even the heavy of heart. High mountain passes are frequented with this invigorating clearness. Trees seem to sparkle in the soft brightness of cool, crisp air, brimming with oxygen and newly cleansed by the saturation of moisture now lifted. Such a promising day is the rare union of a luminous glistening and a placid, calming tinge of chill in the atmosphere. It was on one such radiant day that we boarded the Majestic Prince Charleston, a prim and portly steam-powered ocean liner bound for Hong Kong.

I ascended the gangway with exhilaration tainted with a dread stirred by memories of our tortuous journey on the *Seringapatam,* (memories of watery rancid soup, the hardtack and old horse, the sickness and deaths, and the unrelenting callousness of the sadistic crew of foreign devils). As I handed over our boarding passes, I sensed that Uncle Ān Lè shared my apprehensions, the bird of prey claws clasping our beating hearts as we committed ourselves to a new dungeon of horrors. Adding to our apprehensions was the near recent news of the disastrous demise of the S.S. Central America, the massive loss of lives and the tons of gold vanished to the bottom of the sea. But our fears and old nightmares were laid to rest by a courteous and smiling crew. We were, in fact, treated as if we were dignitaries. Surely, Mr. Guthrie's affiliations and influence had rolled out the red carpet for us. No doubt, the fares for this journey far exceeded those of any passenger boarding the *Seringapatam,* but I couldn't help wondering how much a pile of bagged money really mattered compared to inflicted deaths, severe illness, starvation and imprisonment. Nevertheless, the Majestic Prince Charles was a luxury liner that shone like a diamond compared to the decrepit, decaying *Seringapatam,* a ship that rendered less shine than an old rotted tooth.

The food aboard the luxury liner was served in bountiful feasts of delicious and tempting creations. Beef stew with quartered potatoes, diced carrots, onions and celery with a thick broth worthy of spreading on soft warm slices of French bread or wheat rolls slathered with sweet butter. (I learned to love butter in this manner.) Thick filets of halibut, rock cod, and sea bass were sautéed in lemon sauces, chopped tomato sauces and herbal wine sauces. The menu offered oysters, scallops, mussels, clams, shrimp and prawns of all sizes. On Tuesdays the soup of the day was lentil. I barely tasted two spoonfuls my first Tuesday aboard, but two weeks later I found myself craving the tiny beans stewed in cumin and garlic. Chicken was prepared in an array of variety; hidden in meat pies and sprinkled throughout pasta dishes. The chef served a thick pork chop stuffed with vegetables that filled the dining room with the sound of full mouths uttering, "Mmmm, and oh my, my!" Deserts were always an extravagant affair: rich berry pies and buttery custards, puddings decorated with candied fruits, nuts and sugar coated gumdrops, and a delectable soft chewy substance called chocolate.

Previously, on the day that Zhe had led me to Uncle's hotel room, I confessed to him of my long gone, wild dream of gathering huge nuggets of gold upon my arrival to the Golden Mountain. My foolish dreams had failed to materialize, and in two years of hard work I had barely gathered embarrassing pinches of gold dust. Zhe was quick to point out that as a jeweler's apprentice I handled vast amounts of gold and precious gems. I shrugged, stating that it all belonged to Mr. Guthrie. Zhe gave me a wink and that wry smile of his. Several days later, as I looked out at the sparkling sea from the polished deck of the Majestic Prince Charleston, the image of the shining brick ingots that I had toted for Mr. Guthrie reminded me again what Zhe had told me at the jewelry emporium; "I don't have to own an object to admire its beauty."

The gold and jewels passed through my hands, just as friends like Diego and Ms. Montez passed through my life. I had lost track of Diego during my state of demented grief, and Ms. Montez left California for Australia shortly after introducing me to Mr. Guthrie. Perhaps my life was less about what I acquired and more about a series of passages. Passages of friendship and family, passages of suffering, joy, and wonder, passages of emotions and landscapes, passages of learning and experience, passages of dreams and desires, of faith and bewilderment – even the passages of childhood, through adulthood, old age and then onto a passage through death. My life resembled the gold I had recently drawn into finer and finer wire through the jeweler's press. Having passed through numerous obstacles, I emerged reshaped. As I traced the design of my life I witnessed my own transformation.

Before my eyes, the beauty of dancing diamonds upon the tossing waves of the ocean surrounded me and reached out, touching the golden rimmed horizon of a swirled marble dome. Pearly clouds beneath the blue sky soared beyond the reaches of my imagination. I wondered what passages yet awaited me. I wondered, indeed, what passage was unfolding itself around me at that very moment.

BIBLIOGRAPHY

Absinthe – The Cocaine of the Nineteenth Century, Doris
Laniers, McFarland and Co., Jefferson, N.C., 1998

Absinthe: History in a Bottle, Barnaby Conrad, Chronicle Books,
San Francisco, 1988

Antique Dealers Pocketbook, Lyle Publications, Liverpool,
Terrace, Worthing, Sussex, 1972

California Disasters (1812 – 1899) William B. Secrest, Jr. &
William B. Secrest, Sr., Quill Driver Books - Word Dancer Press,
Sanger, California, 2006

Chinese Calligraphy, an Introduction to its Aesthetic and
Technique, by Chiang Yee, Harvard University Press, 1973.

Chinese Calligraphy: from Pictograph to Ideogram, Edoardo,
Fazzioli, Abbeville Press, New York, 1987

Chinese Fables and Folk Stories, Mary Hayes Davis, American
Book, New York, 1908

The Chinese Have a Word for It (The Complete Guide of
Chinese Thought and Culture) Boyé Lafayette De Mente,
Passport Books, NTC/Contemporary Publishing Froup, Inc.
Chicago, Illinois, 1996

Chinese Tales, (Zhuangzi, Sayings and Parables and Chinese
Ghost and Love Stories), Martin Buber, Humanities Press
International, Atlantic Highlands, N.J., 1991

Everything You Need to Know about Asian American History,
Lan Cao and Himilee Novas, PLUME Penguin Books, USA Inc.,
New York, New York, 1999

The "Fan Kwae" at Canton: Before Treaty Days (1825-1844),
William C. Hunter, Kegan Paul, Trench, London, 1882

Fun with Chinese Characters (The Straits Times Collection 3, Cartoonist: Tan Huay Peng Federal Publiscations, Singapore, Kuala Lumpur, Hong Kong

Folk Songs of the World, Charles Haywood, The John Day Company, New York, 1966.

Gem and Mineral Guides to the U.S.A. (Where and How to Dig, Pan, and Mine Your Won Gems and Minerals) Volume 2:Southwest States, Kathy J Rygle and Stephen F. Pedersen Gemstone Press, Woodstock, VT, 1999

Gold Coins of Europe Since 1800, Hans Schlumberger, Sterling Publishing Co., Inc., New York, 1968

Healing with Medicinal Plants of the West (cultural and scientific basis for their use) Cecilia Garcia and James D. Adams, Jr., Abedus Press, La Crescenta, CA, 2005

A History of Jewellery 1100-1870, Joan Evans, Faber and Faber, London, 1953

Indians of the Feather River – Tales and Legends of the Concow Maidu of California, Donald P. Jewell, Ballena Press, Menlo Park, CA 1987

Jewellery (1837-1901) Margaret Flower, Walker and Company, New York, 1951

The Journal of Wong Ming-Chung, a Chinese Miner (A Dear America Book – My Name is America), Laurence Yep, Scholastic Inc., New York 2000

Land Without Ghosts (Chinese Impressions of America from the Mid-Nineteenth Century to Present), Translated and edited by R. David Arkush and Leo O. Lee, University of California Press, 1989

Lola Montez, Amanda Darling, Stein and Day/Publishers/New York, 1972

The Mad Old Ads, Richard Sutphen, McGraw Hill Book Co., 1966

The Magic Boat and Other Chinese Folk Stories, M. A. Jagendorf, Vanguard Press, N.Y., 1980

Methods of Placer Mining, Garnet Basque, Sunfire Publications, Langley, B.C., 1994

Minerals of the World, Ole Johnsen, Princeton University Press, Princeton, New Jersey, 2000

Mongol Jewelry, Ida Nicholaisen, Editor-in-Chief, /Thames and Hudson Inc., New York, New York, 1995

Mooncakes and Hungry Ghost (Festivals of China) Carol Stepanchuk and Charles Wong, Chin a Books and Periodicals, San Francisco, 1991

Mother Lode Album, Otheto Weston, Stanford University Press, Palo Alto, CA 1948

The Northern Maidu, Marie Potts, Naturegraph Publishers, Happy Camp, CA 1977

Opium Wars (The Addiction of One Empire and the Corruption of Another), W. Travis Hanes III, PH.D. and Frank Sanello, Sourcebooks, Inc. Naperville, Illinois, 2002

The Road to Heaven: Encounters with Chinese Hermits, Bill Porter, Mercury House, San Francisco, 1993

Rooted in Barbarous Soil (People, Culture, and Community in Gold Rush California), Kevin Starr and Richard J. Orsi, editors; University of California Press, Berkeley and Los Angeles, California, 2000.

Ship of Gold in the Deep Blue Sea, Gary Kinder, Vintage Books, New York, 1999

Tales for Big Children: Chinese and Filipino Folk Stories, Susie L. Tan, De La Salle University Press, Malate, Manila, Philippines, 1995

A Thousand Pieces of Gold (My Discovery of China's Character in Its Proverbs, Adeline Yen Mah, Harper San Francsisco, Harper Collins Publishers, Inc., New York, New York, 2002

Traditional Chinese Clothing in Hong Kong and South China. 1840-1980, Valery M. Garrett, Oxford University Press, 1987

The Uncrowned Queen, Life of Lola Montez, Ishbel Ross, Harper and Row, New York, 1972

Understanding Chinese Characters by their Ancestral Forms (Third Edition) Ping-gam Go, Simplex Publications, San Francisco

The Writer's Guide to Everyday Life in the 1800s, Marc McCutcheon, Writers Digest Books, Cincinnati, Ohio, 1993
Best Chinese Idioms, Compiled by Situ Tan, Hai Feng Publishing Company, Tokwawa, Kowloon, Hong Kong, 1986

In 2004, the author traveled to Yosemite National Park and visited local museums in Mariposa, California. This visit initiated his inspiration for writing The Jeweler's Apprentice. The author lives in San Diego.

Walter Black is also the author of two previous novels:
THE UNAMUSEMENT PARK
and
CAPTIVATING THE ESCAPE ARTIST

both available at Lulu.com